RUBY'S DINER

By

Tanya Hilson

WELCOME TO RUBY'S DINER

A diner in Chicago where families and friends come together to enjoy home-cooked meals, laughs, and desserts. But when someone's past catches up to them, other lives around them will be disrupted and destroyed. Sometimes it's hard to move forward when your past is riding your back. This is an emotional and compelling read that pushes its audience to look at their own perceptions of homelessness, drug abuse, alcohol abuse, and human trafficking Deceit, resentment, and revenge cast a long shadow over the employees of this diner, but somethings cannot be swept under the rug. Welcome to Ruby's Diner.

Paperback ISBN: 978-0-578-73390-6

TABLE OF CONTENTS

Welcome to Ruby's Diner 3

Chapter One 6

Chapter Two 11

Chapter Three 19

Chapter Four 28

Chapter Five 32

Chapter Six 44

Chapter Seven 56

Chapter Eight 69

Chapter Nine 75

Chapter Ten 85

Chapter Eleven 100

Chapter Twelve 105

Chapter Thirteen 113

Chapter Fourteen 124

Chapter Fifteen 141

Chapter Sixteen 154

Chapter Seventeen 157

Chapter Eighteen 167

Chapter Nineteen 179

Chapter Twenty 189

Chapter Twenty-One 193

Chapter Twenty-Two 209

Chapter Twenty-Three 219

Chapter Twenty-Four 222

Epilogue 224

Analogue 227

CHAPTER ONE

"Ms. Ruby, we finally did it!" Debbie said as she leaned the broom against the counter and sat down on a barstool.

"Yes, child," Ms. Ruby replied. "Never thought I'd own a restaurant, and what better chef to have cooking for my place other than you?"

Ms. Ruby began to wipe down the countertop. "I remember how you used to have your back porch lit up when you had your barbeques and card parties."

"Well, Ms. Ruby, all I want to say is thank you for the opportunity. I always dreamed of being top chef and people eating my creations."

"Well, I couldn't do it without you, Debbie, and I want you to be more than just the head chef. I would like for you to help me manage the diner too. How do you feel about being the manager?"

"Manager, Ms. Ruby?

"Yes, child, manager. Meaning you'll be in charge, but I'll still be the boss."

Ms. Ruby sat down at the counter and grabbed the hot cup of coffee, sipping on it slowly. "I just thank God for allowing me to be able to open a place like this that also serves the community," she said.

"Well, Ms. Ruby, I'm glad you bought a house right here in the city instead of that farm you always talked about.

"Yeah, I just didn't want to be so far away by myself."

"I wanted to talk to you about that too."

"Talk to me about what, Ms. Ruby?" Debbie said as she walked around to the other side of the counter and poured herself a cup of coffee

"Well, Scooter will be traveling now with the Chicago Bears, and Willie and Vicky moved to Wisconsin. So, I was thinking maybe you can come stay with me. The place is big enough for thy both of us, and you'll be closer to the diner."

"Well, now that sounds good and all, Ms. Ruby, but what if I want to have some male company to keep me company—if you know what I mean."

Debbie leaned over the counter and pulled out a small bottle of cognac from her bra and poured it into her cup of coffee

"Child, you know you're a mess. Trust me, I have already thought about that and those card parties you like to have, so I was thinking you can stay out back in the guest house. It's a three-bedroom guesthouse with two bathrooms, and I have two big Weber grills back there in the yard you can grill on".

"Well, Mr. James did fix the place up, but Ms. Ruby, if you want me to move in to be closer to you, say no more, I'll do it. Now, how much rent will I have to pay?"

Debbie picked up the dustpan and began to sweep the floor of the restaurant.

"Child, the house is already paid for. Scooter made sure of that. The only thing I need from you is to show up as my manager and show out on that grill as my chef."

"Oh now, Ms. Ruby, you know I can do that, " Debbie said.

She pulled out a box from behind the counter and carried it to one of the tables.

"How soon are you looking for me to move in, so I can have my cousin Gail help me pack up the few things I decided to keep? I sold my furniture and beds. I didn't want anything in my house that reminded me of Roscoe. So, all I have is my air mattress, my fold-up table, clothes, pots, pictures, and my TVs."

"The sooner, the better, then you will not have to be traveling from way across town," Ms. Ruby answered. She opened the box of salt and pepper shakers that Debbie placed on the table.

"Ms. Ruby, these tables and booths you bought are lovely. I like the flat-scree TVs too, and the pictures on the wall are beautiful. The football pictures of Scooter are amazing".

Debbie walked around slowly, looking around at each photograph on the walls of the restaurant.

"I see you have pics of some of the greats too. Muhammad Ali, Oprah, Jackie Robinson, Nelson Mandela, Michael Jordan, and Barack and Michelle Obama", she said.

"Yes, all these pictures have something in common." Ms. Ruby joined her in looking at the pictures on the wall.

"What, they're all black?"

They stood side by side, looking at the photos together.

"Yes, they are all black, but they are also 'History Makers." Ms. Ruby walked over to one of Scooter's pictures and touched it, smiling.

"Ok, Ms. Ruby, you got history all up in here."

"And my grandson will be a part of history," Ms. Ruby stood with her arms folded, smiling.

"Oh, I knew that when he was offered a full scholarship to UIC, then the Chicago Bears drafted him too. Yes, that was history in the making there," she paused. "So, Ms. Ruby, did you order the stuff for the kitchen?"

"The stuff for the kitchen will be arriving today. Scooter's assistant ordered all state-of-the-art appliances. New ten-burner range, two new ovens, bigger grills, new deep fryers, walk-in coolers, and a walk-in freezer."

"Ok, Ms. Ruby, you're going to have this place looking like a five star restaurant once you get everything into place".

"We're not done yet, Debbie. I will need you to order the supplies we will need, such as the utensils, napkins, plates, glasses, to-go bags, etc."

"Now, Ms. Ruby, you ain't make me your manager for nothing. I used to work for a place called 'Your Kitchen Needs,' and they supply all that stuff, Ms. Ruby.

"Well, child, get to calling them now, I would like to have our grand opening by Monday." She passed Debbie a checkbook.

A truck pulled up outside the restaurant, and the driver honked to announce their arrival.

"Ms. Ruby, I guess that is the kitchen equipment."

Debbie walked toward the front door of the restaurant, where just outside, men were starting to unload equipment off of the truck.

"Yes, that's it! Unlock the door, Debbie, so they can bring it in." Debbie walked over to the door and unlocked it.

" Hi, I'm looking for a Ms. Ruby."

"That's Ms. Ruby over there. But if you're looking to have some fun after you're done setting up the kitchen, I can show you a good time." Debbie grabbed the broom from behind the door and began dancing with it. "My name is Debbie, and I'm the manager. So, if you guys get thirsty, let me know, and I can quench your thirst," she paused. "I mean, get you something to drink."

"Now, Debbie, let the men do their job. Hi, I'm Ms. Ruby, the owner."

"Hi ma'am, we have a ton of stuff for your kitchen that we need to set up." He held out a clipboard and a pen to Ms. Ruby. "Can you just sign here, please?"

"Thank you, sir. Now I'm trying to open by Monday, will this all be set up and ready for use by then?"

"Ms. Ruby, it's Thursday! Give us until tomorrow, and we'll have your kitchen looking like Gordon Ramsay kitchen," the delivery Man said.

"Well, that sounds great! The inspector will be out Saturday to inspect the place and to make sure we are up to code before we open Monday."

"Yes, ma'am, I understand."

He reached out to take back the clipboard from Ms. Ruby

"After we're done, Ms. Ruby, you will pass the inspection." "Thank you, son, and if you guys need anything, just let us know."

"Now, Ms. Ruby, that's a tall glass of chocolate milk that I wouldn't mind dipping my cookie into," Debbie said.

"Debbie, calm your hot tail down and make them calls for the supplies."

"Oh, I'm on that, Ms. Ruby." She leaned back, licking her lips while watching the men take the equipment to the back of the restaurant.

"I also have interviews to hire some servers, a buser, and another cook. They should be here within the next hour or two."

"Ok, Ms. Ruby, let me call these orders in, and I'll be ready."

CHAPTER TWO

Ms. Debbie walked out of the kitchen.

"Ok, Ms. Ruby, I'm ready for the interviews." She peeked at the men as she walked towards Ms. Ruby.

"Child, didn't I tell you to leave them men alone and let them do their job?"

She sat at a table with a notepad and pen in hand. "Now come on, our fi st interview will be here in a minute.

"What position is this interview for, Ms. Ruby?" "This is for the buser position."

"Ok, Ms. Ruby, now we have to have a code." "A code? A code for what?"

"If you don't like him, I want you to tap my feet, and I'll do the same."

"You're a mess. I tell you—a mess. "

"I'm just saying, Ms. Ruby, especially if they seem lazy, it's a no, go."She pointed her hands repeatedly towards the door.
Ok, here comes the first person," Ms. Ruby said. She lookedup over the rim of her glasses from her seat at the table, feet crossed."Now, Ms. Ruby, where did you find this Urkel-looking characterfrom?" She walked to the front door, smiling and lets the youngman in. "Hi, I'm Debbie, are you here for the buser interview?" She extended her hand out to shake the young man's hand.

Hi ma'am, I'm Lance," he said, stuttering. "Ms. Ruby, this is Lance." She led him over to the table where Ms. Ruby is sitting.

"Hi Lance, you remember me? Please take a seat." "Hi, Ms. Ruby, I remember you from church."

His hands were shaking when he extended his hand out to shake Ms. Ruby's hand, blinking his eyes repeatedly.

"Yes, you know me from church, and I know your grandmother too—Ms. Fisher. "She pushed her glasses up on the bridge of her nose.

"Lance, are your hands and eyes ok?" She watched Lance repeatedly blink his eyes and make hand gestures.

"Yes ma'am, I just have a condition called Tourette Syndrome." "Oh ok, like the movie Deuce Bigalow: Male Gigolo. That's one of my favorite movies."

"Now, Debbie, stop that."

"Ms. Ruby, I'm just saying, now I understand the eye blinking and the hand gestures. If it weren't for that movie, I would've thought something was wrong."

"It's ok. I get teased a lot, but I pay it no mind," Lance said, stuttering.

"Well, we're not into the teasing business here, are we, Debbie?" She pinched Debbie's leg under the table.

"So, Lance, have you ever cleaned before?" She began to take notes.

"I clean my room every day, and I clean my grandma's house too. I wash the dishes. I cut the grass. I mop the floors..." He continued to make hand gestures as he blinked his eyes. The two women asked Lance a few more questions, smiling and nodding during each of his answers.

"That's great, Lance, you have the skills we are looking for. I talked with your grandma and told her I'd give you a try. So, would you like to work here with Debbie and me?"

"Yes, Ms. Ruby, I would like to work here so I can save up money for a new bike and an ant farm." Lance's tics gradually lessen as he grew more comfortable talking with the women.

"So, Lance, how will you be getting to work?" Debbie said. "I have a bike, and I have a chain to lock it up too."

Lance pointed out the window to the bike chained to the tree outside. It had seen better days, the chain was rusty, and the seat had bits of foam spilling out, but it still shone in the morning sunshine, having just been lovingly washed by Lance in anticipation of the interview. "But, I would like to buy myself a new bike."

"So, let me tell you what you'll be doing. You'll be cleaning the tables once people are done eating. Once you clear the tables, you will then take the dirty dishes to the kitchen and run them through the dishwasher," Debbie said.

"Dishwasher, like the one we got at grandma's house." "Well, you can say that, Lance. But this one is a little bigger and faster. Do you think you can handle that, Lance?" Debbie asked. "Yes, ma'am."

Call me, Debbie, I'm not old yet. She looked at Ms. Ruby, smiling. "No off nse, Ms. Ruby."

"None taken, you'll be my age one day, child, if the Lord is willing. Now, Lance, you can start Monday so, be back here at 9 a.m. I'll call your granny to confirm everything."

"Thank you, Ms. Ruby and Ms. Debbie. I'll be the best busboy ever," Lance said, stuttering.

"We know you will."

"I'll be here at 9 a.m. on the dot."

"Ok, Lance. I'll see you Monday at 9 a.m," Mr. Ruby said. "Yes, Lance, we'll see you Monday," Debbie repeated.

Lance left the restaurant smiling ear to ear.

"Well, that went well, and he seems like a nice kid. I'll call his grandma later to let her know we hired him and to get his ID and social security information."

A young woman suddenly stumbled into the restaurant. She appears disoriented, and her clothes looked dirty. She was wearing some faded dingy jeans, a red spotted up t-shirt with some run down gym shoes carrying a backpack. She had a scared, far-away look on her face. This look turned to confusion when she spotted Ms. Ruby and Debbie.

Debbie said whispering, "Ms. Ruby, who is this walking in here?"

"Hello, may we help you?" Debbie said. She walked up to the young lady who has just entered the restaurant. "Are you here for the interview?"

The young lady stood there quietly, looking around her and staring.

"Hello there. I said, are you here for the interview?" She stared at the young lady with a concerned look on her face.

"Debbie, I don't think she is here for an interview. Child, are you ok?" Ms. Rubi said. She walked towards the young lady. "Do you have a name we can call you?

"My name is Ginger Garcia, but people call me Gigi." She looked around, staring at the restaurant.

"Are you lost, Gigi? Do you need some help?" Ms. Ruby said. "I'm hungry! I thought Mr. Pete was here. He usually feeds me, but I'll leave."

"Mr. Pete no longer owns this place, child. I'm the new owner My name is Ms. Ruby, and this is my manager Debbie." "I'm sorry I barged in; I'll be leaving now."

"Now child, you say you hungry! We do not have any food in yet, but we do have some coffee and donuts you can have if you like."

"I have no money."

"Now child, I didn't say you had to pay for anything. Now come have a seat."

Debbie grabbed some napkins and a couple of donuts for Gigi.

"Now Gigi, we have glazed and chocolate, which kind would you like?" "I like both. Can I get one of each, ma'am?"

"You can call me Debbie." She walked around the counter to retrieve the box of donuts and some coffee. "Would you like cream for your coffee? There's sugar on the table if you like that too.

"Thanks, ma'am! I mean, Ms. Debbie. I just like it black."

"I understand, just like I like my men." Debbie leaned back, looking into the kitchen at the men working.

"Now Debbie, ain't nobody say anything about a man. So, Gigi, do you stay around here?" Ms. Ruby sat down at the table next to Gigi. "I used to stay in a house around the corner from here with some other girls but once the police shut it down, I've been staying at the shelter and if they are full, I find me a bench or an abandoned building to sleep. "

"So, what you saying is that you're homeless?" Debbie asked. "Ms. Ruby looked at Debbie.

"Well, I'm just asking! Hey, a closed mouth won't get fed."

"So, are you homeless, child? Do you have family?"

"Yes, I'm homeless." She bit into the first donut, and sip on her coffee. She leaned her head down, squeezing her eyes shut to prevent tears from falling. "I have no family; my mother do not want anything to do with me."

"Why, child! Why would you say your mother wants nothing to do with you?" Ms. Ruby asked.

"She kicked me out over two years ago. I told her that her husband was forcing himself on me."

"Forcing himself on you like how, child?" Ms. Ruby gestured to Gigi to sit closer to her as she shook her head back and forth in disbelief.

"He basically takes it." Gigi sat closer to Ms. Ruby, and gave her a small, sad smile. "I remember to this day, the day she put me out. One night my mom got drunk as usual, and she fell asleep like she always do. I was on the front room couch watching the Wendy Williams Show, and he came walking in the front door and sat on the couch next to me. He was smoking on a cigarette, drinking on some brown liquor. "

"'So, what's this you watching?' he said, and he started to rub on my legs. I pushed his hand back and said, you see what I'm looking at. He went to touch me again and I got up but when I tried to leave, he grabbed my arm and pulled me back. That's when I fell on top of him and that's when my mother walked in. "

"He started hollering at me saying, 'Girl didn't I tell you to leave me alone with your hot pussy ass?' then he pushed me off him. My mother was like, 'What the fuck is going on?' I was like, 'I was watching TV and he come in here feeling on my legs. I told him to stop and I got up but he pulled me back and that's when I fell on his lap.' She was like 'BITCH, stop lying!' then she slapped me across the face and told me to get out." Tears began to flow down Gigi's face

"She believed him and not me and I'm her only daughter. She believed him. She believed him." She trailed off, repeating the phrase, and tears began to flow down her face. "Ever since then, I been on the streets. I have a high school diploma, but it's like you need a college degree to get a real job. That's when I met Mean Mug."

"Mean Mug! Who's that? And what type of a name is Mean Mug?" Debbie asked

"It was my pimp's name, until the police raided the house and took him to jail."

"So, Gigi, what you saying is that you're a street walker? A party girl? A hoe?"

"Debbie, no time for jokes now. Can't you see the child is in pain? Look, child, I don't know you, and I don't know what you been through, but I know without God, you wouldn't be here to tell us your story. I believe things happen for a reason, and I believe you walking in here was for a reason. I tell you what, I'm doing some hiring today, and if you'd like, I can give you a job as a server. The only thing you will have to do is take the guests' orders and give them to the cook. You will provide customer service to the guests in a professional manner. Do you think that is something you can handle?"

"Are you serious, Ms. Ruby?" Gigi frowned, sadly. "Even after hearing I'm a party girl, as Debbie put it?"

"Look, child, I'm not here to judge you but here to help you. Luke 6:37 says, 'Judge not, and ye shall not be judged: condemn not, and ye shall not be condemned: forgive, and ye shall be forgiven.' Now if you think you can handle the server position, I'll give you a try, but if you think it's too much . . . "

"Yes, I will take it, Ms. Ruby. "Gigi stood up and gave Ms. Ruby a hug. "Anything is better than sleeping with men I don't know for food."

"We'll be opening Monday, but before you can start you will need to have a picture ID and a social security card Debbie can put into the system so you can get paid. Now, you'll make twelve dollars an hour plus tips, and you'll be paid weekly."

"I have a picture ID, but no social security card. I haven't seen my social security card in a while, but I can try to get one."

"Well, the social security offic is down the street. If you like, I can walk down there with you, and help you fill out the paperwork." Debbie offered

"You'd do that for me, Debbie?"

"I may joke around, but I have a heart. Gigi, do you mind me asking how old you are?"

"Debbie, I was thinking the same thing." Ms. Ruby said.

"I'm twenty-one years old, but I'll be twenty-two on Christmas."

"A Christmas baby! Ok, you're of legal age to work. Glad we got that established." Debbie took the card out of Gigi's hand, and passed it to Ms. Ruby. "Yup, her ID says she's twenty-one."

"Thanks, ID inspector. "Ms. Ruby said. She grabbed for the ID.

"Ms. Ruby, it's going on 1 p.m. The fellows and I are going to take a quick lunch break and we'll be back to finish up," the Delivery Man said.

"That sounds great! So how is everything coming along? I didn't want to be walking back there being all in y'all way."

"We got it going. As I stated, we should be finished by tomorrow." You'll have people eating in here by your opening day.

"I got something for you to eat." Debbie stuck her tongue out, licking and biting at her lips.

"Debbie!"

"Ms. Ruby, I'm talking about these donuts." She bit into a donut seductively.

"Mmm-hmm, that's all you better be talking about. Debbie, now you go down there with Gigi to the social security offic and bring back some Harold's Chicken too." Ms. Ruby bent down taking the money out of the leg of her pantyhose and passed it to Debbie. "I'm going to read a few scriptures of my Bible, and we have one more interview at 3 p.m. for the other cook position."

"Ok, Ms. Ruby, it shouldn't take no longer than an hour. The social security offic is only two blocks away and they usually get you in and out if you only need a copy of your card."

CHAPTER THREE

"We back, Ms. Ruby." Debbie said as she walked into the diner with a pan full of chicken, and placed it on the counter. "I told you it wouldn't take long. There wasn't too many people waiting on social security cards, but it was a lot of people waiting to fi d out why they checks were cut short. I tell you this new president we got is cutting out everything."

"Yes, he is, child. Until people learn to get up and go vote this will be the outcome for every election. People need to stop saying their vote don't matter. How would they know if they do not get out and vote? Then they wonder why their social security checks, food stamps, and health benefits are being cut because they choose not to get out and vote."

"I hear you, Ms. Ruby. I do make sure I vote. Right now, I want to wash my hands and put this chicken in my belly."

"It sure smells good. So, Gigi, you finally got your card?

"I did, Ms. Ruby. I gave it to Debbie to complete the paperwork."

"Ok, that's good. The only thing you will have to do now is fill out this application so we may put it in our records. You go on and have some of that chicken, then fill out the application.

"Thanks again, Ms. Ruby, for this opportunity. I never had a job, or anyone to really care for me. I appreciate this; I really do." Gigi grabbed a chicken leg, and bit into it like a pit bull.

"No problem, child, eat up. If you like something to drink, I have water and ginger ale in the cooler behind the counter."

"I tell you them other chicken joints ain't got nothing on Harold's; this mild sauce is fye. I tell you what, Ms. Ruby, I'm going to make this BBQ sauce recipe my great-great-grandma passed down and mark my words, I bet we can bottle it and sell it." Debbie said.

"If you're talking about the BBQ sauce you be putting on your food, yeah we can sell that. I always thought that was something you bought from the store."

"Nah Ms. Ruby, that there is a family secret, but I think now is the time to let the secret out." She licked the mild sauce off her lips. "Ms. Ruby, I'm done with the application." Gigi passed the paper to Ms. Ruby. "So, when do I start?"

"The grand opening is Monday. Can you start tomorrow so Debbie can train you?"

"Yes, ma'am, I can be here tomorrow.

"I already bought shirts and aprons; you will take two of each with you. I will provide hairnets, and make sure you cut them nails of yours down too. Now tell me, what size shirt would you like?"

"You can give me a small."

"Now Gigi, this is a place of business, so no need to be wearing that tight stuff," Debbie continued. "Ms. Ruby, give her a medium."

"I agree with Debbie. A small will be too tight for you. Here take this medium and go try it on in the bathroom." Gigi left and returned a few minutes later with the shirt on.

"See that shirt looks just fine on you, Gigi." Debbie said

"I agree with Debbie. A small would've been too tight for you."
"It do fit me nice. Thanks again for giving me a job and I will be here bright and early at 8 a.m. Monday. Ms. Ruby, do you mind if I take a few pieces of chicken and a ginger ale back to the shelter with me? I have to be there before 7 p.m. to get a bed."

"I tell you what, Debbie and I have one more interview and the guys are almost done in the back. Once we're done with the interview, you can come stay with me tonight. "

"Ms. Ruby." Debbie nudged Ms. Ruby's arm and dropped her voice to a whisper. "You don't know her like that to be letting her stay at your home."

"Look Debbie, I got this," Ms. Ruby said. "Now Gigi, finish up eating and we should be leaving after the interview."

"Ms. Ruby, are you sure about this?" Debbie said, whispering. "Sure, about what?"

"About letting a complete stranger stay at your home?"

"Look at the child, Debbie. Do you really think she's out to hurt me or you?"

"No, she don't seem like that type."

"Correct, she seems like the type of young lady God walked in here to get help and we're going to do just that, help her."

A tall brown-skinned man walked into the diner smiling. He was wearing a white polo shirt, a pair of dark denim Levi jeans, and blue loafers. "Hello, I'm looking for Ms. Ruby. I'm Robert but everybody calls me Rob. I'm here for the cook position," said the man.

"Hi, I'm Ms. Ruby." Ms. Ruby walked up to the tall man and shook his hand. "Robert you say?"

"Yes, it's Robert Washington, but everybody calls me Rob." "Hi, I'm Debbie—the manager of the place." Debbie walked around Robert, looking at him up and down. "You're very tall to be a cook. I'm going to need a ladder to interview you, huh? Or should I just climb up?"

"Debbie . . ."

"I know, Ms. Ruby. Behave." Debbie sat at the table and gestured for Robert to do the same. "Have a seat, Mr. Washington."

"So, Mr. Washington—" Ms. Ruby asked. "You can call me

Rob, ma'am."

"Ok, so Rob, can you tell me if you have experience in the kitchen?"

"Yes, ma'am I do. I just recently worked for a place called the Ham Bone Joint. I worked there as the cook for five years. But the owner recently lost the place due to back taxes. Before then, I cooked on the ship. Here is my resume."

"The ship as in boat?" Debbie asked

"I wouldn't say a boat but somewhat bigger. I was a Navy Seal and I worked in the kitchen on the USNS as a cook." Robert said, smiling.

"A Navy man, huh? So, you can serve and protect us?" Debbie looked over the resume that Ms. Ruby passed her. "I'm just meddling." "A military cook. I remember when my husband was an airman and the stories, he used to tell me about that kitchen he used to cook in. Rest his soul." Ms. Ruby looked up to the ceiling, shaking her head with a smile on her face.

The two women asked him a few more questions, smiling and nodding as they went along. Rob answers each question with confidence and charm. Before long, they all looked like old friends

"So, Rob, your resume looks impressive. We will be serving things such as burgers, steaks, chops, chicken, some appetizers, pizza, soup, etc. I'll be the head cook as well as the manager and you'll be working with me in the kitchen. Now we're having our grand opening Monday and the restaurant will open at 9 a.m," Debbie said.

"Well, Debbie seems to like you, which is hard for her to do when it comes to some people. I looked over your resume and you seem to have the skills we are looking for. I'm with Debbie, can you start Monday?"

"Yes, Ms. Ruby, I can start Monday. What time would you like for me to be here?"

"8 a.m. will be great! You can help Debbie make sure everything is in place before we open. The guys are in the back now finishing up but will be done by Friday. I have my inspectors coming in Saturday. Would it be ok if you came in Saturday to help put up the food and kitchen supplies?"

"Yes, Ms. Ruby, I can be here Saturday." Robert responded. "Great! We'll be seeing you Saturday at 8 a.m. Before doing so, I will need your state ID or driver's license and social security card so I can put you into the system for you to receive your paychecks."

"Ms. Ruby, may I ask what the pay rate is for this position?"

"Well since you are an experienced cook, I will start you off with fifteen dollars an hour. We will be closed on Sunday for that is the Lord's Day."

"Ms. Ruby, that works for me." He dug around in his wallet, and pulled out his ID and social security card, handing it to Debbie. One of the men from the delivery truck came in from the kitchen. He was sweaty and out of breath from the day's hard work. Debbie pursed her lips as she looked at him, then headed into the back to take a copy of Rob's forms.

"Ms. Ruby, we're done here for the day and will be returning tomorrow to finish up. What time will you be here tomorrow?" the Delivery Man said.

"Well son, I have an interview tomorrow morning so, we should be here by 9 a.m. We'll be seeing you then." Ms. Ruby said.

The Delivery Man and his crew left. A few minutes later, Debbie appeared from the kitchen. "Ms. Ruby, I reached out to my cousins and they will be moving my things for me Saturday evening after they get off of work.

"Sounds great! How about you come over to the place when we leave so you can see where you'll be staying. I'm only ten minutes from here once you jump on the E-way."

"Ok, Ms. Ruby, I can do that. I can grab a change of clothes on the way to your house. Look, Ms. Ruby..." Debbie got closer to Ms. Ruby, watching over her shoulder. "... are you sure about letting Gigi stay with you for the night?"

"If I weren't sure, I wouldn't have asked her." She touched Debbie's shoulder, looking her in the eyes. "Gigi, we're about to leave, do you need to go pick up any clothes?"

"Ms. Ruby all I have and own is in this bag, so, I'm ok. I just need to get to the laundromat to wash them." She held the bag close to her.

"I have a washing machine and dryer at home you can use to wash your clothes."

"Thanks, Ms. Ruby, I really appreciate you helping me out."
"Debbie grabbed the keys off the counter so we can lockup.

***

"Well ladies, this is my home. I just ask that you leave your shoes at the front door, so my carpet won't have shoe or dirt tracks."
"Whoa, whoa, whoa! Ms. Ruby, you living like them rich folks from that TV show, Lifestyles of the Rich and Famous. OMG this house is beautiful. I can imagine how the guest house looks. I mean, my new place." Debbie began to roam Ms. Ruby house from room to room like a kid.

"Your house is beautiful, Ms. Ruby." Gigi stood in one place, looking around her, and holding her bag to her chest.

"Thank you! Now you can sleep in the room in the back by the kitchen and Debbie you could sleep in the room across from Gigi." Ms. Ruby said. "Now ladies, if you'd like to shower or take a bath, there are bathrooms in both rooms. Both have a Jacuzzi and walk-in shower. There's plenty of towels and soap. Gigi, you could put your clothes in the washer downstairs in the basement. I will give you one of my grandson's jerseys to put on until your clothes get done washing, if you like."

"That will be fine, Ms. Ruby. Thank you!" She set her bag down.

"Let me show you the room you will be sleeping in, and if you need anything else, let me know. The basement is here downstairs." She flicked a switch, turning the basement lights on. "I'll grab that Jersey for you. Now go on ahead, child, and get comfortable. I have Cable TV too, if you'd like to turn the TV on." Ms. Ruby grabbed the remote control by the TV sitting on the dresser, passing it to Gigi.

"Thanks, Ms. Ruby, but I think I just would like to take a nice, long, hot bath and write as I wash my clothes."

" Write? What are you writing? A diary?"

"I have a diary I keep, Ms. Ruby, but I like to write music."

Gigi pulled out a notepad from her bag, holding it close to her chest.

"Music?"

"Ms. Ruby, I guess the room across from here is my room?" Debbie asked as she stood in the doorway, looking at Gigi and Ms. Ruby. "Yes, Debbie, that's the room. Get comfortable. I'll be over there in a few minutes after I get Gigi settled."

"Is that a waterbed I see?" Debbie walks in the room across from Gigi's.

"So, you say you write music?" Ms. Ruby sat down on the seat in the room.

"I just write sometimes."

"Well, child, I think writing is therapeutic. There's bubble bath if you like under the sink in the bathroom. Let me grab that jersey for you." She left the room, returning a few moments later with a Chicago Bears jersey, and left it on the bed for Gigi before she left the room again, closing the door. She went across the hallway and knocked on Debbie's door before entering.

"Ms. Ruby, this waterbed feels good. What made you want to get a waterbed?"

"That was Scooter's idea. It has a thermometer on the side of it if you would like to adjust the temperature of the bed."

"You fancy, huh?" Debbie walks over to the table that sits next to the bed. She digs around in her duffl bag for a moment before pulling out a bottle of Moscato. "I gotta tell you, this is living."

"Now where that wine come from?" Ms. Ruby asked.

"I grabbed it when we stopped to get me a change of clothes. I'm going to take me a nice warm bubble bath as I sip on my Moscato, watching the Steve Wilkos show I missed today. I see that TV in the bathroom hanging on the wall, over the tub. What is it—waterproof?"

"No, child, the TV is built within the wall. That was Scooter's idea."

"Well, he got it right, alright. I need ice." "It's on the door of the refrigerator?"

"Ms. Ruby, you hear that?" Debbie walked toward the kitchen.

"Hear what, child?" Ms. Ruby followed behind Debbie. "You haven't had anything to drink yet, and you're hearing things."

Debbie stood in the doorway of Ms. Ruby's room with a glass of ice. "Do you hear the singing?"

"I hear it now, child. That's Gigi. She said she likes to write music."

"She sounds good! Ok, we have a singer in the house."

"Look, Debbie, the child been through some things, so let's just try to help her out because that's the right thing to do. From here on out, do not call her a party girl or a call girl. Imagine being in her shoes."

"I got this, Ms. Ruby. I will take her under my wing. Now you get you some rest so we can finish up tomorrow. The only thing we will have to do is clean up after the workers and finish setting the tables up. I put in the orders, and some items will be delivered tomorrow. We got this. I looked at the guest house when you were talking to Gigi, and it is lovely. After we are done tomorrow, I will start moving my things in."

"Great!"

"I see that the guest house is fully furnished. It's nice too." "Ok, child, I'm going to shower and read a few scriptures before I go to bed. If you need anything to eat, the fridge is full of food. Check on Gigi to see if she needs anything."

Debbie walked out into the hallway and approached the door to Gigi's room. She knocked on the door lightly. After a few moments of no response, she opened the door and peeked in the room. She tiptoed back out and returned to Ms. Ruby's room, standing in her doorway.

"Ms. Ruby, she's asleep, and snoring like a cow."

"That was quick! The child must being tired."

"Yeah, she sounds tired, the way she's snoring. Let me close her door back. I'll see you in the morning, Ms. Ruby."

CHAPTER FOUR

Debbie walked into the kitchen and sat down at the royal-blue and white marble island. "I smell bacon."

"Good morning, Debbie. I just thought I'd cook some bacon, eggs, toast, and grits before we leave. So, how'd you sleep?"

"Ms. Ruby, I never slept in a waterbed before, and it felt great. And the massage from the recliner, I had to remind myself I was in somebody else's house." Debbie began to laugh, rubbing her arms around herself in a sexy way.

"Child, would you like some coffee?" Ms. Ruby grabbed the coffee pot from the counter

"Yes, coffee will be nice.

"Good morning, ladies! It smells good in here. It's been a long time since I woke up to someone cooking breakfast." Gigi said.

"Morning, snoring beauty." Debbie poured creamer into her coffee

"Morning, Gigi! Did you sleep ok? I cooked breakfast. Would you like me to make you a plate?"

"That will be nice, Ms. Ruby." Gigi sat down across from Debbie.

"Ms. Ruby, what about—"

"I'm making you a plate too, Debbie." Ms. Ruby interrupted her. Then she turned to Gigi, "Would you like something to drink?

I have coffee, orange juice, and milk.

"I would love some OJ, Ms. Ruby."

"Look in the fridge and grab the orange juice. There are cups in the cabinet over the sink." Ms. Ruby placed a plate in front of Debbie, and a plate on the counter for Gigi.

"So, Gigi, we heard you singing last night, and I must say you sound good, girl. How long have you been singing? Ms. Ruby said something about you like to write music."

Gigi sat down in front of her plate and picked up a piece of bacon. "Yes, I love writing music and poetry."

Ms. Ruby tapped Gigi's hand to put the bacon down. "Grace first, Gigi.

"It's been so long since I said Grace. I haven't been grateful lately for anything." She looked unhappily. "I have a mom that doesn't love me."

"You do have things to be grateful for. You are breathing and alive. It's some folks that didn't wake up today, but here you are warm-blooded and breathing."

"Sorry, Ms. Ruby, it's just been a long time since I prayed." "Well, I'm here to teach you, now repeat after me: God is good."

Gigi bowed her head uncertainly. "God is Good." "God is Great."

"God is Great."

"Let us thank God for this food," Ms. Ruby said. "Let us thank God for this food." Gigi repeated. "Amen." Debbie said.

"Amen." Gigi said as well.

"Now was that hard?" Ms. Ruby asked.

"Nope! Everything looks good, Ms. Ruby," Gigi answered smiling. Gigi grabbed a piece of bacon with one hand, and a fork with the other, digging into the eggs.

"Gigi, now I know we'll be leaving in a few, but you don't have to devour your food down like that. Slow down!"

Gigi stopped eating quickly and slowed down as she chewed on her food.

"Take your time; no need to rush. We have an hour before we have to leave, and we are only ten minutes away. Take your time, child." Ms. Ruby sat down at the island next to Gigi.

"Ms. Ruby, these grits are good. Not everybody can make grits." Debbie put another spoonful of grits in her mouth. "I have an idea, Ms. Ruby. How about we put grits and shrimp on the menu the same as they do down south?"

"Shrimp and grits are good." Gigi bit into a piece of buttery toast. "When I went to Louisiana for Mardi Gras, that was my first-time tasting shrimp and grits."

"I always wanted to go to Louisiana for Mardi Gras. So, how was it? Who did you go with?" Debbie asked.

"Mean Mug took a few girls and me down there to party." Gigi smirked.

"Now, child, you don't have to talk about that. Go on and eat your food so you can get dressed."

"My clothes . . . I forgot to wash my clothes." Gigi put her face in her hands.

"I washed them for you, child, when I came into the room early to check on you. I saw your bag still sitting on the floor, so I took your clothes and put them in the washer and dryer. They should be all done now," Ms. Ruby said.

"Ms. Ruby, you did that for me? Thank you!"

"You're welcome child, but I will say you need to get more clothes if that's all you have."

"Well, now that I have a job, I should be able to grab some new clothes and some shoes. Thanks again, ladies, for giving me a chance. I'm about to get dressed." Gigi got up, scraping the scraps on her plate into the garbage disposal.

"Just put the plate in the dishwasher, Gigi." "Ok."

"I guess you're right, Ms. Ruby. She do seem like she's been through a lot. I wonder if she can give me some penis tips." Debbie gestured as she sucked on a piece of bacon.

"Debbie!"

"I'm just joking, Ms. Ruby. I will never ask her that. Now if she volunteers to tell me..." Debbie got up from her chair.

"Child, go get dressed." Ms. Ruby picked up Debbie's plate and her own and scraped the scraps off into the garbage disposal

CHAPTER FIVE

"Open the door Debbie; you have the key." They all stood around at the front door of the diner.

"I'm reaching for the keys now in my bag." She rummaged around in her purse for a minute, pulling out all sorts of things in her search for the keys. Ms. Ruby stared at her in a combination of surprise and curiosity.

"Child, you need a suitcase."

Debbie opened the door, and the alarm went off. Ms. Ruby walked over to the alarm box sitting on the wall behind the counter and turned it off

"Debbie, I forgot to give you the code. I'll give it to you later." "Ok, Ms. Ruby." Debbie walked behind the counter and took her sweater off, hanging it on a hook on the wall

"Look, I'm going to get ready for this interview. In the meantime, Debbie, show Gigi how to work the register while you wait on the delivery. The guys should be here shortly to finish up in the kitchen." Ms. Ruby took her shawl off and hung it up on the hook next to Debbie's sweater.

"I'm ready to start, Ms. Debbie, when you are."

"So, Gigi, this shouldn't be too hard because you already know how to count money, right?" Debbie rubbed her fingers together

"If I don't know how to do anything else, Ms. Debbie, I know how to count."

"Oh, I'm quite sure you know how to count money." Debbie began to do ballerina squats.

"Debbie!" Ms. Ruby said.

"Now Ms. Ruby, have a sense of humor. I'm just messing." "Oh, I get it now, you real funny, Ms. Debbie." Gigi began to press buttons on the cash register, getting familiar with the various operations.

Debbie watched her from the counter, looking at her phone now and then, laughing occasionally. A little while later, there was a knock at the door.

"The delivery man is here." Ms. Ruby walked to the front door, and unlocked it to let the Delivery Man in. The Delivery Man walked in, wearing an overall suit with a tool belt that hangs from his side.

"Hi again, ma'am, we're here to finish the kitchen up," the Delivery Man said. He stepped inside with two other workers, carrying tools and equipment.

"You guys are right on time," Ms. Ruby said.

"Yes, they are." Debbie pushed Gigi out of the way, walking from behind the counter to stand next to Ms. Ruby.

"You remember my manager, Debbie."

"Morning, Miss." The man reached for Debbie's right hand, giving it a soft kiss.

"Oh, you're a handyman and a gentleman, now that's what I like." Debbie stood looking like Ms. Celie from The Color Purple, with a smile on her face, blushing.

"We shouldn't be long, Ms. Ruby; we already got things in place." The men turned and walked back towards the kitchen.

"Yes, lord, we're right on schedule." Ms. Ruby walked behind the counter to put on a pot of coffee. "Would you guys like a cup of coffee?

"That will be just fine, Ms. Ruby. Thank you!" The Delivery

Man said and then disappeared to the back.

"I see you all worked up, Ms. Debbie." Gigi reached under the counter for her purse. "Do you need a liner?" "A liner! What the hell is a liner?"

Gigi pulled something from out of her bag. "A panty liner." "Now that's funny, a liner," Ms. Ruby said.

"Ok, ok, you got one in." Debbie smirks at Gigi, as she walked back behind the register. "Anyways, are you familiar with the register now?"

"Yes, Ms. Debbie, you taught me well. If I need any help, I'll let you know."

"That's right! Because I'm the manager," Debbie said with a French accent.

There was a knock at the front door.

"There's our stuff," Debbie said. She walked to the front door.

A UPS Man stood in the doorway, with a dolly full of boxes.

"Hi ma'am, I have some packages for this location. Can you sign here, please?"

"Sure!"

"Where would you like for me to put them?"

"You could unload them here." Debbie pointed to a corner by the front door. "We'll take it from here. Thank you!"

After that the UPS Man left. "Hmm, I'm shocked, Debbie." "Shocked at what?"

"Shocked that you didn't try to flirt with him too," said Ms. Ruby.

"Now, Ms. Ruby, I love me some men, but what I don't do is married men. I saw that band on his finger.

"I know that's right." Ms. Ruby helped to put away supplies.

"Now that delivery man in the back, I didn't see a ring, and he seems like he's such a gentleman." Debbie sat down at the table, unloading the supplies as Ms. Ruby and Gigi helped to put them up.

"Just because he doesn't have on a ring doesn't mean he's not married," Gigi said.

"Gigi, you should know, I mean, I know." Debbie began to look over the boxes. "Now come over here and help me put these supplies up."

"Well, I can't argue with her on that one. There's a lot of married men who don't wear their rings just to cheat," Ms. Ruby said.

"Yeah, I know firsthand about cheating men, sneaky men, straight men, gay men," Debbie said.

"Yeah, me too. Those are the same men Mean Mug made me have sex with. I will say this, though; I used to love getting the guys who just wanted to talk and curl up like a baby. You know—the ones I didn't have to have sex with."

"You do not have to talk about that, child," Ms. Ruby said. "No, it's ok, Ms. Ruby! "Gigi grabbed a stack of napkin holders, placing them on the tables. "Sometimes I need to talk and let it out. I mean I write in my diary, but sometimes it's good to talk to real people who will not judge you." Gigi gave Debbie a smirk.

"Matthew 7:1 says, 'Do not judge, or you too will be judged.' Now child, ain't no judging over here. We all have a past; unfortunately, you got tangled up in a web. You're not in that web anymore. You are free. If you need to talk, I'm here for you." Ms. Ruby loaded the cooler on the counter with soda.

"Gigi, I'm here too if you need to talk. Trust me, you're not the only one who's been in a web." Debbie pulled out silverware holders and placed them on the table. "I was in a relationship where I thought everything was going ok. I mean we played cards together, we cooked together, we shopped together, we watched movies together. Then I found out..."

"You found out what, Ms. Debbie?" Gigi said. She then walked over to the table where Debbie was sitting, grabbing the condiments and placing them behind the counter.

"I found out he was living a double life."

"I think it was more than that," Ms. Ruby closed the lid of the cooler.

"I found out he was cheating."

"Cheating, Ms. Debbie, how did you find out?

"I was having a card party and BBQ, and my next-door neighbor invited her cousin who came in from out of town to the party. We were all having fun—drinking, smoking, eating."

"Yeah and keeping me up all night," Ms. Ruby said. "Anyways, the cousin asked if they could use my bathroom, and the next thing you know, he came back out with a picture of my man asking me how I know Roscoe. At first, I was like, 'I don't talk to hens about my man, and why the hell are you asking me questions about my man?' And that's when he through The Gap Band at me."

"The Gap Band, Ms. Debbie?"

"I said it was more to it," Ms. Ruby said.

"He dropped the bomb on me."

"Ok, ok, I get it now. The song from the group The Gap Band."
"He told me that my man was his man too."

"No, he didn't!" Gigi was shocked. "Yes, he did!" Ms. Ruby said.

"So, he was cheating on you with a man? Not just a man, but your neighbor's cousin? So, what did you do after that?" Gigi grabbed some plastic to-go bags and placed them under the counter.

"I called Roscoe and had the speakerphone on. I was talking all nice, and he was asking me if I miss big daddy, and I was like 'Yeah.' Then he was like, 'What did you win?' and then Jamie—that's the cousin—he was like, 'She won a whole lot of information'." "Whaaat! Then what'd your dude say?" Gigi asked.

36

"He was trying to play it off like he didn't know who was on the phone. That's when I told him it's over, and his shit will be gone, and there is no need to come back to my place."

"She sure did!" Ms. Ruby said.

"What you do with his things, Ms. Debbie?" "I grilled them," the ladies laughed.

There was a knock at the door.

"That should be the lady for the server position." Ms. Ruby stood up. "Gigi, please open the door and let her in."

Gigi walked to the door, letting the woman in. The lady walked in, wearing a pair of cowboy boots with a summer dress and a straw hat.

"Hi, I'm here for the interview with a Ms. Ruby. My name is Connie."

Gigi stood and looked at the lady.

"Hi Connie. I'm Ms. Ruby, and this is Gigi and Debbie." Ms. Ruby walked towards the front door to shake Connie's hand.

"You drink coffee Connie?" Ms. Ruby guided Connie to the table.

"Yes, ma'am."

"Gigi, please get us two cups of coffee." Gigi poured two cups of coffee and brought them to the table

"So, Connie, how is your day going? Was your commute ok?" Ms. Ruby pulled out some paperwork.

"My day is going okay, ma'am, and my commute was fine as well. It only took me fifteen minutes to get here.

"Well, that's good your commute is close. So, I see on your resume you've served before."

"Yes, ma'am, I have served on and off for about twenty years now. I just moved to Chicago a few years ago from Peoria, Illinois."

"Peoria, that's like a suburb or something?" Debbie walked

over and sat at the table with Ms. Ruby and Connie.

"This is Debbie. She's the manager of the diner." Ms. Ruby pointed out.

"Nice to meet you, Debbie."

"So, what brought you to Chicago?" Debbie picked up Connie's resume, looking it over.

"Well, after my husband died, I decided to sell my house and move to the city to be closer to my daughter. My daughter attends Loyola University. She's studying to become an Oncologist. She currently lives on campus, but she comes home on some weekends too."

"Sorry to hear about your husband." Ms. Ruby said.

"Yes, sorry to hear about your husband." Debbie paused. "So, what's an Oncologist?"

"That's someone who treats cancer patients."

"Oh, ok, that's where the money at." Debbie asked.

"She didn't go to school just for the money. My husband battled cancer for several years. When she finished high school, she wanted to become an Oncologist to cure her dad." Connie's eyes began to tear up.

"It's ok, child! Ms. Ruby grabbed a napkin from the napkin holder and passed it to Connie. "My husband and my daughter died, so I do understand your pain. But what I can also tell you, is it will get better with time, and you will always have memories."

"Thank you, ma'am!"

"Call me, Ms. Ruby!" Ms. Ruby asked her a few more questions. The two women got along well quickly, and even Debbie seemed to like her. After only a few minutes, Ms. Ruby smiled and gathered her paperwork. "Can you start Monday?"

"I'm with Ms. Ruby on this one, and your resume speaks for itself. Our grand opening is Monday, and if you would like to take the position, it's yours." Debbie got up from the table and extended her hand to shake Connie's.

"Monday will be fine with me.

"Ok, all we will need now is two forms of ID, Connie, for documentation." Ms. Ruby sip on her cup of coffee

"I have my social security card and state ID." Connie reached into her purse and passed Ms. Ruby her social security card and ID. Ms. Ruby turned and passed it to Debbie.

"Here Debbie, take this to the offic and make a copy. Now, Connie, since you have previous experience, I will pay you twelve dollars an hour plus tips. The diner will be open six days a week, Monday through Saturday from 9 a.m. to 6 p.m. Closed Sundays for that's God's day. I'll be giving you two shirts and two aprons. I require that your nails are cut short, and hairnets are to be worn every day. What size shirts would you like?"

"A large will be ok for me, Ms. Ruby." Connie said smiling.

Debbie returned from the back. "Here you go Connie, I made copies. I look forward to working with you. I'm quite sure you know how to work a cash register, but we'll be here Saturday at 9 a.m. for our first staff meeting. The meeting will give you a chance to meet the other new employees. Breakfast will be provided."

"That's fine with me, Debbie." Connie stood up and grabbed the shirts and aprons off the table. "I'm right down the street, and I'm excited to be working with you guys."

"Would you like a bag for your shirts, Connie?"

"No, Ms. Ruby, I'm fine! I'll just put them on the back seat of my car. No need to waste a plastic bag."

"Oh ok, I see you're into recycling, I recycle too. Hennessy bottles, beer cans, Moscato bottles..." Debbie said.

"Now, Debbie, Connie's talking about plastic, not no liquor bottles. Don't mind Debbie. You'll get used to her." She stood up from the table, smiling. "We'll see you tomorrow."

Connie left the diner. And a moment later, the Delivery Man appeared from the kitchen.

"Ms. Ruby, we are all done here in the back. You have a beautiful- looking place here, ma'am, and if you ever need a handyman, this is my card. Please call me." The Delivery Man pulled out a business card from his shirt pocket, passing it to Ms. Ruby.

"I'll take that." Debbie took the card out of his hand before Ms. Ruby could take it and examine it.

"So, your name is Caesar—Caesar Palace? Now ain't that a hotel name in Vegas? Your mother really named you that? I got to see your ID." Debbie stood there, with her hand out.

"Never mind her, Caesar. I think it's a powerful name." Ms. Ruby said.

"So, what made her name you Caesar Palace?"

"My mother was out with some friends one night playing the slot machines at Caesar's Palace, and she went into labor and had me right there on the casino floor. My last name is Palace, and my mom named me Caesar. So, that's how I got my name."

"Ok, I get it now. You look like a Caesar too: strong, and powerful." Debbie slipped his business card into her bra. "I could be your Cleopatra."

"Never mind her, Caesar, she can be a comedian at times. Thank you for everything, and if you like, you and your workers can come to the grand opening on Monday."

"I don't know about the fellows; I may have them on some jobs. But I most definitel will be here for your grand opening, Ms. Ruby". Caesar stared into Debbie's eyes.

"Now, are you sure you coming for the opening, or for Debbie?"

Ms. Ruby walked Caesar towards the door.

"Both. Your grand opening and a sweet treat. "Caesar opened the door to leave, looking back at Debbie with a smile.

"Ok, Ms. Debbie, I see you. He said he would most definitely be coming back for a sweet treat. Look at you up in here, pulling it," Gigi said.

"Girl, don't let this age fool you." Debbie answered.

"I see they got it looking nice back there. It looks like a state-of-the-art kitchen. We took care of a lot today, and the restaurant looks like it's all good to go." Ms. Ruby said.

"Yes, it looks beautiful! I turned everything on just to see if it worked, and it lit up. I love the digital fryers and grills. The food will be delivered tomorrow and the inspection too. Once we get through that, Ms. Ruby, we good to open Monday."

"I'm so excited, my first job. Thanks again, Ms. Ruby!" Gigi hugged Ms. Ruby.

"I'm excited too, child, and no need to thank me. God said, help those who are least fortunate, and they will be blessed. I just do what my heart tells me, and it told me that you needed the help. Anyways, I want to catch my gospel show that's coming on tonight so, let's get ready to leave."

"Sounds good to me. I'm going to go home and finish grabbing some things to bring back to my new guest house. My cousin already took care of the storage for me, and then I'll be back at your house tonight, Ms. Ruby." Debbie grabbed her sweater and purse.

"Well, I guess I'll head back to the shelter and see you ladies Monday for the grand opening." Gigi walked behind the counter to grab her purse/bag.

"Child, I been so busy and forgot to ask you if you would like to stay at my house. I mean I have the room if you like. I just ask that you obey my rules, which are keeping my house clean and come in at a decent hour or don't come home at all. You have to learn responsibilities too, so I will be charging you for rent, which will be one hundred dollars a week, which will include utilities. If you'd like to rent something on the Cable channels, I ask that you let me know first, and of course, you will be responsible for paying for the rental. If you could respect those rules, you are welcome to stay." Ms. Ruby walked behind the counter to grab her shawl and purse.

"I would love that, Ms. Ruby! I promise I will respect your rules, your home, and pay rent. I'm going to use the bathroom really quick before we leave." Gigi started singing The Pointer Sisters', I'm so Excited" as she walked to the bathroom.

"That girl must have an old soul. She knows all the old songs. Now, Ms. Ruby! I know Gigi seems sweet and all, and you are trying to help her, but are you sure? I mean sure, sure about letting her stay with you? It was different when you said she was just going to spend a night, but allowing a stranger to stay at your home, Ms. Ruby..."

"The child needs a place to lay her head, and she seems harmless. She also reminds me of my daughter." She put her shawl on. "Plus, Proverbs: 11:25 says, 'A generous person will prosper; whoever refreshes others will be refreshed'."

"You're right, Ms. Ruby! Now, do I have to pay rent too, Ms. Ruby? Because I know the house is paid for." Debbie started to laugh and pulled a tube of lipstick out of her purse and put it on.

"No, Debbie! I just told her that so she could have a sense of responsibility. The money I will put up in an account for her, but she will not know that. Once she is ready to get on her feet and move into her own place, she'll have this security to do so." Ms. Ruby said.

"That's a good idea, Ms. Ruby. A good idea. You are a blessing to many and to me." Debbie put her arm around Ms. Ruby's shoulder and kissed her on the cheek. Then she turned and hollered for Gigi.

"Gigi! We're leaving! Please spray, it doesn't take that long to do a number one." She and Ms. Ruby both chuckled. Gigi came out of the bathroom, and all three ladies left.

CHAPTER SIX

Saturday

"Gigi, thank you last night for helping me to put up my things. I guess Ms. Ruby was right, everybody can use some help. Thank you for sharing your music with me too. You can write and sing. Gigi, that's a gift, and we have to do something with it." Debbie said.

"No problem, Ms. Debbie, I didn't mind at all. I'm glad you enjoyed reading my music."

"The other employees should be here soon, Debbie, so can you start with cooking the breakfast? There's some eggs, bacon, Mississippi sausage, hash browns, and grits in those two grocery bags on the counter. There's also some bread and butter I put in the cooler." Ms. Ruby said.

"Ms. Ruby, when did you have time to get breakfast?" Debbie asked.

"Child, I got this out of my basement freezer. When Scooter comes home, he always likes for me to cook him a big meal, so I keep a freezer full of food."

"I do the same thing, Ms. Ruby. Don't let there be a sale on chicken, beef, or pork—because my freezer will be jam-packed." Debbie grabbed the bags, heading towards the kitchen.

"Scooter! So that's your grandson's name, Ms. Ruby?" Gigi

put her backpack under the counter.

"Yes, that's my grandson's name. His real name is Calvin, but we call him Scooter."

"So, what made you all start calling him that?"

"When he was little, instead of walking, he always scooted on the floor, so we start calling him Scooter." Ms. Ruby walked over to the counter, reaching under and grabbing some buffet kits. "Gigi can you take these to the back and open them up and rinse them out? I know they're new, but I still like to clean things before I use them."

Gigi grabbed the kits and took them to the back.

"Ms. Ruby, this grill cooks too good." Debbie poked her head out of the kitchen and looked at Ms. Ruby. "It fires right up. The new burners work just as fine too.

"Ok, I have Gigi rinsing off the pans for the food and I'm setting up the tables. The inspector should be here in a few hours, so make sure you clean everything back up." Ms. Ruby grabbed the two coffee pots, putting them on the coffee maker to bre

"Here are the pans, Ms. Ruby, all clean and ready for use. Where would you like for me to set them?" Gigi walked over to Ms. Ruby.

"Set them here on the table. Then go grab that pitcher from behind the counter and fill it up with water so I can put it in the pans to keep the food warm."

"Ok, Ms. Ruby!"

"And grab them burners too." "Burners! What are burners?"

"Those silver round cans under the counter. There should be four." Gigi grabbed the burners and walks them over to Ms. Ruby, who placed them under the pans.

"Gigi help me push this table together with that table." Ms.Ruby stood, placing her hands on each corner of the table.

"Ms. Ruby, I can do this by myself. How about you just have

45

a seat and a cup of coffee and relax?" Gigi pushed the two tables together, placing the chairs under them. Ms. Ruby nodded her head and took a seat at the table as Gigi went to get her a cup of coffee. A moment later, there was a knock on the door, and Gigi walked over to open it.

"Good morning Ms. Connie, nice to see you again." Gigi let Connie in, locking the door behind her.

"Good morning to you too. Gigi, right?"

"Yes, it's Gigi!" Gigi extended her arm to shake Connie's hand.

"Ok, I just wanted to make sure." Connie shook Gigi's hand with a pleasant smile.

"Hi Connie!" Ms. Ruby raised her cup of coffee in greeting. "Come have a seat. Gigi, please grab the coffee container on the side of the coffee pot and fill it up with coffee so Connie can get som

"Yes, Ms. Ruby!" Gigi poured the coffee into the container

"I see you have it smelling good and looking nice in here, Ms. Ruby. I love how the tables are already set up with the plates, glasses, cream and sugar, condiments, and wrapped-up silverware. Nice idea to go with the black cloth napkins, it cuts down on pollution and trees." Connie took her sweater off, placing it on the back of her seat.

"Thank you, Connie! I couldn't have done it without Debbie and Gigi." Ms. Ruby sip on her cup of coffee, smiling. "So, are you ready to meet the crew? They should be here shortly."

"Yes, I'm excited to see who I'll be working with." Connie opened the package of creamer and poured it into her coffee. There was a sound of a truck backing up outside.

"I see the meat truck pulling up, Ms. Ruby." Debbie rang the food pick-up bell. "Gigi, open the door and let them in. I'll be out there soon as I finish washing my hands." Debbie poured liquid soap on her hands washing them.

"Yes, I see he is packing boxes on the dolly." Ms. Ruby said.

Gigi opened the door for the Meat Man as Ms. Ruby, grabbed the coffee container, pouring more coffee into her cup. Debbie came from behind the counter carrying a note pad and pen.

"Hi Connie!" She continued walking to the front door to greet the Meat Man. "Good morning, sir! I'm Debbie, the store manager. So, what do we have here?"

"Good morning, Miss! I have a few packages here and more on the truck."

"Great! I just would like to mark off what I ordered.

"Well, right here I have some poultry, chicken wings, chicken legs, chicken breast, chicken quarters. I also have some roast beef, corned beef, beef burgers, gyros—both chicken and beef—and beef polishes. The fish and the pork are on the truck. I'll get that as soon as I unload these. Where would you like for me to put the boxes, Miss?"

"Gigi, please show him to the kitchen and have him unload the boxes next to the coolers." Debbie marked in the notebook.

"Did you order enough food, child?" Ms. Ruby asked.

"It sounds like she did to me, and he has more on the truck. I take it this place is going to be rolling." Connie said and sat with her legs crossed, sipping on her coffee

"Here is the rest of the meat, miss, I'll take it to the back." The Meat Man pushed the dolly to the back.

"Wait there, Mr. Meat Man, you moving too fast." Debbie stepped in front of the dolly. "Remember, I would like to check off what I ordered before you leave, and I need to look at the fish to make sure it's good." Debbie grabbed a butter knife off the table and cut the plastic ribbon off the box, opened the lid, and looked through the fish. "Debbie, what are you doing?" Ms. Ruby stared at Debbie with a confused look on her face.

"I'm making sure the fish is good. I remember when I worked for a catering company, we received some fish and I didn't lift the lid like I'm doing now, and come to find out, the fish was no good. So, I'm just checking to make sure we're good, Ms. Ruby. We don't need no lawsuits here. Ok, you're good to go." Debbie moves out of his way.

"And that is why she's the manager."

"Ms. Debbie, would you like for me to unload the meat into the cooler?" Gigi asked.

"No that's ok, I'm going to have the new cook do that once we are all done with the breakfast meeting. But what you could do is help me grab the pans of food so we may sit them in the chafers to keep them warm."

"You're all set, miss." the Meat Man said.

The Meat Man walked towards the front door, pushing the dolly. "You ladies have a nice day." The Meat Man left through the front door.

"Debbie, would you like my help as well?" Connie continued to sip on her coffee

"You know what, Connie? Yes, that would be nice. Can you help Gigi with the food so I may clean the kitchen back up before the inspector gets here? He should be here in a few hours." Debbie finished up the kitchen and returned to the table with the others, pouring herself some coffee

"I see Lance is outside chaining his bike up to the tree." Ms. Ruby moved her head shoulder to shoulder, looking out the window at Lance.

"Connie, that's our bus boy, Lance. He has Tourette Syndrome, so bear with him."

"I'm familiar with Tourette Syndrome."

"You've seen Deuce Bigalow too?" Debbie added a packet of sugar to her coffee

"Are you talking about the movie with Rob Schneider? That is one of my favorite movies. I have a cousin of who has Tourette

Syndrome, and she teaches sign language. She's happily married with two kids, and one of the smartest women I know."

Suddenly, Lance walked in.

"Hi Lance, I spoke with your grandmother earlier, and you are all set to start working Monday." Ms. Ruby said. She walked over to greet him. "Walk over here and have a seat, the meeting should start in a little while. We're just waiting on one more. Would you like something to drink?"

She headed towards the cooler.

"Milk, Ms. Ruby!" Lance shouted.

"Milk it is." Ms. Ruby said. She grabbed a gallon of milk out of the cooler, pouring Lance a cup.

"Here comes Mr. Washington." Debbie walked towards the front door. "Good morning Mr. Washington, glad you could make it. The other new employees are sitting at the table. Please join them. Care for some coffee?" she locked the door and put up the Closed sign.

"Call me Rob, Debbie. And yes, coffee will be nice.

"We have coffee, cream, and sugar on the table." Debbie walked back over to the table, taking a seat.

"Here's your milk, Lance." She set the glass of milk down in front of Lance and grabbed her cup of coffee. "Hi Rob, glad you made it."

She stood looking over the table, holding her coffee in both hands.

"Hello all, and welcome to Ruby's Diner. I would like to thank you all for showing up to your first breakfast meeting. I would like to talk over a few things before we eat, but first, I would like for you all to introduce yourselves starting with Ms. Debbie first, then we will go around the table."

"Hi again all, I'm Debbie and I'm the restaurant's manager. All I ask from you guys is to come to work on time, and give 100 percent customer service, and keep them coming back. I also ask that we all work as a team to keep this place running. If someone needs help, just ask. That's what I'm here for." Debbie stood up, holding the coffee cup and hitting it with a spoon as if it were a wine glass.

"Connie stood up. Hi I'm Connie, and I will be serving our guests." Connie sat with her hands folded in her lap.

"I'm Gigi, and I'm a server as well."

"Hi, I'm Lance and I'm the bus boy." Lance stuttered.

"Hi all I'm Robert Washington, but you guys could call me Rob. I'm the sous-chef and I will be pushing the food out."

"Pushing the food out?" Lance yelled. His fingers fumbled against his sides as he spoke. Rob looked in shock, and Debbie stood up quickly.

"Lance, that means Rob will be cooking the food and making sure he gets it out to Connie and Gigi so they may serve the guests."

Ms. Ruby sat down next to Rob and tapped him on his knee under the table to get his attention. She leaned in and whispered in his ear as Debbie talked to everyone. "He has Tourette Syndrome, so bear with him."

"Ok, now I understand," he said stuttering. "He is going to be the one hitting the bell saying "READY!" just like on TV."

"Yup Lance, you are right, that's exactly what he will be doing." Debbie set her cup of coffee on the table. "Also, Rob, we just got our meat in. After breakfast, I would like for you to unload it in the cooler. Gigi, I would like for you to roll the rest of the silverware and sit them behind the to-go booth. Lance, I will take you to the back so I can show you how the new dishwasher works and where you can find the broom and mop."

"Ok." Lance said.

"Connie, Ms. Ruby said she'll show you around and show you how to work the register. Also, we received our new menus and I will be giving you one each to take home so you can know what's on the menu. I will show Lance what he will be doing and Rob, you and I will discuss the menu after you are done in the cooler. There are tags in the office on my desk for you to use to label and date the meat.

***

An Hour Later, Debbie walked towards the front with Rob.

"Rob, you packed the hell out that freezer and put the meat away nice and neat in the cooler. Plus, you tagged the meat too with the expiration dates. Now, that's what I'm talking about. Thank you! Great job. I guess that's the military part in you."

"No problem, Debbie, I'm glad to be a part of the team. Well, if you don't need anything else, I'm going to be heading out. I have something to take care of."

"Nope, we are all good, and set to go. Thanks again, Rob. I'll see you Monday morning at 8 a.m. We'll be opening the doors at 9 a.m. Please look over the menu. I'll show you then how we will be plating the food. I'll be making some demo plates, so it will be easy."

"Thanks, Rob, for all your help. I'll see you Monday." Ms. Ruby said. She stood behind the counter, waving goodbye.

"I see that Lance left. Well bye, ladies, and enjoy your day." Rob said and then he left.

"Thanks, Ms. Ruby, for showing me how to work the register. I will look over the menu tonight and I look forward to seeing you ladies Monday." Connie walked over to the table, grabbing her purse and sweater off the chair. "I'm going to head out too, it's Bingo night."

"Did you say Bingo? I love Bingo. Maybe the next time you go, we could go together."

"That sounds fine with me, Debbie. I'll let you know when the next Bingo game will be. Bye ladies!" Connie walked out the door. As she was leaving, the Health Inspector walked in.

"Hi, I'm looking for Ms. Ruby. I'm the health inspector."

"Hi, I'm Ms. Ruby." She walked towards the Health Inspector, extending her hand. "And your name?"

"I'm Inspector Russo, Ms. Ruby. It's finally nice to meet you. So, you're Scooter's grandmother?" He shook Ms. Ruby's hand. "Must be nice to raise a superstar like Scooter."

"Yes, Scooter is my grandson. Would you like something to drink, Mr. Russo?" Ms. Ruby walked behind the counter. Debbie walked behind the counter to join Ms. Ruby.

"This is my chef, Debbie. Debbie, this is the health inspector, Mr. Russo."

"I would love some water, Ms. Ruby." The Inspector took a seat at a barstool at the counter. "I will be going over this form with you that will explain all I will be doing and if everything turns out ok, you are good to go."

"Hi Mr. Russo, nice to meet you." Debbie poured out the leftover coffee and washed out the coffee pot

"Hi Debbie." He drank down the glass of water.

"Would you like more water, Mr. Russo?" Ms. Ruby asked as he chugged the water down.

"No, I'm ok, Ms. Ruby, but thank you. So, Debbie you're the chef, I take it you have your food sanitation license?" Mr. Russo pulled out a clipboard with forms attached to them.

"Yessir, I do." Debbie dried her hands off with the towel that sat next to the sink. "I have it right here." She grabbed her purse from under the counter, and pulled out a folded-up paper, passing it to the Inspector.

"This here looks good. So, Debbie where did you go to school?" The Inspector marked on his form.

"I got my degree from KKC—Kennedy King College—on the

Southside of Chicago in Englewood. Class of 2010."

"Ok, one of the best Culinary Programs in the city of Chicago. I know the director of the program there: Ms. Smith. She's such a nice lady too."

"Yes, I remember Ms. Smith." Debbie bended over, placing her elbows on the counter, fumbling with her fingers. "She is a very sweet old lady."

"So, Ms. Ruby, I see you had your fire inspection already." The inspector pulled out a tablet, scrolling through it.

"Yes, Mr. Russo, Scooter's assistant took care of all that," she said and then looked at Gigi. "Can you please clean the breakfast table off and break the tables apart and reset them?

"Reset them?" Gigi looked at Ms. Ruby, confused.

"Make sure you put new plates, silverware, and cups on the tables after you split them apart."

"Yes, Ms. Ruby." Gigi placed her Apple phone in her back pocket.

"So, can one of you ladies show me to the back?" The inspector slid off the barstool

"Sure, Debbie can show you around while I help Gigi." Ms. Ruby walked over to the table and put out the burners.

"Right this way, Mr. Russo," Debbie said. The two walked together to the back.

"Ms. Ruby, what is he here to inspect?" Gigi asked.

"It's a city thing. They need to make sure everything is up to code before we can open to the public. So, how you feeling, Gigi? Are you ok? You just seem quiet." Ms. Ruby said.

"I'm ok, I just miss my mom sometimes."

"You say it's been two years since you've seen her. How about you try giving her a call?"

"I tried before over and over, but she would just hang up.

When I tried the last time, her phone was disconnected."

"What about brothers or sisters or grandmama?" Ms. Ruby grabbed the dish container off another table and began placing the empty cups and plates into it.

"My granny stays down south in this one house with about twenty of my cousins and my momma two sisters, so no, I didn't want to go down there. I have a brother on my father's side, but he is currently locked up for drugs. I used to go see him until they shipped him away to California. I write him at times, but I have no return address for him to write me back."

"Now you do: 555 W. Oak Park Ave." Ms. Ruby picked up the dishes, walking them to the counter. "Gigi, you can throw everything else away."

Debbie and Inspector Russo came walking out back to the counter. Gigi grabbed the dish container from Ms. Ruby and took it to the back.

"I'll take that to the kitchen, Ms. Ruby, and run these through the dishwasher." Gigi said.

"Thank you, Gigi! So, Mr. Russo, how did the inspection go?" Ms. Ruby stood by behind the counter with Debbie as the Inspector sat back down on the barstool.

"Ms. Ruby, everything passed. You have a fine place here Ms. Ruby, and from talking to Debbie, I can't wait to taste what's on the menu. Debbie, what you call it, the food you say you put your foot in?" The Inspector said.

"Soul food!" Debbie reached for the paper the Inspector passed her.

"Yes, soul food. Well that's the form saying you passed. I recommend that you put this up for documentation along with your sanitation license. Congratulations, ladies, you can officiall open." Mr. Russo slid off the barstool and grabbed his tablet and notepad.

"I'll see you soon for lunch," he said and walked out.

"We passed, we passed!" Debbie started to dance as if she were in a school dancing band.

"What's going on up here?" Gigi said when she walked out from the back, drying her hands on a towel. "The usual! Debbie being herself." Debbie was doing the Robot dance.

"I see you still in them Soul Train days, huh, Ms. Debbie?" Gigi and Ms. Ruby laughed.

"Girl, don't let this age fool you." Debbie busted down, doing a split. "Help me up, Gigi. Help me UPPPP!"

"Well, I guess we can lock up and head home." Ms. Ruby grabbed her sweater off the hook

CHAPTER SEVEN

The Grand Opening

"Good morning, all." Debbie yelled. She stood talking to the new staff. She was wearing a royal-blue chef uniform, Chicago Bears Crocs, and sporting a Chicago Bears chef hat.

"Good morning, Ms. Debbie." Lance stuttered.

"So, are you guys ready for the grand opening?" Debbie stood, clapping.

"Yes, Ms. Debbie!" Everybody said at the same time.

"I love the get-up, Debbie." Connie sip on a coffee, smiling.

"What you know about football, Debbie?" Rob sat in the chair, leaning back, his hand rubbing his goatee.

"Trust me, Rob, I may know more than you think about football." Debbie pretended to be posing with a football.

"Have a seat, child." Ms. Ruby told Debbie, and then she walked up, placing a box of donuts down on the table. "Look I bought some donuts for you guys to have. Before we get started, feel free to get some."

"Can I have two, Ms. Ruby?" Lance grabbed for the donuts in the box.

"Of course, Lance, get as many as you want. But remember, others have to get some too."

"Sharing is caring," Lance said. He bit into a chocolate long boy donut.

"It's good to know you guys are all ready. Remember, before you start, always clock in. I believe Debbie showed all you guys how to clock in and clock out. You will get a thirty-minute lunch break and lunch will be free on me this week just until you guys receive your first paycheck, and that should be a week from now, right, Debbie?" Ms. Ruby said.

"Yes, ma'am," she said.

"Let's just have some fun, and if anyone needs help with anything, just ask me or Debbie. Remember, have fun. Now, go wash your hands so we can get ready to serve our guests." Ms. Ruby said.

"Ms. Ruby, where are the remotes for the TVs?" Debbie stood up, stretching.

"They're in the drawer under the register." Ms. Ruby walked over to unlock the front door.

A Few Hours Later, Debbie came walking out of the kitchen to the counter and filled up a pitcher with ice water

"Ms. Ruby, it's packed up in here."

"Ms. Debbie, you and Rob got the food looking and smelling good." Gigi opened the register. "That Shrimp Mac & Cheese looks good. I have to try that."

"If you want something to eat, just let Debbie or Rob know. Again, I will provide lunch for you guys until you receive your first paycheck then after, you guys will get 50 percent off meals. All drinks are free except the canned sodas, bottled water or canned Arizona's, those are for customers unless you buy them."

"Thanks, Ms. Ruby!"

"That man know he drinks a lot of water?" Debbie said as she filled the pitcher up. "He's fast too, Ms. Ruby. You made a good decision by hiring him, but I think he kind of got a nervous problem."

"Why you say that, Debbie?" Ms. Ruby looked puzzled.

"You know I have the back door open for the cool breeze and there's some kids out back playing with fireworks and when they go off—the fireworks—Rob jumps or twitches. I asked him was he ok, and he said he's good, but I think he has a nervous problem if you ask me."

"Now don't you go trying to diagnose the man." Ms. Ruby put cash in an envelope, sealing it up. "I'll take the pitcher of water to Rob. Then I have to go to the offic to drop this cash in the safe. Plus, it looks like you may have a guest coming in."

"Hi again, Ms. Debbie." Caesar said. He walked up to the counter and took a seat. "I see your guys' grand opening is coming along great."

Debbie was blushing. "Hi Caesar, I'm surprised to see you. Would you like a cup of coffee?" She cleaned the counter after a guest. "Yes, coffee will be fine, if I could get one of them scones to go with it."

"I don't think that will be a problem." Debbie poured him a cup of coffee, smiling. "Which scone would you like?

"I would like the one like you." "Like me!"

"Yes, the caramel cinnamon scone. Caramel on the outside and sweet on the inside." Caesar poured sugar into his coffee as he looked up at Debbie.

"Ok, Caesar, I see you know what you want, and like what you see." Debbie lifted the cover off the scones, grabbing a scone with some tongs, and placed it on a saucer plate in front of Caesar. Just at that moment, the bell on the counter rang.

"Corned beef well dipped with extra hot peppers and cheese fries: up!" Rob said. He placed a plate with a corned beef sandwich and fries in the hot window.

"Sounds like my food is up." Connie closed the cash register and washed her hands.

"You right Debbie about Rob and his water, the man drinks water like a fish." Ms. Ruby walked to the counter and reached down to grab a thing of towels. "I'm going to take these in the back to Rob and Lance..." Ms. Ruby tapped Debbie's foot with her shoe. ". . . and help Lance with drying the dishes."

"Would you like something to eat besides a scone, Caesar?" Debbie topped off his coffe

"We had a job across town so I picked up something, but I would love to take some carry-out for tonight."

"Carry-out, huh? So, what, you ain't got no woman at home to cook for you?"

"Actually, I do have a woman at home, her name is Chaka. She's my daughter. So, no woman or girlfriend." Caesar bit into his scone, sipping on the coffee

"A daughter!" Debbie laid some napkins down in front of Caesar.

"I'm a widower."

"Oh, sorry to hear that." Debbie placed a cup under the soda machine, filling it up with orange soda. "What happened to her, if you don't mind me asking?"

"No, I don't mind. My wife died during childbirth. We had a beautiful daughter and I named her Chaka, which means 'Life.' She's seven years old but think she's twenty-seven."

"Oh, I understand, I used to be that age."

"So, what about you?" Caesar looked over the menu. "Do you have someone special in your life?"

"Not anymore!"

"Are you a widow too?" Caesar set the menu down.

"No, I just came out of a deceitful relationship some time ago." Debbie took a sip of the orange soda.

Rob rang the bell on the counter and said, "One fried chicken dinner and one catfish dinner: Up!

"Thanks, Rob!" Gigi said. She trayed the food, adding a bowl of clam chowder to it. "You got it rocking out here. People rubbing their bellies asking for the take-out menu. Ms. Debbie, these customers are loving the menu." She picked up the tray and carried it to her table.

"Debbie, would it be ok if I stepped out back for to vapor? It's slowing down now, and my tables are ok." Connie grabbed her purse from under the counter and pulled out a smoke vaporizer. "I already asked Gigi to keep an eye out for my tables."

"That's fine, just remember to wash your hands when you're done."

Connie nodded and then walked to the back.

"Sorry about that, Caesar, so, where were we?"

"You were saying you were in a deceitful relationship. Deceitful like how?

"Let's just say I found out he likes some of the same things I liked, like men's genitals."

"Awe, damn! All I can say to that is, I'm 100 percent man, and I love women."

"Well, that's good to know."

"I suppose it is, especially since I would like to ask you out. I was thinking a standup comedy show and some dinner."

"Are you asking me out, Caesar?" Debbie stood there blushing and smiling at the same time.

"Yes, I am! Debbie, would it be ok if I take you out Saturday night?" Caesar grabbed her hand on the counter. "I promise to be the gentleman my mommy taught me to be."

"Well, I guess Saturday night will be fine. We close at 6 p.m. and that will give me time to get dressed and meet you somewhere. Just let me know the place, and I'll be there."

"I could pick you up instead if you'd like, Debbie." Caesar

glancing at the menu.

"No that's ok, plus I just moved and feel more comfortable meeting at the restaurant first.

"Understandable! You have my number from my business card. Would it be ok if I got yours so, I may text the restaurant address to you?" Caesar pulled out his cell phone.

"That was slick." Debbie gave Caesar a smirk. "I suppose, since you will need to text me the address." She grabbed Caesar's phone and put her number in it.

"Great! Now that we are done with that, I would love to order the smothered rice and chicken for myself, and my daughter will have the fried shrimp dinner with fries."

"I'll put that in now." Debbie walked to the register to place the order.

Twenty Minutes Later, Debbie placed the bag down on the counter in front of Caesar. "Here's your dinner, Caesar! Nice and hot." "Would you care for any ketchup, cocktail sauce, or hot sauce?"

She bent over to grab plastic silverware.

"Now, this smells good. Cocktail sauce would be nice." Debbie grabbed some and puts it in his take-out bag. "Thank you, and I'll see you Saturday." Caesar said before he left.

"You over here flirting again, Debbie?" Ms. Ruby grabbed a pack of napkins, refilling the napkin holder on the counter while Debbie did the two-step dance, brushing her shoulders off

"I got a date; I got a date." Debbie swung her hips side to side. "Caesar asked me out, Ms. Ruby."

"Ms. Ruby, I'm going to put me an order in since we slowed down some. Will that be ok?" Gigi said.

"Yes, that will be fine. Just ring in what you would like so Rob can get the order. While you're back there, tell Lance to come here." "I will, Ms. Ruby, soon as I put this Shrimp Mac & Cheese in. My mouth been thirsty for this all day." Gigi put her order in.

Lance walked from the kitchen to the front and yelled, "Ms. Ruby, Gigi said you wanted to see me." He stood, drying his hands off on a towel. "Did I do something, Ms. Ruby?" he said stuttering as he fumbled with his hands.

"No, Lance, you didn't do anything. As a matter of fact, you are doing a good job, but I would like for you to take a lunch break." Ms. Ruby grabbed the towel out his hands. "Let Debbie know what you would like to eat and she'll order it for you."

"What would you like, Lance?" Debbie asked him as she stood at the register.

"I want chicken and fries."

"Would you like chicken dinner or—"

Lance interrupted her, in a straight voice, without stuttering or hollering. "I would like the chicken tenders with fries, Ms. Debbie. And can I have a Coke?"

Debbie looked confused as she put the order in.

"I only like milk with my breakfast," he said stuttering.

"Debbie, looking at Lance, this the new Deuce Bigalow," Debbie mumbled under her breath. "Lance, your food should be ready in a few minutes. Go have a seat over there with your Coke and I will bring it to you."

"Ok, like Gigi and Connie." Lance walked to the table sipping on his Coke.

A Few Minutes Later, Rob hit the food bell. "Chicken Tenders, up!"

Debbie grabbed Lance's food and walked it over to his table.

As she did so, the front door opened, and a man walked in.

"Connie, can you please seat our guest?" Debbie set the plate of chicken tenders in front of Lance.

Thanks, Ms. Debbie." Lance grabbed the ketchup and squeezed it all over the fries.

"Hi, welcome to Ruby's Diner, will it just be one today?"

Connie reached down and grabbed a menu from the host stand.

"Yes, just one." The man looked at the time on his watch, as Connie walked him to a table, placing the menu next to the empty plate. She stood next to the table to take his order.

"Hi, I'm Connie, may I start you off with something to drink?"

The guest picked up the menu, looking it over. "Yes, I would love a raspberry iced tea, if you have it."

"That, I think I can help you with." She walked away and returned with a glass of raspberry iced tea and a glass of ice water. "I noticed you looking at your watch before I seated you, are you under any time constraints?"

"I see you observe pretty well. Actually, I am under a time constraint, so is there something you can recommend?" He sip on the ice water.

"Everything is pretty good here, but you look like you're a steak man. So, I recommend the smothered T-bone steak. It's a T-Bone smothered with onions, bell peppers, and mushrooms in a savory gravy served with homemade loaded mashed potatoes, and broccoli. It's served with garlic bread, too."

"Connie you hit it on the button! I am a steak man. Everything you just mentioned sounds good to me. So, can I get that cooked medium-rare? I would also like to try the shrimp scampi bowl, and your Southern fried chicken plate." He passed the menu back to Connie.

"That's a lot of food. Will others be joining you?" Connie wrote the order down.

"No, just me." He took out a pen and a small notepad from his inside jacket pocket.

"I'll put that in for you now, sir." Connie walked away towards the counter where Ms. Ruby and Debbie were both sitting at the counter. On the other hand, Gigi and Lance were cleaning and wiping down tables.

"That should be the last guest of the day Connie." Debbie looked over some paperwork with Ms. Ruby.

"Correct! After this customer I'll be done. He ordered a lot of food though for it to just be him." Connie put in the guest's order.

"What'd he order?" Ms. Ruby asked. "Steak, shrimp, and chicken."

"Sounds like more money to me." Debbie glanced over at the guest. Then she gestures to Ms. Ruby to turn around. In an excited, low voice she said, "Wait! Ms. Ruby do you know who that is?"

"Child, who is he?" She turned her head slightly to get a look at the man.

"Ok Debbie, you got me curious now." Connie leaned her elbows on the counter and peered over at the man.

"That's the Chicago food critic, Antonio Giovanni." Debbie announced.

"You're right, Debbie, that is him."

Debbie looked for Gigi and said, "Gigi, Connie's customer is a known food critic! He just ordered a few meals. I want all of us to keep busy, but I want all of us to make sure he is ok by asking if he needs anything. I'll let Rob know what's going on. In the meantime, just do what you guys are doing, resetting the tables and rolling silverware." Debbie walked to the back to inform Rob of what was happening. Ms. Ruby walked over to the table to speak with the guest. "Hello, and welcome to Ruby's Diner." Ms. Ruby smiled generously to the man. "I'm Ms. Ruby." She extended her hand out to shake the man's hand.

"So, you're the famous Ms. Ruby." He looked up at Ms. Ruby

and shook her hand.

"You know something I don't know, sir." Ms. Ruby looked at him mysteriously.

"Who don't know you? After that press conference where your grandson mentions your name and how much he loves you." The guest smiled up at Ms. Ruby.

"That's my Scooter." Ms. Ruby looked over at Scooter's picture. "Well, I just wanted to say welcome, and I hope you enjoy your meal. Everything cooked here are my head cook Debbie's home recipes so I'm quite sure you will enjoy."

"You say Chef Debbie?" The man looks puzzled. "I never heard of Chef Debbie."

"Once you get her food in your belly, you'll know her then." Ms. Ruby patted her stomach. "Enjoy your meal."

An Hour and a Half Later, Connie handed the man his check and a to-go bag. "I'm glad you enjoyed everything."

"Yes, everything was great." He looked at the check. "Can you have Chef Debbie stop by?" He passed Connie his credit card to pay for the bill.

"Sure!" Connie took his credit card and walked to the counter where Debbie and Rob sat.

"The food critic would like to talk with you." Connie swiped the credit card.

"That's Mr. Giovanni. Let me say hi as well." Rob said and then followed Debbie over to the table. "Mr. Giovanni, how the hell have you been?" He said smiling.

"Mr. Washington!" Mr. Giovanni stood up, smiling, to shake Rob's hand. "Wow, this where you been hiding? It's been a few years."

"Yes, it has. So, how is Tommy and the wife?" Robs stood with his arms folded over his chest.

"Everyone is doing fine. Tommy just had fraternal twins

65

about a month ago. And my wife is doing fine as well, being a new grandmother and all."

Debbie stood looking on with a smile.

"That's good to know." Rob paused. "Mr. Giovanni, this is Debbie, the head cook and the manager of Ruby's Diner.

Debbie smiled at the inspector with a nervous look on her face.

"Nice to meet you, Debbie." He shook her hand." So, you're the one behind the menu and I see who's on the grill? Your food was amazing. I love the plating of the food and the presentation of it. Everything was flavorful." He said smiling

"Thank you, Mr. Giovanni! The menu consists of recipes my granny used to cook for my cousins and I when we were growing up. As I got older, she showed me how to cook and here we are."

"I see she taught you well." He placed a fifty-dollar bill as a tip on the table. "Rob, it was nice to see you again. I'll see you guys around." And with that being said, he exited the restaurant.

"Rob, how in the hell do you know Mr. Giovanni?" Debbie walked over to the door, locking it. Rob walked back behind the counter and got a cup of water. He leaned against the counter, sipping on it.

"I attend meetings for ex-military veterans who suffer from PTSD."

Debbie walked behind the counter to the register, opened it, and began counting money. "What's that?" Debbie continued to count the bills. Rob continued sipping the water.

"It's a disorder in which a person has difficult recovering after experiencing or witnessing a terrifying event."

"Damn, that sound like some deep, emotional, scary shit. So, Mr. Giovanni—he attends the meetings too?"

"No, but his son does, and that's how I met him."

"Oh, so you know his son? How do you know him?" She

continued counting money, tapping away at the calculator.

"He was one of my Seals."

"Like the movie Navy Seals? I loved that movie with Dennis Haysbert. I love his voice."

"You can say that, but this was no movie." A blank stare comes across his face. "I lost men. I was Tommy's lieutenant in Afghanistan. We got ambushed and Tommy was shot, along with me and a few more men from our squad."

"You been shot before, Rob?" Debbie looked shocked as she stuffed the money in a yellow zip-up pouch

"Shot, stabbed, and held hostage." Rob pulled up his shirt, displaying his wounds. "After they ambushed us, I was able to make it to the pickup spot, but I tried to go back to rescue others, but was caught and held hostage for a few days until I was rescued. Tommy was paralyzed from the waist on down. I received a medal and was honorably discharged. I attend the meetings to help with the flashbacks and dreams I still have at times.

"Now I see." Debbie nodded and closed the register. "Now you see?" Rob asked confused.

"I noticed when the kids were playing with the fireworks you were kind of jumpy."

"Sorry about that."

"No need to be sorry. You been through some scary shit and I will say I salute you." Debbie put her right hand on her forehead, giving Rob a salute. Ms. Ruby appeared from the back with Lance.

"Well, it's almost closing time. Lance, clock out. Your granny is expecting you to be on your way soon." "I clocked out, Ms. Ruby. Thank you," Lance shouted. "Ms. Debbie and Rob, the food was good. Thanks, Gigi, for helping me today. I'll see you all tomorrow." Lance walked out the front door, unchaining his bike from the tree.

"He seems like a good kid. I'm going to head on to the back

and clean up the grill and then I'll be leaving." Rob walked to the back. "I made some good tips today." Gigi sat at the counter, pulling money out her apron and counting it.

"Yes, the tips were good." Connie sat next to Gigi, counting her tips too.

"Well, there will be plenty more tomorrow." Ms. Ruby grabbed her sweater off the hook

Hollering in the back at Rob, Debbie dropped the money in the safe and grabbed the keys. "Rob, we're about to leave in a few. Are you done?" Rob didn't answer.

"I'll get him, Ms. Ruby. You and Gigi can go to the car. I'll set the alarm and lock up." Debbie left and walked to the offic and then into the kitchen.

"Rob, we're about to leave and lock up. You ready?" Debbie walked into the kitchen, putting on her sweater. She looked around, and saw Rob standing in the corner of the kitchen, sweating, and shaking badly.

"Are you ok, Rob?" She walked up to him and grabbed his shoulder. "Rob, Rob, what's wrong? What's wrong?" She waved her hands in front of his face. A few moments passed before Rob snapped out of it.

"I'm sorry, Debbie! I just had a flashback. I guess talking about what happened triggered something." Rob said shaking. He took out a bottle of pills, opened them, and swallowed a few. "I'm ok, that's what the meds are for—to help with the PTSD. Please keep this to yourself, Debbie."

Debbie looked concerned, "I will, Rob! I just want to make sure, you are alright."

"I'm good." He took a deep breath. "I just need a cold beer and a remote."

Afterward, Rob left as Debbie set the alarm and locked the door.

CHAPTER EIGHT

On Saturday, Debbie and Ms. Ruby sat at the counter as two police officers walked in, sitting at the counter across from the

"Hello, ladies," both officers sai

"This place looks way different than what it looked like before," said one of the officers. He scanned the place like the Terminato

"Yes, it looks beautiful. I see they knocked down a few walls," said the other officer He sat on the barstool with folded arms. Debbie got up and walked out from behind the counter.

"Hi officers I'm Debbie the manager, and that's Ms. Ruby." Debbie looked over at Ms. Ruby. "We're the new owners. May I get you anything to drink?"

"Yes, can we get two coffees?" The office looked back over at Ms. Ruby. "So, your Scooter's grandmother? What a talented kid," he said smiling.

"Hopefully, that arm of his will get us to the Super Bowl," the officer sai

"So, would you officer like to see the menu?" Debbie grabbed two menus from the side of the host stand.

"I have a taste for some of that fried chicken the food critic was talking about on the news earlier," the office said as he rubbed his belly.

Next to him, the other office looked over the menu. "That

sounds good, but I'll have the buffalo chicken wrap with extra blue cheese crumbles."

Debbie began writing their order down on her notepad, "Ok, and what two sides would you like with your fried chicken, Office Lopez?" He looked back down at the menu.

"I'll do the red beans and rice," he said.

"Office Reed, and for your side, what will you like?" "I thought it came with fries," officer Reed sai

"You could get fries or any other side on the menu. Some may be an upcharge depending on the side."

"I'll do the smothered cheese fries with extra bacon and green scallions," officer Reed answere

"You officer care for anything to drink besides coffee? It's on me." Ms. Ruby walked over to the soda machine.

"A Coke would be great," officer Lopez sai

"A Coke will be fine for me too, ma'am," office Reed said. "Just call me Ms. Ruby." She placed Cokes in front of the Officer with two straws.

"Ms. Ruby, can you put my order in? I'm going to lunch. Rob said it was ok," Lance said smoothly.

"Sure Lance, what would you like?" She walked over to the register to put Lance's order in.

"I would like a double cheeseburger, Ms. Ruby, with some curly fries." His fingers fumbled at his sides

"Ok, I'll let Rob know. It should be up in a few, Lance. What would you like to drink?"

"I'll have a Dr. Pepper. I'll be back, I'm going to wash my hands." Lance walked to the back.

"So, how is the food?" Debbie walked over to the officer and topped off their drinks. "Is everything to your tasting?"

"This chicken hitting." Lopez bites into the chicken leg. "This taste like that New Orleans Southern fried chicken."

"And the buffalo wrap is good too. Can I get a small to-go box, Debbie?" Reed said and sat up, patting his belly.

"This one is on me, Reed." Lopez gave Debbie his credit card. "Can I get a to-go box, as well as a slice of that Red Velvet cake?"

Debbie walked away to get the boxes and dessert. Connie walked from the back to the host stand as two men walked in. The taller guy was wearing a pair of black jeans, a red Miami vice looking shirt with a red brim hat as the shorter looking guy was wearing a neck full of gold chains and a black and white Adidas track suit, black Addidas jumpers, sporting a gold mohawk haircut. "Hello fellows, welcome to Ruby's Diner. Just two?"

Connie reached down under the booth to grab menus.

"Yes, Becky with the red hair," One of the guys said. He stood looking Connie up and down.

"It's Connie! Follow me, please." Connie seated the two of them at a table. She stood at the head of the table. "May I get you guys anything to drink?"

"This place sure looks nice." He looked around. "I'll have a cup of water for now until I get my food. I'll have a Sprite, with my food."

"And you, sir?" She focused on the other man.

"They call me Mean Mug, and you could just pour yourself right in this cup and I'll drink it all up." He spread his legs grabbing his junk and gestured for Connie to sit down.

"I'm good, I'm married." She looked at him with a smirk. "Anything to drink for you, sir?" she asked irritated.

"I do married, fat, ugly, and even the pregnant ones. "He sat back putting his leg up on the booth seat. "I don't care as long as you can breathe and make money," he chuckled. "I'll have a sweet tea."

Connie walked away

"Thank you, officer and hope to see you soon." Ms. Ruby and

Debbie wiped down the counters.

"You will, Ms. Ruby." The officers exite

"I can't stand an asshole. Oops sorry, Ms. Ruby." Connie looking agitated. She placed an order on the register.

"Ms. Ruby, I reset the tables in the back, and cleaned the ladies' room." Gigi walked over to the soda machine, grabbed a cup, and filled it up with grape soda. She took a seat at the counter

"I hope they hurry up and eat, then leave." She grabbed four cups, filling two with water, and one with iced tea. She carried two cups in one hand and one in the other over to the table where Mean Mug was sitting.

"What's wrong with Connie?" Gigi sipped on the soda, looking through her phone.

"Her customers at Table Five got her irritated trying to hit on her." Gigi turned around to take a look at Connie's guests and dropped the glass of soda as she turned and ran in the back. With hardly a moment of hesitation, Ms. Ruby and Debbie followed her.

"Ms. Ruby turned around. Lance, grab the broom and dustpan and sweep this glass up. Once you do that, mop and put the wet sign out after you're done." Ms. Ruby walked in her offic where Gigi stood shaking.

"Gigi, what's wrong?" Debbie gestured to Gigi to have a seat. "Why did you run back here like that?"

"Yes, child, what's wrong?"

Gigi was still shaky as tears filled her eyes. "That's him! That's Mean Mug—the pimp I told you about. How did he get out? I hope he didn't see me."

"Child, calm down. He ain't going to do anything to you up in here." Ms. Ruby pulled a 38 Special out of her desk drawer, placing it on top of the desk. "I've dealt with his kind before."

"Ms. Ruby, where in the hell you get a gun from?" Debbie said surprisedly.

"Look, I have to leave out the back. He cannot see me, Ms. Ruby," Gigi said nervously. "I have to go." She stood up quickly.

"Where you going to go?" Ms. Ruby stood up. "You are ok here. Debbie, let Rob know what's going on so he can keep an eye out and make sure Lance cleaned that glass and soda up."

Debbie immediately left.

"Look I have a lot of cop friends and trust me; I have a good lawyer. If he ever tries to bother you again, he will be locked up. You have nothing to worry about." Ms. Ruby sat down next to Gigi, patting Gigi's knee. "Now you can stay back here 'till he leaves. "Ms. Ruby walked to the front.

"Connie, are they almost done?" Ms. Ruby looked over at the guests in the restaurant.

"Yes, I'm getting them some to-go bags now, Ms. Ruby, and closing out their check."

Ms. Ruby grabbed the to-go bags and heads over to the table where Mean Mug was sitting. "Hello gentlemen, I hope you enjoyed your meals." She placed the to-go bags on the table. "Is there anything else we can get for you?"

"No ma'am, the food was good." Mean Mug stood up picking his teeth with the toothpick in his mouth as he started walking towards the door. "We'll be back." He stopped and turned around looking at Ms. Ruby. "Oh, and tell Gigi, I said I'll be seeing her around."

They walked out. Ms. Ruby's eyes stared at both men until they got in their car. She walked over and locked the door and stood there for a moment, with her arms crossed, until they pulled away and drove off. She turned back around; her eyebrows still furrowed in anger. "He said to tell Gigi he'll see her around," she told Debbie.

"He looks like a Mean Mug. How in the hell did she get involved with him?"

"Because dudes like that prey on young girls like Gigi. A young lady in the street with nowhere to go. No job, no money, no food. I got this though, Ms. Ruby. He will not be a problem up in here." Rob stared out the window, at the spot where their Cadillac had been parked. He shook his head. "I handled worse."

"Gigi, come on out. He's gone."

"Is Gigi ok?" Lance asked as he stood fumbling his fingers

"She's ok, Lance. She's just not feeling too good," Debbie said. Gigi walked from the back, slowly peeking around the corner. "Ms. Debbie said you not feeling too good, Gigi. You ok?" "I'm ok, Lance, I just need to get home and rest."

"Yeah me too. I'm about to leave and go home after I put this mop bucket away. I hope you feel better." Lance pushed the bucket to the back.

"I knew he was trouble when I laid eyes on him." Connie's hands were shaking as she placed the silverware she rolled in the bin.

"Rob, is everything ok in the back?" Debbie asked.

"Kitchen's clean, meat's labeled, grill's clean. Lance took care of the dishes and I had him mop the cooler and freezer."

"Good, and it's clean out here and I dropped off the money. Let's all clock out so I can lock up. I have a date." Debbie grabbed the keys out the drawer.

"You ready, Ms. Ruby?"

"Yes, child. I'm ready to go home too. It's a marathon of Martin coming on. I love me some Martin Lawrence."

"That sounds good, Ms. Ruby. You mind if I watch it with you?" Gigi grabbed her purse from under the counter. Debbie set the alarm and locked the door as they all head out.

CHAPTER NINE

"Good morning, Debbie." Ms. Ruby greeted Debbie as she came strolling through the front door of the diner. Ms. Ruby sat at the counter, filling up the sugar caddies

"And what a wonderful Monday morning it is." She hung her sweater on the hook, smiling ear to ear.

"I know that smile." Connie loaded the sugar caddies on a tray. "So, I take it your date and weekend went well."

"I take it that it did too, for I haven't seen you all weekend." Ms. Ruby helped to place the caddies on the tray. "I came to the guest house looking for you yesterday to go to church and you wasn't there."

"No, I wasn't there, Ms. Ruby." Debbie poured her a cup of coffee. "I ended up spending the weekend helping Caesar.

"Girl, helping him to do what?" Connie grabbed herself a cup of coffee, leaning on the counter and waiting on Debbie to tell all the dirt.

"Fast tail I tell you, a mess." Ms. Ruby shook her head.

"No, Ms. Ruby, it wasn't like that." She poured cream into her coffee. "It was like something I never experienced before on a date." She stirred her coffee

"Mmm-hmm, so how was it?" Ms. Ruby asked. "Yes, girl, spill it." Connie sipped on her coffee

"Ok, so when we left here Saturday..." Debbie poured sugar

into her coffee as she spoke. ". . . I went home and got in that nice Jacuzzi sipping on some Moscato and Caesar called while I was in the Jacuzzi giving me the address of the restaurant we were going to meet at. He never told me the name, but just gave me the address."

"But when I tell you it was beautiful, OMG it was. I pulled up, stepping out my car looking like Jill Scott and when I say all eyes on me, I mean, all eyes were on me. I walked into the restaurant and Caesar was there standing with a bouquet of roses looking like Morris Chestnut but them sexy eyes of his blew up when he saw all this."

"He escorted me to my seat. He pulled my chair out. He asked me if I like seafood and of course I told the truth: YES."

Ms. Ruby and Connie laugh.

"He already had a bottle of Moscato, but it wasn't the Moscato they sell at the corner store. This was some expensive wine. He asked if I'd care for some wine and of course, I told him the truth again: YES. Then he grabbed my wine glass and poured me some. The waitress came over and asked if we would like to order appetizers and Caesar took the wheel and ordered the appetizers for us."

"What did he order? Girl, spill the beans," Connie said.

"Girl, he ordered steamed mussels with white wine and garlic, stuffed crawfish with mushrooms, and cheesy crab dip." Debbie leaned back against the counter, hugging her cup of coffee with both hands, looking up in the air and smiling.

"That sounds like it was tasty. Did y'all even have room for dinner?" Ms. Ruby grabbed the creamer containers and filled them up. "What did you two order for dinner?"

"For dinner he ordered me a whole lobster and it came split and cracked. He also ordered me shrimp scampi, with a baked potato, and broccoli. The food was beautiful, look I got the pictures!" Debbie pulled her cell phone out and showed Ms. Ruby and Debbie the pictures of the food.

"You took pictures while he was at the table?" Connie said. "Girl, no! He had a phone call to take and excused himself from the table. When he left, that's when I pulled my phone out and took the pictures." Debbie laughed.

"Yes, that looks good." Connie looked over Debbie's shoulder as she flipped through the pictures

"Looks expensive too," Ms. Ruby said.

Gigi appeared from the back and grabs the sugar caddies.

"What y'all looking at?"

"Hi Gigi. Oh, just pictures of some new food recipes I want to try." Debbie showed Gigi the pictures too before putting the phone back in the side pocket of her chef pants. "We're about to open, Gigi, can you make sure all the tables are set? Make sure they're not missing any condiments or silverware."

"So, finish telling me what happened, Debbie, before we open." Connie filled up the cooler with bottled water

"He came back to the table looking kind of worried. I was like, "Is everything ok?" and he said that was his babysitter on the phone, and his daughter is throwing up, and not feeling well. He then asked if he could get a rain check. And I couldn't say no with him staring at me with them sexy, brown eyes. Girl, he had me melting."

"I told him of course, and that I look forward to it. That's when our food arrived but Caesar told the server to wrap it up because he has an emergency and we had to leave. The waiter came back wrapping our food up. He then placed the bill in front of Caesar and Caesar give him his credit card."

"Oh, my Lawd, every move he made was sexy. I couldn't keep my eyes off his juicy lips." She shivered. "He then put a fifty-dollar bill down for a tip and pulled my seat out for me to get up. Girl, I was surprised by this brother here. He walked me out to the valet and waited with me until my car pulled up. He said, "I'll give you a call once I find out what's going on with my Chaka," and gave me a kiss on the cheek.

"And damn, he smelled good. I got in my car and came home. Your lights were off, Ms. Ruby, so I didn't want to wake you and Gigi up by coming through the house, so I just went through the back. Remember, you gave me the key to the gate? I got home and took my clothes off. Poured me a glass of wine and fell asleep watching TV.

"So, if you came home, why didn't I see you when I came to wake you up for church?" Ms. Ruby placed donuts in the dessert container.

"Caesar called and broke my sleep letting me know his daughter was ok. He was so apologetic and asked if he could take me out to breakfast, and I agreed. He picked me up and we spent damn near the whole day together. Ms. Ruby, I know what you're going to say, and I will make it up next Sunday. It's just been so long since I've been asked out. We had a nice time too. He picked me and took me to this Chicken and Waffl place for breakfast. We just talked and talked."

"Mm-hmm. Well, you better be ready for church next week," Ms. Ruby said.

"I'm all done," Gigi interrupted. She placed the caddy tray back under the counter. "Would you like for me to open the doors now, Ms. Ruby?"

Ms. Ruby looked up at the clock. "We have five minutes, why not?"

Gigi unlocked the door.

"Connie walks up. Is she ok, Ms. Ruby?"

"Well, she didn't say too much last night. She sat in the family room with me for a minute watching Martin. Then she went in her room to write in her notepad. I think she was doing that music stuff, because she was singing too."

"She'll be ok. I've been in that situation before I got married. Had a no-good–ass boyfriend—excuse my mouth, Ms. Ruby—He used to beat the hell out of me and make me do things with other men," Connie said with a menacing look on her face.

"I can't believe it! You, Connie?" Debbie asked.

"Drugs make you do stupid things. But when I was raped, that's what brought me back to reality because I got pregnant from the rape. I went to have an abortion, but when I got there and got on that table, I couldn't do it."

"My mother and father gave me another chance and put me in rehab and I never looked back. Two years later, I met my husband and he adopted my daughter. So, if no one else understands the things she's been inflicted to do to survive, I do.

"Wow Connie, that's some deep sh—," Debbie exclaimed.

"Don't you say it," Ms. Ruby said.

"I was going to say that was some deep stuff she had to go through."

"Mmm-hmm."

A few hours had passed and Rob walked from the kitchen to the front of the restaurant where Ms. Ruby and Debbie were sitting doing paperwork.

"Debbie, here is the list for the order we need to place for the freezer and the cooler." Rob passed Debbie a clipboard.

"Rob, can you make me a gyro plate? I'm going to eat some now and take some home for later so, hook a sister up."

"Sure, no problem, Gigi. Would you like it the same way? extra gyro sauce and onions, and your pita bread toasted?"

"Yes! Thanks, Rob." Gigi walked over to one of her guests to assist them.

"Ok, Rob, remembering orders like that," Debbie said.

"Rob, before you go make Gigi's food, can you hang this on

top of the front door? I forgot about it earlier." Ms. Ruby passed Rob a bag. "I'm just not tall enough to reach the hook."

"Sure thing, Ms. Ruby." Rob pulled a door chime out the bag. "What a good idea." Rob walked to the door, hanging the chime on the hook.

"That will alert us when someone walks in. Lance!" Ms. Ruby said.

Lance was placing plates and cups in the dish bin when she called him. He stopped to look at her. "Yes, Ms. Ruby?"

"Can you check the men's bathroom for me and make sure it's clean and has toilet paper in there? Once you do that, you can clock out for the day."

"Ok, Ms. Ruby."

Lance walked off carrying the dish bin to the back

"You know, Ms. Ruby, Gigi let me read her music and I must say—the girl got a gift. She can write and sing," Debbie said.

"Yeah, I know she has talent. It's sad how people try to block one's blessing by keeping them down."

"She should try to get on that show called Your Big Chance."

Connie walked over to the table. "I've seen that show. It's a nice show. Ladies, will it be ok if I head out? I'm done with my tables and I rolled an extra bin of silverware too."

"Yes, that's fine, Connie. Thanks for rolling the extra bin," Debbie said.

"Good night, see you tomorrow." The door chimed as Connie walked out.

"So, you were saying, Your Big Chance?" Ms. Ruby flipped through the paperwork. "What type of show is that?" Ms. Ruby bundled receipts with rubber bands and put them in a long yellow envelope.

"It's a singing show somewhat like The Voice but unlike The

Voice, this show only uses local-talent celebrities to be the judges. It could be producers, agents, rappers, singers...," Debbie said.

"That sounds like that would be something she'd be interested in. What would she need to do to get on there?" Ms. Ruby said.

The bell chimed as the door opened.

"I clocked out Ms. Ruby. Bye, Ms. Debbie." Lance exited. "He's a nice kid. He's been doing a good job." Ms. Ruby said. Rob hit the food bell and placed a plate in the hot window.

"Gyro plate: up!"

Gigi grabbed her food and sat with Debbie and Ms. Ruby.

"Let me get a piece of that." Debbie took a fork, grabbing a piece of the gyro meat off of Gigi's plate. The bell chimed as the door opens again.

"I'll get the door." Debbie walked over to greet the guest. A short, chubby, round man and a short, old, grey-headed lady walked in. "Hi, welcome to Ruby's Diner. Would you like a table or a booth?"

Debbie grabbed two menus.

"Hi I'm Pastor Charles Clark of We Are One: New Covenant Missionary Baptist Church." He spoke in a pastoring voice, tapping the host stand with his hand as if he were giving a sermon. "Because we are all one in the body of the Lord. Can I get an Amen? This is my First Lady, Ms. Henriette Clark." The Pastor looked around the diner. "Some members of my congregation told us about your place, so, we decided to stop in not only to see how the food is, but to welcome you to our neighborhood."

"Well, thank you both for deciding to visit our establishment. I hope you two enjoy the food. You care for a booth or a table?" Debbie said.

"How's about we do a table?" The Pastor hit his stomach. "I don't think this six-pack will fit behind a booth," they all laughed

"Yes, a table. Charles's stomach hasn't fit in a booth in a

while," First Lady chuckled, "It's sure beautiful in here. It looks way better than it looked before when Mr. Pete had this place."

"Yes, it is nice. I love the beautiful pictures on the wall. That's all history there. I see you have pictures of our new quarterback Calvin Walker. That boy there has a gift. Hopefully, he will get us to the Super Bowl," the Pastor said.

"Yes, he's the grandson of the owner, Ms. Ruby." Debbie answered.

Ms. Ruby walked over to the table.

"So, I see you know my grandson, Scooter. Hi, I'm Ms. Ruby, the owner. Welcome to our diner." The Pastor stood up.

"Hi Ms. Ruby. I'm Charles Clark Pastor of We Are One: New Covenant Missionary Baptist Church." He extended his hand. "And this is my wife First Lady Henriette Clark." The Pastor sat back down.

"Ms. Ruby, you have a beautiful diner here. The tables are set lovely and I love the pictures on the walls," First Lady said.

"Yes, and the flat screens too. I tell you what..." The pastor shook his head up and down, looking at the menu. "...this menu looks so tempting, y'all might have to get a wheelbarrow to push me up out of here."

"Yes, it sure looks nice," First Lady said.

"Well, Debbie will take care of you two. Enjoy! And thanks again for coming in." Ms. Ruby walked back to the table, grabbing her paperwork. "Gigi, tell Debbie I'm putting this paperwork up and I'll be in the office

"Here are your drinks." Debbie placed two cups of water on the table along with a ginger ale and a coffee. "Are you all set to order?" Debbie pulled out her notepad.

"I would love to try the stuffed chicken," First Lady said

"And what would you like for your two sides?" Debbie asked.

"I'll try the mixed greens with the candy yams." First Lady

said.

"Ok! And for you, Pastor?"

The pastor sat, still looking over the menu. "I can't make up my mind, it all looks good." He flipped through the menu. "Ok, I will order the lamb chops and for my sides, I will have the mashed potatoes with gravy and the sautéed spinach." He passed Debbie the menu then grabbed it back. "Let me order the rib tips too, why not?" "And this is why we don't eat at the booths, First Lady looked shaking her head. Debbie laughed.

"And Debbie, please bring some to-go boxes." The Lady passed the menu to Debbie.

"Sure thing!" Debbie walked to the register to place the order. An Hour Later, Debbie topped off their cups of water

"How we doing over here?" Debbie asked.

"These were the best lamb chops I have tasted in a long time." The Pastor cut into the chop. "I will have to tell my whole congregation about this place."

"Yes, and the dressing in the stuffed chicken was seasoned to perfection. The food has plenty of flavor but Debbie as you can see, this is why I asked for to-go boxes," First Lady said.

"And that wheelbarrow." Pastor leaned back in the chair, patting his stomach.

"I'm glad you enjoyed it." Debbie placed to-go boxes on the table. "Do you care to have any desserts?"

"No, Debbie. I think we had enough. The bill will be fine."

Debbie pulled the bill out of her apron and placed it in the receipt holder. The Pastor placed his credit card in the receipt holder and passed it back to Debbie. She went to ring their order at the register and returned a moment later. "Here is your credit card, Pastor." She handed him his card back.

"I also brought you a slice each of my peach cobbler. It's on the house." She placed the desserts in a to-go bag.

"Debbie, thank you! That is very generous of you," First Lady said. "Yes, it is." The Pastor grabbed the dessert out the bag and opened the lid to put his nose in it, smelling the aroma.

"I'll be having this tonight before I go to bed." The Pastor placed the dessert back in the to-go bag and grabbed both bags as he helped the Lady out of her seat, locking arms with her.

"We'll be seeing you soon. Pastor and first lady leave out

Debbie walked wobbling back behind the counter, rubbing her stomach and laughing. "Let me clean this table then we can get out of here."

CHAPTER TEN

A few weeks later passed and Debbie was talking on her cell phone and sitting at the counter, sipping on some coffee as Connie sat across from her eating lunch.

"Ok, baby, that's great news. I can't wait to tell her. I'll see you tonight." Debbie hung up.

"What got you all excited over there, Debbie?" Connie cut into her salad. "I see you smiling ear to ear."

"My Caesar got me excited." Debbie stared at Caesar's picture on her phone.

"I was eavesdropping, so I knew that already," she chuckled. "You guys been seeing each other a lot lately.

"Yes, we have." Debbie got up to walk behind the counter and refilled her coffe

"So, where you two going tonight?" Connie poured salad dressing on her salad. "And you can't wait to tell who what?"

"And I thought I was nosy, you nosy too" Debbie removed the top from the cake dish and grabbed a slice of cinnamon apple crumb cake. "Since you all up in my business, Miss Ear Hustler, Caesar is taking me to the Arie Crown Theater to go see that new play called Back Porch Secrets." Debbie bit into the cake and resumed talking with food in her mouth. "Girl, I read the book and it was good. That damn Bobby made me want to jump into the book and kick his ass.

The play has a star cast too, so it should be good. It received five-star reviews."

"My girlfriend Nancy and her husband went to go see that play and she said she loved it. So, who is this 'she,' and what is she going to be excited about?" Connie was still being nosy as she bit into a piece of garlic bread.

"I knew it."

"You knew what?"

"I knew white hens were just as nosy as black hens," she laughed. "Anyways Ms. Lucy, 'she' is Gigi.

"I'm nothing like Lucy or Ethel—now they are what you call some real nosy hens," she chuckled. "But what is Gigi going to be excited about?"

Debbie laughed, "Gigi was over at my house one night watching the BET Awards with me. I was on the phone talking to Caesar and Gigi started singing that song 'Rise Up' by Andra Day and Caesar heard her and was like, 'She sounds good.' I then was telling him that Ms. Ruby and I said she should try to audition for that show Your Big Chance and he was like, 'She should' too.

"I hear her singing around here, but I didn't know she could sing like your saying she could," Connie said.

"Yeah, the girl can sing, sang. Anyways, you know he do the remodeling thing and he is doing some remodeling for the set of Your Big Chance."

"That's awesome!" Connie walked over to the coffee pot to top off her coffe

"Caesar's brother is also the casting director for the show and said he could get Gigi a spot to audition. She will be auditioning within a few weeks. I can't wait to tell her. "

"Well, here she comes." Connie grabbed her dishes and placed them in the dish window.

"I see some of my regulars coming in too, so let me get them started. Let me know what happens, Debbie." Connie walked towards the front door, waving at Gigi as she walked past towards Debbie. "Hey Debbie, I got Ms. Ruby's medicine. Where she at? In the office? Gigi walked behind the counter to wash her hands."

"Yes, she's back there talking on the phone. When you give Ms. Ruby her meds, come back up here. I got some good news to tell you," Debbie said.

"What news, Debbie? You can tell me now." Gigi sat next to Debbie.

"Girl, go give Ms. Ruby her meds, I'm not going nowhere," Debbie said.

After a few minutes, Gigi returned, looking excited.

"So, what is it, Debbie? You finally decided to let me do your hair? Gigi giggled as she grabbed a glass and filled it up with Nehi strawberry soda and leaned on the counter.

"Girl ain't nothing wrong with my snatch back." Debbie played with her hair. "I see you trying to ride my Beyoncé hairstyle." Debbie looked at her reflection in her phone, touching her hair

"Yeah, the style she wore when she played in Cadillac Records. Don't nobody wear rollers no more, Ms. Debbie, I'm just saying." She sipped on the strawberry soda. "You should let me hook you up, Ms. Debbie. I used to do all the girls' hair before we had to go entertain Johns, if you know what I mean." Gigi's facial expression changed.

"Girl, no need to be remembering all that. Look, I was just on the phone with Caesar and I was telling him a while back that you should try to get on the show called Your Big Chance and he agreed."

"How do Caesar know that I sing?"

"He heard you the night you were over my house watching the BET Awards. I told him you write your own music too."

"Ok, Ms. Debbie, I'm confused. What do Caesar have to do

with the news you said you had to tell me?"

"Your Big Chance is having auditions and we think you should audition. Not just Caesar and I, but Ms. Ruby too."

Ms. Ruby came out of her offic and walked over to the counter to pour herself some coffee and grabbed a slice of sweet potato pie. She then joined the two ladies at the counter. "Ms. Ruby too" what, Debbie? I heard you say my name." Ms. Ruby sipped on the coffee

"I was telling Gigi that we all think she should audition for the show Your Big Chance."

"Oh yeah, that singing show you were telling me about where they turn regular folks into singing stars." Ms. Ruby bit into the pie.

"I hear y'all, but it's hard to get on that show. Plus, I would need a whole makeover and those makeovers are expensive. You have to send a portfolio in and from there they will call you back to tell you if you made it to audition. One, I don't have the money for the makeover and two, I don't have a computer or laptop to put a portfolio together." Gigi paced back in forth behind the counter as she talked to Debbie and Ms. Ruby. Connie walked up to put her guest's order in.

"So, Gigi, are you excited. What day do you go audition?" Connie placed the order.

"That would've been nice, but I don't have the fashions or the portfolio for the audition, plus it's hard to get on that show," Gigi said.

"Debbie, I thought you said..."

Debbie cut her off, "Gigi, if you'd be quiet for a minute, I can tell you the news." Debbie looked at Connie with a smirk. "I was trying to tell you that Caesar's brother is the Casting Director for the show, and he said he got you a spot to audition. You audition is in a few weeks at the McCormick Place on the twenty-first. Now these auditions are by appointment only and your appointment is at 5 p.m. Caesar said you just go in and give them your name and portfolio and go from there."

"Ms. Debbie, stop playing," Gigi yelled. She ran from behind the counter and grabbed Debbie. "Are you serious, Debbie? I have an audition in a few weeks? I'll need a portfolio. OMG, who could I get to help me with that? I don't have a camera. Professional pictures cost a lot of money. I need makeup."

Debbie grabbed Gigi buy the shoulder's. "As Ms. Ruby would say, "Peace be still." I can help you with getting your makeup done. My cousin Gail son, Quincy—aka Quita—does makeup. She has her own beauty shop, where they do hair, makeup and nails. I can have her take care of all that for you for free. She owes me. As far as pictures, you can call Sears or another place that takes professional pictures and get some prices and I can help you pay for them, since I'm going to be your manager, right, Gigi?"

"My manager?" Gigi laughed. "I guess so, Ms. Debbie."

"Or she could just ask me since I used to be a photographer."

Connie grabbed two glasses, filling them with ice

"Connie you used to be a photographer too? I see you have many hats under your belt."

"Before my husband got sick that was my profession. After he was diagnosed and I couldn't afford a home nurse anymore due to the medical bills, I started taking care of him myself. I was able to set up a work studio from home and tend to my husband at the same time," Connie said.

"Wow, Connie, the things you'll do for love," Debbie said. "Connie, you'd do that for me? I mean, I can pay you to do the photoshoot," Gigi said.

"I would love to do it and Gigi; you do not have to pay me anything. Now once you get that singing contract, you can hire me as your photographer and put me on to more artist." Connie grabbed her guests' drinks.

"Sounds like a plan, I can most definitely do that, Connie."

Connie smiled and walked off to her guests' table

"So, Debbie, when could you ask your cousin about the makeup?" Ms. Ruby asked.

"Manager Debbie, you meant to say."

"Girl, what you know about managing anything besides food and drinks?" Ms. Ruby chuckled.

"Ms. Ruby, anything that deals with money that can make me money, I know how to manage it. Plus, Gigi's had enough bad luck in her life, and I won't steer her wrong. I guess you rubbing off on me, Ms. Ruby. Plus, that girl can SING."

"Ok, Ms. Debbie. Now, if I make it, I'll need one of those managers who can get me booked to perform at places like the United Center, the Staples Center, and of course Carnegie Hall."

"What you mean if you make it? You'll make it, child; have faith, you'll see. I keep telling folks, a mustard seed of faith is all you need. After that audition, trust the world will know your name, Gigi Garcia. Sounding like a Selena mixed with a Mary J. Blige. God didn't give you that voice for nothing," Ms. Ruby said.

"I got a table coming in. Thanks, Ms. Debbie. Thanks, Ms. Ruby. I can't wait."

"What got Gigi all happy?" Rob sat at the barstool with a plate of ribs and fries.

"She got an audition for a singing show in a few weeks," Ms. Ruby said.

"Well, the girl can sing." He bit into the ribs, licking the sauce off his fingers. This sauce Debbie made is fy

"Rob, Connie got her table's food. Gigi just got a table but they only going to want some desserts. Once those two tables are done, we can leave," Debbie said.

"Rob, you're ok with mopping the coolers since Lance is out sick?" Ms. Ruby asked.

"Ms. Ruby, I already took care of the coolers and the freezers. I did the bathrooms too, so we all good. I just need to wash them few dishes up from them last two tables and we can close up."

A week later, Ms. Ruby and Debbie were having lunch at one of the diner's tables.

"We been busy all day, I'm glad we finally got a chance to sit down and put something in our stomachs." Ms. Ruby bites into the corned beef sandwich.

"Yes, it's been a crowd especially since we put them new lunch specials on the menu." Debbie bit into the chicken gizzard. "Look at her." Debbie looked Gigi's way as Gigi pulled her notepad from apron. "She keeps that notepad on her now, writing her heart away."

"That young lady has a story to tell, watch what I tell you," Ms. Ruby said.

"Well she has two more weeks before her audition. All she's been doing around here and at the house is singing and writing. Caesar came over last night and the girl sang that Minnie Riperton song for us, you know the one she sang on Soul Train "Lovin You," and blew us away. You was there when Minnie sang it on Soul Train, Ms. Ruby. You know, in your younger days," Debbie chuckled.

"Yeah, I remember them days and I remember auditioning to become a dancer for Soul Train. I used to love me some Don Cornelius."

"You auditioned to dance for Soul Train?" Debbie looked at Ms. Ruby with a surprised expression on her face.

"These legs ain't always had the arthritis, child. Back then I was a dancing machine." Ms. Ruby started to dance in her seat.

"So, did you make the audition?" Debbie asked.

"Nope, my skin wasn't light enough. They were looking to cast light-skinned black women, if you get my drift."

The doorbell chimed. Four women walked in wearing big

church hats. They huddled together, talking and giggling amongst themselves near the host stand. Debbie audibly sighed when they walked in.

Debbie whispered to Ms. Ruby, "It's the church hens." She walked over to greet them. "Hi sisters, what a beautiful day the Lord has made. Let me say it again: What a beautiful day the Lord has made. Just four?" Debbie reached under the booth to grabbing menus and walked the ladies to a big round table.

"Yes, just us today, Debbie. Sister Linda won't be joining us. She had to go to the dentist to get that abscess taken care of, "Sister Betty said.

"I'm glad she did, because every time she opened her mouth, it smelled like straight halitosis," Sister Haddy said.

"And girl, when she was singing at choir rehearsal, I kept passing her breath mints. When you used to it, you can't tell," Sister Loretta said.

"Well, unlike y'all, I had to let her know the truth. I mean we were in the ladies' room freshening up before service last week and she was talking, and all that breath blew my wig back. I said, Sister Linda, I'm not being funny, but it smells like you have something rotten in your mouth. She blew her breath in her hands and damn near choked herself," Sister Mary said.

The Sisters all laughed.

"Ok Sisters, enough about the stinky breath. Are we having the same drinks today, Sisters?" Debbie asked. "Yes!" all the ladies said at the same time.

Debbie walked to the counter to get the drinks as Connie sits at the barstool, counting her tips drinking water from her favorite reusable bottle. "I tell you some church folks can be messy. That whole table full of hens over there—all they do when they come in here is talk about the other church folks." Debbie filled the cups up with ice.

"Girl, it's the same in all churches to me. It's always somebody who think they're better than others but have the most skeletons. I had an auntie like that when I was younger—rest her soul—but she used to talk about everybody that walked in the church. But here it is, she was married but sleeping with the vicar," Connie said.

"A vicar?" Debbie asked confused.

"That's what you Baptist folks call deacons."

"Oh, Ok. Your auntie was a bad girl, I see. Sleeping with the deacon—I mean, vicar. Did her husband ever find out?" "Hell, he was sleeping with the vicar too."

"Girl, shut your mouth. Now, that's some real R. Kelly-in- the-closet shit. Let me drop these hens' drinks off and take their orders so I can get them up out of here." Debbie walked away.

"Lance walks out the back with the dish bin. Connie, I think something is wrong with Rob. He's not saying anything." Connie got up and went to the kitchen to check on Rob. Lance got the dish bin and went to bus tables. Debbie walked over to the counter to put the ladies' orders in.

"Rob, the last order, make sure the catfish is fried hard." "Have a seat here, Rob, I'll get you some water."

"Rob, you ok? Debbie grabbed a basket of bread from the warmer.

"I'm ok, Debbie, just got a little dizzy."

"He had a blackout, "Connie whispered. She grabbed a towel for Rob, wetting it with cold water and rubbing his forehead with it before placing the towel around his neck.

"Rob, how about you go home, and I can finish for the day.

Debbie walked into the kitchen placing her hand on his shoulder.

"Are you sure, Debbie? I do need to go get my meds from the

pharmacy."

"You mean to tell me you been without your meds? No wonder you're having these spells. Have you eaten anything today?"

"I had some coffee and a donut when I started.

"And you do not have any real food on your stomach neither. I'll fini h up and let Ms. Ruby know your leaving and you're not feeling well. Connie, grab Rob's jacket from the back," Debbie said.

Connie walked over to the wall to grab rob jacket of the hook passing it to Rob. He put on his jacket and leaves out the front door. "I'm going to start cooking these ladies' food, Connie. Please keep an eye on them for me for refills," Debbie said

"Where Rob going?" Ms. Ruby asked. She walked up to the counter.

"I sent him home, Ms. Ruby. He had another spell, "Debbie explained.

"Again? He's been having them all week," Ms. Ruby said with a concern look on her face.

"That's because he haven't been taking his meds, Ms. Ruby. He takes them meds for the PTSD, and he's got high blood pressure," Connie added.

"I knew about the meds for the PTSD, but I didn't know he was taking meds for his blood pressure too," Ms. Ruby said.

"He'll be alright."

Debbie leaned her head out the kitchen window as she cooked, offering a reassuring smile as she spoke

"Rob left," Lance said stuttering. Lance walked up to the counter to grab the dirty dishes and placed them in the dish bin. "Is he ok?"

"He's a little under the weather but he'll be just fine. He just needs to get some rest."

Lance shouted loudly over his shoulder as he walked to the

back. "That's how I was feeling last week. I was sick and needed to rest. But I feel way better now."

"Everything ok over here, ladies? Do we need any refills or more bread? Chef Debbie is putting your meals together now. It shouldn't be long," Connie said.

"Honey, is everything ok? Why is the boy yelling like that?" Sister Betty asked.

"Almost blew my eardrums out," Sister Loretta exclaimed.

Ms. Ruby walked over to the table with the ladies. "Good evening, ladies. Hope you're enjoying yourselves so far. Your food should be up shortly, and I hope you enjoy as always." Ms. Ruby walked off and turned around swiftly. "And by the way, that boy's name is Lance and he has a condition called Tourette Syndrome."

"Connie walked off, giggling to herself.

"Did I just hear Ms. Ruby do a whole twist?" Gigi unloaded the empty sugar caddies on the counter and grabbed the sugar packets, filling them up

"Yes, she did," Connie said.

"Now child, y'all know I don't say much but them "hens," as Debbie calls them, be getting on my nerves. Every time they come in here, that's all you hear them doing, talking about folks. Gigi, grabs their food out the window and helps Connie take it over there." Ms. Ruby grabbed the money out the register and counted it before placing it in a pouch and walking it to the office Debbie washed her hands as Gigi and Connie sat at the counter filling up the sugar caddies

"They should be done in a few. So, Gigi, did you decide what you're going to sing at the audition?" Debbie asked.

"Yeah Gigi, have you thought about that yet?" Connie poured herself a cup of coffee

"I was thinking of singing something I wrote myself, called 'Spoken Dreams'." Gigi pulled out her notepad.

"Now that would be a risky move, Gigi." Debbie held a cup in front of Connie, gesturing her to pour her a cup of coffee. "I've seen some folks try to go on that show and sing their own songs they have written, and they end up being the same ones who don't win. You have to sing something that everyone knows. Like "Halo" by Beyoncé or that song by Adele—you know, the one everybody used to sing."

"Debbie, you talking about "Someone like You." That's was my song." Connie started to sway her head back and forth, snapping her fingers off-beat and singing Adel

"Let's leave the singing for Gigi." Debbie leaned on the counter sipping on her coffee. Ms. Ruby walked behind the counter to change out the receipt paper.

"I know, Ms. Debbie, but like Ms. Ruby says, 'Have a mustard seed of faith'."

"That's all it takes. Now, what y'all talking about?" Ms. Ruby asked.

"I want to sing a song I wrote for the audition, but Debbie thinks I should sing a song everybody is familiar with. What you think, Ms. Ruby?"

"I think you knows best. If you think your song can win, then sing it."

"All I'm saying is that some have tried, and never won the record deal." Debbie got up to grab to-go boxes and the bill and walked back over to the ladies.

"Debbie, you read my mind." Sister Haddy reached for one of the to-go boxes that Debbie had placed on the table with the bill. "I'm going to take the rest of this here home and warm it up tonight when my show comes on."

"Now Sister Haddy, you watch a lot of shows, which one are you talking about now?" Sister Mary grabbed a to-go box.

"She talking about them housewives' girls." Loretta pulled out a credit card. "Here Debbie, this will be for the table."

Debbie took the card and headed back behind the counter to the register.

"Gigi, sing your song. You're the only one who knows it best," Ms. Ruby said.

"I agree with Ms. Ruby. You wrote the words; your voice will take care of the rest," Connie added.

"I see y'all still on that. Sing your song, Gigi, if you think it will get you to the semifinals. That's all I'm saying." Debbie paused. "Finally, they are about to leave."

The ladies got up from the table but before they left, Debbie passed Sister Loretta her credit card back. "Thank you, ladies. See you next week. Tell Sister Linda I said I hope she's feeling better. Enjoy your evening, ladies."

"They finally gone, huh?" Ms. Ruby asked

"Yes, now time to get our drink on. Lance, come out here and bus the last few tables so we can get out of here." Debbie ran the end-of-day report on the register.

"Get y'all drink on. So, what you doing tonight—Caesar? Lawd, I didn't mean to say it like that," Ms. Ruby chuckled.

"No, me and the girls are going back to my place to have a few cocktails. My cousin Quincy is going to do Gigi's hair for her portfolio, and Connie is going to do the photoshoot while we photo-drink."

Connie and Gigi both laughed at Debbie as they counted their tips.

"My cousin said he was going to meet us here, but I don't see a missed call or anything from him. I told him what time. Let me call him." Debbie pulled out her cell phone and dials Quincy's number. She stood there as the phone rang. Quincy entered the diner, rolling a glittery purple suitcase and carrying a Louis Vuitton duffl bag. Debbie had her back turned to the door, and didn't see Quincy walked in.

97

"Hey girl, what's going on?"

"Quincy, where you at? I thought you said you were going to meet me up here at the diner so you could do Gigi's hair for her portfolio."

"Honey, I'm right behind you."

The ladies all laughed.

"Hi Quincy, it's nice to see you again," Ms. Ruby said.

Quincy bended down to give her a hug. "Hi Ms. Ruby, I see you got it looking nice up in here. I see you have fine-ass pictures of your grandson on the walls too. Only if he were..." He paused and smiled at Ms. Ruby playfully. "...I'm just playing, Ms. Ruby. I don't do young meat. I like that old, rough meat."

"Yeah you two are related. Y'all a mess, I tell you," Ms. Ruby said. "Quincy, this is Gigi, and Connie."

"Honey, I love that bag Connie said. I bet that cost you an arm and a leg." "Nah, girl, I got this as a gift from my firefighte friend. I let him pull on my arms and legs, and it pops out goodies like this."

They all laughed.

"Quincy, why the hell are you lugging around a suitcase? A shiny one at that," Debbie asked.

"Girl, this is my on-the-go salon on wheels. Whenever I have to go to a client's house, this is what I take because it has everything in it, I need—from makeup, to nails, to wigs. You name it, I got it. My duffl bag has my pajamas because we having a sleepover. You did say you have a Jacuzzi, right, Cuz?"

"Yes Quincy, I have a Jacuzzi. Let me drop this money off and make sure Lance mopped up back here, then we can leave." Debbie went to the back.

"Gigi, your hair is beautiful already, but I can make it look glamorous," Quincy began to vogue. "Girl, I got the right color and style for you." He rubbed his hands through Gigi's hair. "And Connie,

I don't discriminate, I do white girls' hair too. I'll hook you up. I tell you what, you take a few pictures of me in my new Versace pajamas so I can send them to my policemen friend. Maybe then, he'll want to arrest me." Quincy frowned, looking like Shanaynay from Martin.

"Quincy, you're too funny," Gigi said. "Call me Quita, girl. You family."

CHAPTER ELEVEN

"Well, this is my home, Connie." Ms. Ruby gave Connie a tour of her home. "Here's the wine opener. Y'all lucky I had one, I received this as a housewarming gift."

"Ms. Ruby, your house is beautiful. Thanks for the wine opener."

"You're welcome, child. Now I'm going to video chat with my grandson for a few. Then I'm going to watch a classic and go to bed." Ms. Ruby walked Connie to the back of the house, letting her out. "Have fun!"

"I'm back!" Connie passed the corkscrew to Debbie. "Ms. Ruby has a beautiful house."

"Yes, I love it," Gigi said.

"These sangria daiquiris are going to be good." Debbie blended ice with the bottle of sangria.

"Girl, hurry it up. I been wanting a cocktail all day." Quincy combed through Gigi's hair. "Gigi, since you remind me of La La Anthony, I got a style for you."

"She does put you in the mind of La La." Connie set up the camera equipment.

"What you know about La La?" Debbie poured the drinks. "One, I love Carmelo Anthony, and two, I watch Power."

Connie adjusted her camera lens.

"So, Quincy, what you have in mind?" Gigi rubbed her fingers through her hair.

"You'll see." He grabbed a glass of sangria. "I'm going to do a short and a long style so you will have two differe t ones for your portfolio."

"Gigi, trust me, my nephew can do hair in his sleep, so he will have you looking glamorous." Debbie passed Connie a glass of sangria.

"Oh, I'm not doubting he can't, I'm just excited. This will be my first time taking professional pictures." She looked in the mirror that's hanging on the door.

"Girl, you were right, this daiquiri is good." Connie continue sipping on her drink.

"Yes, girl, I must agree." Quincy tapped Connie's cup with his. "So, Gigi, how long you been singing?" He worked on trimming Gigi's split ends.

"I always sang, it's just something I like to do. It's like, I can hear a song once and can sing it back. But I enjoy writing my own music."

"That's good that you write you own music, especially if it's something people will want to hear instead of having to hire someone to write songs for you. That's extra coins you don't have to spend."

"You're right, Nephew, that do make sense."

"So, Gigi, I know your mother must be excited about you auditioning, huh?"

"My mom doesn't know." Gigi smirked. "I haven't spoken to my mother in over two years."

"Quincy, it's a long story." Debbie blended more sangria. "I don't think Gigi wants to go into that."

"It's ok, Ms. Debbie, it's time I stop holding it in."

"Now, I don't want you up in here crying over things, it's not that serious."

"Nah, I'm good, Q." Gigi looked at him up in the mirror.

"Well, girl, spill the beans," Quincy said.

"I think it's time for round two." Connie lifted her cup up. "Well, my mom went and married this man, and everything seemed to be cool at first until he started trying to come at me

"Come at you! Come at you how, girl?" He looked at her through the reflection in the mirror

"He used to flirt with me, then it went from flirting to him touching me and pushing himself on me."

"Girl, shut your mouth."

"That's what I said when she finally told me." Debbie poured round two.

"I hate a nasty motherfucker," Connie said.

"Ok, Connie, I never heard you use that word. It's the liquor talking already."

"Nah, I'm just saying, I hate when a man pushes up on women when they know that's not what she wants. No means no."

"So, girl, what happened next?"

"One day I was sitting on the couch watching TV and he came in there sitting on the couch with me. He then began to feel up my legs, and I was pushing his hands away. I tried to get up and he grabbed me, and when he grabbed me, I fell on his lap and my mom walked in," Gigi said.

"Quincy, girl, then what?"

He placed the flat iron on the holder

"When she walked in, he started hollering, talking about how I jumped on him trying to give him a lap dance." "Girl, no he didn't. Then what?"

"I was trying to tell my mom he was lying and that he'd been trying to flirt and sleep with me. She then asked why didn't I say anything to her before if he was trying to sleep with me. I told her I tried but she was too drunk or high to remember. She believed him over me and told me to get out."

"No mother should put a man before their own daughter."

Connie sipped on the drink.

"Yeah, that there wasn't cool for her to do. Trust and believe, she'll realize that one day," Debbie said.

"I'm a mother. I know she has to be wondering what's going on with you. I know she's really thinking in the back of her head she fucked up."

"Google, play Jamie Foxx, "Blame It on the Alcohol.""

The music started to play on the background and Connie got up dancing.

"Girl, it's going to be ok. Things fall back in place for a reason and your place is coming. If you can sing, the way I'm going to have you looking, that record deal will be yours. So, can you sing for us what you're going to sing at the audition?" Quincy asked.

"Sure!"

"Auntie, turn that down for a minute so I can hear Gigi while the curling iron heat up." Quincy took a drink, and Gigi stood up and began to sing her song. After a few moments, tears began to roll down all their faces.

"Gigi, that is beautiful. It matches your story, especially the part when you say, "I was that bird that felt alone, who was pushed out my nest and kicked out my home." Girl you got this," Quincy said. "Ms. Ruby was right, Gigi. Sing your song." Debbie walked over to Gigi and gave her a hug, and Connie followed.

"I love it," Connie said tearfully. "How can a mother do that to their child? Abandon them . . .?"

"I'm ok now that I can talk about it. Quincy, I hope you're right about things falling back in place."

Quincy was singing. "It will all work out for the good of them who love the Lord." He paused. "That their song comes from the Reverend Milton Brunson and the Thompson Community Singers of Chicago." Quincy grabbed Gigi's chin gently. "It will work out."

"I like you, Quincy. You can come spend a night at my house anytime." Connie said.

"Next time, girl night at your house." Quincy touched Gigi's hair softly. "Ok Gigi, turn around and look in the mirror."

"Oh, my freaking God, it looks beautiful. My hair never looked this good before," Gigi said.

"I told you, my nephew can do this in his sleep," Debbie said. "Gigi, it's beautiful. You really look like La La now." Connie grabbed her camera and begins snapping pictures. "Look, I just want you to act natural. Act like I'm not even here"

"What you doing, Connie? I hope those aren't for the portfolio," Debbie said.

"That's exactly what they are for. This shows her in everyday life." Connie continued to snap pictures. "Now Gigi, pull out your notebook and sat here on the couch with one leg folded behind you."

"Ok Connie, do your thing. I see you in your zone."

"Once I do these, Gigi can change into her other clothes then I'll snap those."

"And Connie, don't forget about me. I'm going to go change into my pajamas. Auntie, let me get towels so I can shower really quick." I'll do the jacuzzi another time.

"I have towels in the linen cabinet in the bathroom, Nephew," Debbie said.

"Ok, Auntie, while I'm taking my shower can you make another pitcher of sangria?" Quincy walked off into the bathroom and turns around and looks at Gigi. "Gigi, you got this."

CHAPTER TWELVE

"Gigi, these are beautiful." Ms. Ruby looked through the portfolio. "Connie, you did a good job. And Debbie, your nephew really got her hair looking good. Maybe he could do something to this here." Ms. Ruby patted her hair.

"Yes, they both did a good job. Thanks again, Connie," Gigi said.

"And Ms. Ruby, you were right about Gigi singing her on song.

She sang it for all us and she had us all crying. It's a beautiful song," Debbie said.

"Like I said, can't nobody tell her story but Gigi," Ms. Ruby said.

The doorbell chimed and suddenly Scooter entered.

"Look what the wind blew up in here," Debbie walked out from behind the counter to hug Scooter. Ms. Ruby turned around to see who Debbie was talking about.

"Scooter!" She stood up to hug him. "I was just talking to you last night on the phone. Why didn't you tell me you were coming?" "I wanted to surprise you, Grandma." Scooter kissed her on the cheek. "How you been doing though, Ms. Debbie? I see you got it smelling good up in here like you used to have it smelling over there at the old building we use to stay in."

"I'm doing good, Scooter. It's sure nice to see you again." She hugged him again before pulling out her cell phone and snapping pictures of the two of them together.

"We had a team meeting today at Soldier Field and I thought I'd surprise you after I was done, Grandma. Plus, I want some of Debbie's famous fried chicken," Scooter said.

"You're Calvin Walker aka Scooter! Most touchdowns in high school history as a quarterback. Two MVPs and All-American," Lance said stuttering. He walked up to shake Scooter's hand.

"I see I have a fan here, Grandma. You must be Lance, my grandma told me all about you." Scooter hit Lance in the arm playfully. "I've seen you play on TV. Is Soldier Field really that big? I've never seen the stadium!"

"Yes, Lance, it's a big stadium. I tell you what, on opening day, I will give you tickets and front row seats too. How would you like that?"

"I'd love it!," Lance shouted.

"Ok, I'll give my grandma the tickets."

"Hello, and what about me?" Debbie looked at Scooter with her arms folded across her chest, rolling her eyes.

"Now how can I forget about you, Debbie?" Scooter asked. "Ms. Debbie, can you take a picture of me and Scooter?" "Sure, Lance, then you have to get back to work. Those tables in the back need to be cleaned and reset." "Ok."

Debbie took a picture of Lance and Scooter as they smiled before her.

"Thanks, Scooter! It was nice to meet you," Lance stuttered "Nice to meet you too, Lance," Scooter said.

"Scooter, this is Connie, one of the servers."

"Hi Connie, my grandma talks highly of you too." He shook her hand.

"And this is Gigi," Ms. Ruby said.

"Now Grandma, you hid this secret from me. You didn't tell me how beautiful Ms. Garcia was."

Gigi was shocked, "You know my name?"

"My grandma told me your name and she talks highly about you too, but she never talked about how fine you are.

"Ok Scooter, I'm getting jealous," Debbie said. "Ms. Debbie, you know you will always be my girl." "Thank you for the compliment." Gigi blushed. "So, do you like football?"

"I know it's a game where people get hit a lot."

Scooter giggled. "Oh, it's a lot more to it. I'm about to order me something to eat, would it be ok if you joined me?"

Gigi looked at Ms. Ruby and Debbie.

"I don't see why not. Debbie and Connie can handle the floor," Ms. Ruby said

"Rob is off, so I'll cook your food. What would you like for your sides?" Debbie asked.

"I would like greens and Mac. Gigi, what are you having?" I'll have the fettuccini alfredo pasta. Thanks, Ms. Debbie."

"Well, I'll let you young folks talk. I'll be in my offic if you need me." Ms. Ruby walked away to her offic

"So, Gigi, you like working here?" Scooter gazed at Gigi as he fumbled with the menu. Gigi blushed as she noticed Scooter staring at her with a smile.

"I love it, and I love your grandma for giving me a job and a place to live."

"You know my grandma is all I got, and we don't keep secrets from each other. She told me your situation because I wasn't liking the fact that a stranger was staying at my granny's home. If you understand what I mean."

I most definitely understand that, but she was persistent," Gigi said.

"That's my grandma for you. She's always had a big heart. Hey, I'm sorry that you had to go through that stuff with your mom's husband. I can't stand dudes like that. It's good you got away, but I know you may still be missing your mom. I know I miss mine."

"Yeah, Ms. Ruby told me about your mom. Sorry, Scooter."

"Nothing to be sorry about. I know she's still with me or I wouldn't be playing football again. Look, my mom is gone, and I will never be able to see her here on this earth again, but your mom is still alive. Maybe one day you should try talking to her again. I know you still think about her no matter how mad you may be. She's your mom."

"I tried, but she didn't want to talk. All she cares about is him and getting high," Gigi said.

"That's why I say try again. Sometimes when people on drugs or drinking, they don't be thinking clearly. All their thinking about is chasing that high. I know, I was chasing a high too but a different high. I was popping pills, prescriptions pills, opioids after I got shot. My grandma and coach tried to help me but I wasn't trying to hear none of that at the time," Scooter said. "All I wanted to do was feel numb. I didn't want to feel the pain so to not feel that, I popped pills. My coach noticed first, then told my grandma. That's when I ended up going to rehab and that's what saved my life and got me back playing football. All I'm saying, Gigi, is anything is possible."

Debbie placed a plate of food in the hot window and rings the food bell. "Fried chicken: up! Alfredo: up!"

Gigi got up and grabbed the food, placing the plates on the counter. "Can I get you something to drink, Scooter?" She grabbed two glasses and filled them up with ice

"Sure! A Coke would be nice."

"Finally, they're leaving." Connie opened the register, placing money into it.

"You ok, Connie?" Gigi asked.

"I'm good! It's just irritating how old men be all down my shirt invading my body. I don't do seniors; I like them younger than that."

Scooter chuckled.

"That was my last table. I'm about to go take pictures of this lady and her five dogs," Connie said

"Ok, so you got back into the photography thing?" Gigi asked. "After I did your portfolio, it's like it gave me my groove back.

I haven't did this since my husband died and I got you to thank Gigi. I'll see you later and nice meeting you Scooter. I'll see you at home opener." Connie clocked out and went to say goodbye to Debbie and Ms. Ruby.

"I like Connie. She's a cool white chick," Gigi said. "So, she did your portfolio? What type of portfolio?"

"It's a picture portfolio she did for me for my audition I'm doing this weekend," Gigi said.

"Audition for what?" Scooter was intrigued. "It's an audition for the show Your Big Chance."

"Oh, now that's dope. I love that show and how they showcase local talent. Congratulations!" Scooter gave Gigi a hug. "So, what are you singing for the audition?"

"It's something I wrote."

"So, you not only sing, you write your own songs too? Now that's some straight Alicia Keys there. So, how long have you been writing your own music?"

"For some time now. It helps me to cope with my feelings due to some things I been through."

"So, it's therapeutic for you." "Yes, it is."

"That's dope! Whatever works for you that will get you through."

"Look at you sounding like your grandma." Gigi bumped him with her elbow.

"Yes, she rubs off easily." He bit into the chicken

"You're blessed to have someone to love you like she does. She talks about you all the time. I used to get that from my mom until she met her husband. I mean everything was ok. He seemed cool from the beginning, then it was like a 360 just happened out the blue. First, she started drinking and she never drank like she do now. I mean she'd have some wine with her girlfriends but now it's wine, vodka, gin, and blow."

"I think you need to go see her," Scooter said.

"I don't know where she moved to and I don't know any of his family and my mom's family stay down south."

"Look, if you really want to find her, I can help you do so." "How could you do that, Scooter?"

"One of the players on the team, their father owns a PI business," Scooter mentioned.

"PI?" Gigi asked.

"Private investigator business."

"Ok. How much does he charge for that?"

"I tell you what, how about you come see me practice tomorrow and we can talk to him then? This will be on the house; he owes me one."

"Why does he owe you?"

"He bet me he could hit every target in practice with the football, and let's just say I hit them all and he didn't."

"That will be nice if you could get him to do it. I mean I do want to know if she's ok."

"So, I'll pick you up here tomorrow morning..." Scooter finished up the last bite of his food. "...for practice and Saturday, I'll escort you to your audition, if that'd be ok with you." Scooter looked Gigi in the eyes.

"I would like that," Gigi said blushing.

"I'm going to go back here and tell my grandma I'm about to go. I have to meet some of the guys at the gym. I'll be seeing you soon, Gigi." He walked off to the back

"I see y'all over here looking all cute." Debbie walked from the kitchen to the counter. "Scooter is a nice kid, Gigi. He has a good heart."

"Yeah, I can tell he's a cool dude. He gets that from Ms. Ruby," Gigi said.

"So, what you and Ms. Ruby's grandson talking about?"

Connie walked around the counter to pour herself a cup of coffee

"Connie, it's official you are hereby now labeled 'the white hen'."

Gigi started to laugh.

"Spill the beans, Gigi." Debbie filled up a cup with sweet tea. "He asked me if I would like to go to practice with him tomorrow and he asked if he could escort me to the audition."

"Ok, so that means you're going to be rolling up in style. The boy drives a blue and orange Lamborghini. Look, it's out front."

Gigi and Connie ran to the window looking out at Scooter's car.

"Damn that's nice. I would love to snap that," Connie said. "That's his car for real, Ms. Debbie?"

"Yeah, one of them," Debbie said.

"Ok Scooter, I guess Gigi can have tomorrow off so you can take her to meet this PI guy." Ms. Ruby walked from the back with Scooter, walking him to the front door.

"It was nice meeting you, Connie. Nice seeing you again, Debbie—the chicken was banging. I'll be picking you up tomorrow, Ms. Gigi. Goodnight ladies." And with that Scooter walked out.

"Ms. Ruby, what'd he ask you about tomorrow?" Gigi asked.

"He said he wanted to take you to see this guy, but I know my Scooter. He wants to take you around the guys so he can show you off.

"Well, it's not no date or nothing, just business." "I know my grandson; it's going to be a date."

"Girl, I wish I could go. I would love to be on that field looking at all them tight asses in them shorts," Connie said.

"Oh Connie, we going to be there on opening night. So, we will get to look at plenty of tight asses," Debbie said. "Y'all too fast for my speed," Ms. Ruby said. The doorbell chimes, and Caesar walked in.

"Hey baby, I didn't know you were coming up here," Debbie walked around from behind the counter to hug Caesar.

"I wanted to stop by and give you this for the play tonight."

Caesar passed her a Nordstrom bag and an Aldo bag.

"Hey Caesar, I see somebody been shopping," Gigi said. "Yeah, I see." Debbie peeked inside the Nordstrom bag.

"Look at it when you get home, baby. I'll be by to pick you up around 7 p.m. tonight. The play starts at 8 p.m., so please be ready at Seven o'clock, and let me get a piece of that apple pie too, with a sweet tea, Caesar said.

"Baby, you can get whatever you like." Debbie grabbed his cheeks, kissing him on the lips. She then grabbed the slice of pie, and put it in a small to-go container for him.

"It was nice seeing you again, ladies. I'll see you tonight." Caesar walked out.

"I guess it's me and you tonight, Ms. Ruby. Let's rent A Raisin in the Sun with Puff Daddy Combs and eat popcorn," Gigi said

"Ok, sounds like a plan to me. Let's lock up and leave," Ms. Ruby said.

CHAPTER THIRTEEN

Gigi and Scooter walked into the diner.

"That was some intense practice," Gigi said.

"Oh, that was nothing compared to what we normally do. Coach let us off easy since it got hot," Scooter replied

"I see y'all made it back. So, Gigi, how was it being out there with all that testosterone?" Debbie asked.

"It was something different, I must say," Gigi answered

"Y'all hungry?" Debbie stood at the register.

"I could eat something. How about a chicken Caesar for me, with extra chicken," Scooter said.

"What you having, Gigi?" Debbie asked.

"I'll have what Scooter is having, with some garlic bread."

Debbie rang their order in. "Rob, when you're done with them orders, come out here so you can meet Ms. Ruby's grandson."

"I'll be out there in a few. Salads take no time to make. I have the garlic bread on the grill now," Rob said.

"Where is my grandma, Debbie?" Scooter took a seat at the barstool.

"She's at my nephew's shop getting her hair done. She said she's going to see Gigi audition. Connie took her so she could get her hair done too. What y'all drinking?" Debbie filled up two glasses with ice.

"I'll have a unsweetened tea with lemons, Debbie," Scooter said.

"I'll have a sweet tea with lemon," Gigi added.

The food bell rang. "Two chicken salads: up!" Rob yelled.

Debbie grabbed the food out the window, and placed the plates in front of Scooter and Gigi.

"So, my grandma wants to go see you audition too, huh?" Scooter asked.

"Yes, we were talking about it after you picked Gigi up this morning. Hell, we're all going to show our support," Debbie answered.

"That's really nice of you all. I would love for you guys to be there," Gigi said.

"We will, front and center. We could all ride together," Scooter told her.

"How we all going to fit in that little car, Calvin?

"Ok, I see y'all on a first-name basis?" Debbie was surprised. "No, we can all ride in the Range Rover. There will be more than enough room."

Rob walked from the kitchen to the diner. "What up, man? I'm Rob, the cook." He then walked up to Scooter and shook his hand. "You a bad boy. I see your numbers."

"Awe, there will be more of those to come. I told my grandma that I'll get you guys some tickets for the season opener."

"Now man, that will be cool. I try to make a game at least once a year but them damn tickets be high as hell."

"I tell you what, Rob, I can get you season tickets for this year if you like."

Rob stood smiling ear to ear excitedly. "Hell yeah, I like." "You can take Lance to some of the games if it wouldn't be a problem."

"You talking about Lance? Nah, that won't be a problem at all. Well, thanks again, man. It was nice to finally meet you in person."

114

Rob walked back to the kitchen. The doorbell chimed, and Connie walked in, carrying a bag of groceries.

"We're back." She set the bag on the counter. "You like my hair, Debbie?"

"It's cute Connie. I see you to Ms. Ruby, what'd you do, put a rinse in your hair?"

"Hey Grandma." Scooter got up to give her a hug. "Let me not touch your hair now. I know how you black women get when you get y'all hair done."

"Hey baby. You like it?" Ms. Ruby posed. "I love it. Who did it again?"

Debbie's nephew. He has a whole salon," Ms. Ruby said. "Well, he did a good job. I'm about to head out. I have some play films to look at. I'll call you later, Grandma. See you later, Gigi." Scooter kissed Gigi on the cheek. "Ms. Debbie and Connie, see you soon."

"So, Gigi, what was that about?" Debbie asked. "What!" Gigi yelled.

"You know what. The kiss on the cheek, what." "He kissed me."

"I didn't see you stopping him. Hell, I wouldn't stop him neither. That young man is fine and smart. I'm just saying," Debbie said.

"Yes, he is," Connie added.

"Oh, and rich. He's a catch, Gigi, and Ms. Ruby raised him right," Debbie said.

"I see y'all over here playing matchmaker," Ms. Ruby commented.

"I don't think we need to try to match them up, Scooter already did that," Connie said.

Debbie walked like she'd got swag like Scooter. "I'll see you tonight, Gigi," she laughed. "So, what y'all got planned tonight?"

"Oh nothing, we going to Skype each other while I practice my song," Gigi said.

"Ain't nothing to practice, you got that song down pat," Debbie said.

"I think she just like hearing us say it to boost her confidence.

Ms. Ruby patted Gigi on the shoulder. "I see we all have the same stylist." Ms. Ruby touched Gigi's hair. "Quincy did a 360 on all our head."

"Gigi, tell 'em! We're going to be performing all over the world, Debbie said.

"What you mean we going to be performing?" Ms. Ruby looked at Debbie through the rims of her glasses. "Unless you can sing like Gigi, you will be behind the scenes," she laughed.

"I'm good with that, as long as I make sure Gigi gets the right contract, royalties, and tours." Debbie suggested.

"And as Quincy say, the coins." Connie snapped her fingers. "That's the plan, Debbie." Gigi scrolled through her phone.

After a moment, the doorbell chimed. The Pastor walked in, but the woman on his arm wasn't the first lady. The Pastor looked around nervously. He repeatedly looked over his shoulder as they waited to be seated.

"You got a guest, Debbie." Connie went about making a fresh pot of coffee

Debbie whispered, "Lawd, now who the hell is this THOT?"

I'm about to go in the office I have to make a call." Ms. Ruby got up from the stool.

"I'm going to sit here and finish writing this song I been working on." Gigi pulled her notepad out her backpack.

"I see you got guest Connie looking towards the door. I'll get that." Debbie grabbed her apron and walked to the door, putting it on.

"Good evening, Pastor, will it just be two today?"

116

"Good evening, young lady. Yes, it will just be two. Can we please get a table all the way in the back corner? You know, for a private meeting." He stood, scoping out the place.

"Sure, Pastor." Debbie grabbed menus and walked the Pastor to the back of restaurant. She placed them on the table as they sit down. "May I get you something to drink?"

"I would like to get a coffee."

"And for you, ma'am?"

"She'll have the same."

Debbie walked off

"I don't believe this short fat, round body, I'll-pay-you-on-Tuesday–looking ass man had the audacity to bring another woman in here. Now I see why them church hens be talking about him." Debbie grabbed two cups and rinsed them out, filling them up with coffee. "Then he had the raisins to ask me to sit him in the back in the corner." Debbie shook her head.

"The raisins?" Connie asked. She looked puzzled as she walks to the register, cashing her guest's check out.

"Yes, girl the raisins. When a man walk, pay attention to how he walks." Debbie set the coffee cups on saucer. "If a man got some big boys down there, he walk with a swag. That right there will let you know if he is working with something. But if a man walks and it look like his legs is rubbing up there by the raisins, that means you're going to get a branch instead of a trunk, if you know what I mean."

"Oh, Ms. Debbie, you nasty," Gigi said.

"Girl, I just know the anatomy of a man, and I know those are raisins down there." Debbie laughed as she walked off with her coffee

"Debbie need her own talk show," Connie said.

"I can see her doing the Wendy Williams thing," Gigi giggled. "She'd have so many women mad, because she'd be telling the truth."

"I can see her and Quincy doing a show. Imagine them two."

"Yeah you right. I can see that," Gigi said.

"Do you believe Mr. Raisin net ordered the chick the same thing he orders his wife when they come in here." Debbie put an order in on the register. "Gigi, tell Lance to come out here and grab them few dishes from the tables in the back."

Gigi did was she was told and walked to the back.

"Rob, make sure that steak is medium-well, I forgot to put that in," Debbie yelled.

Rob hit the food bell. "Heard!"

"Ms. Debbie, I cleaned the tables off in the back. I wanted to know if you could send the picture you took of me and Scooter," Lance said.

"How you want me to send it, Lance? You have an email?" Debbie asked.

"No, I have a new phone I bought with my check." Lance put the dish bin in the window. He pulled his new cell phone out to show Debbie.

"Ok, Lance, you have an iPhone, huh? Do you know how to work it or do you need any help?" Connie grabbed a slice of strawberry cheesecake from the cooler.

"It's the iPhone X. I don't need any help, Ms. Connie. I know how to work it just like my computer," Lance stuttered.

"Ok, Lance, give me your number, and I will send you the picture," Debbie said.

"Thanks, Ms. Debbie. I can't wait to show my friend." Lance waited for the picture. After a few moments, he smiled. "Got it!" He grabbed the dish bin and headed to the kitchen.

"Steak medium-well: up! Stuffed chicken: up!" Rob yelled

Debbie grabbed the food from the window and walked it over to the Pastor. "I have your food here." She placed the stuffed chicken in front of the lady and the steak in front of the Pastor. She balanced the now-empty platter on her hip. "I have some A1 steak sauce here for you, Pastor. Is there anything else I may get for you two?"

"I think we are just fine." The Pastor cut into the steak. "Mmm-hmm, this here steak looks good and smells good too." He cut a piece of the steak, placing it in his mouth.

"If we need anything, I'll let you know." Debbie walked away, placing the food tray back in the window. While Connie scrolled through her phone at the counter, sipping on a cup of coffee

"Ms. Ruby's back there taking a nap. She looking tired," Gigi said.

"Yeah, she had a long day," Connie answered.

"Ms. Debbie, do you have a stamp I could get? I would've asked Ms. Ruby, but she dozed off," Gigi asked

"Yeah, look in that corner drawer where I keep the stationary stuff. There should be some up in there. So, what you need a stamp for?" Debbie grabbed a bag of salt-and-sour chips off the rack and poured a Coke. She sat on the barstool next to Connie.

"I'm writing my brother." Gigi looked through the drawer.

"That's nice. I bet he'll be happy to hear from you," Connie said.

"Once that table leaves, we're done for the day. Plus, Ms. Ruby needs to get home to her own bed."

The doorbell chimed and First Lady walked in with Sister Mary.

"I told you that GPS app works." Sister Mary said.

First Lady looked towards the back of the diner and walked over to the table where the Pastor was sitting with the other woman.

"What the Hell is going on in here? First Lady stood at the head of the table, taking her earrings and wig off. "Sister Mary, hold my stuff.

"Baby, baby, this is not what you think." The Pastor stood up.

"And I thought the reality shows I be watching be good."

Sister Mary said as she pulled out her phone and stood recording everything.

"I don't want to hear that "baby" shit." First Lady reached in her jacket pocket and pulled out Vaseline, putting it on her face.

"This is all uncalled for, baby." The Pastor tried to grab the Vaseline. "The young lady just needed someone to talk to and I thought I'd give her some pastor advice. That's all, baby."

Debbie, Connie, and Gigi looked on in amazement from the barstools.

"Advice, my ass! He was trying to get them raisins wet," Debbie said.

Connie and Gigi laughed as they all watch. The Pastor's Lady Friend stood up quickly.

"Look heifer, your so-called husband's been coming to me for years. Don't act like this is brand new to you. You know your husband like hoes. When he's not with you, he's with me spending them church offerings.

"The shit just hit the fan." Debbie looked on, munching on the chips like they were popcorn.

"First Lady, I told you he was spending money on other women." Sister Mary continued to record on her phone. Before the Pastor could open his mouth, First Lady knocked him upside his head before reaching over him to try to swing at the Pastor's Lady Friend. The Pastor held First Lady, and talked to his Lady Friend at the table, pleading with her.

"Please just leave, please. She carries a gun in her purse."

"Honey, it ain't that serious. Fighting you will mess up my hair and nails your husband just paid to have done with them church tithes." The Pastor's Lady Friend strutted off swiftly and turned around. "He'll be back, trust me."

"I don't believe you around here buying ass with the church money. You got me up in church and in here looking like a damn fool. But no more." First Lady grabbed her wig back from Sister Mary and put it on. "I'm done with your short-dick ass." She reached into her purse.

"Please baby, don't shoot me. I'm sorry, baby. I love you. Please don't shoot."

First Lady pulled something out of her purse. "It's not that serious. I'd rather get my money now, as opposed to waiting for you to die. I want a divorce." She placed papers in his hand.

"You been served!" Sister Mary laughed and continued to record on her phone.

"Come on, Sister Mary, I got some dirty clothes and shoes to throw out at home." First Lady and Sister Mary walked out together.

"Here's your check, Pastor." Debbie, passed him the check. The Pastor pulled some cash out of his wallet and dropped it on the table.

"Keep the change," he said and then walked out.

Gigi was surprised. "OMG, I can't believe that just happened. Now, that was some real Jerry Springer right there."

"If Pastor would've let his wife loose, she would have whooped that woman's ass. She was heated to the point you could see the steam coming out her nose and ears," Connie said.

"Something told me he was going to get caught up one day the way people be in here talking about his affairs. But wait, what got me is when the First Lady took off her wig and whipped out the Vaseline and started putting it on her face." Debbie bended over laughing so hard, as tears of laughter began to roll down her face. "I'm going to have Lance clean this table while I run the end-of-day on the register, then we can leave."

"I'll get Ms. Ruby up." Gigi walked to the back.

"I've never seen anything like that up close and personal." Connie got up and grabbed the dirty cups from the counter and put them in the dish bin as Lance walked by. "That was so real."

"Girl, yes it was. I was telling Ms. Ruby," Debbie said.

"I see I slept through all the action. I just been feeling tired lately. I got a headache and took some Tylenol and dozed off." Ms. Ruby sat on barstool.

"I used to get migraines, Ms. Ruby." Connie reached under the counter to grab her bag. "Do it hurt really bad, Ms. Ruby?"

"You might want to go see about that, Ms. Ruby," Debbie said. "Yeah, Ms. Ruby, how long have you had migraines?"

Rob and Lance walked in the front with the ladies.

"We all set in the back and cleaned up," Rob said.

"Ms. Ruby, I mopped out the freezer and cooler. It's pizza and game night at my cousin's house. I'll see you guys later." Lance unlocked the door and exited, his hands fumbling.

"Speaking of pizza, I guess I will order that for me and my lady friend," Rob said.

"Lady friend, huh?" Debbie said.

"Yeah, she's someone I been seeing from the meetings I attend. She's coming over to my house and we're going to watch The Best Man: Part 2."

"That movie was good. And I must say Morris Chestnut was looking fine," Connie said

"Yeah, Morris can get it." Debbie grabbed her bag, and then grabbed Ms. Ruby's purse and passed it to her. "What Beyoncé say in her song "Drunk in Love"? We will be all night, and I'll be grinding on that wood, I'm swerving on that." Debbie did the belly dance.

"Girl, you too much. I don't think Caesar would like that," Ms. Ruby said.

Rob cleared his throat. "Yeah, I agree with Ms. Ruby," He

laughed. "I don't think Caesar would like that."

"Caesar can be my Jay-Z and I can give him my Becky." Debbie opened her mouth, making a smacking sound with her tongue. Rob shook his head, and they all left as Debbie set the alarm.

CHAPTER FOURTEEN

"Girl, I'm excited like it's me that's going up there to audition," Debbie said.

The four women walked into the diner, turned the alarm off, and grabbed two coffee pots to put them on to brew

"I'm nervous and excited." Gigi sat on barstool next to Ms. Ruby. "Ms. Debbie, I think I'll have a coffee today, too.

"Girl, you will be just fine." Ms. Ruby walked to the register and put the starting money in it. "The way I been hearing you sing around the house."

"And up in here too," Debbie added.

"You got it. Mustard seed, child. Just keep thinking "mustard seed," Ms. Ruby said.

The doorbell chimed and Connie entered. "Hey ladies." She walked behind the counter and placed her bag under it. She sees the coffee and sighs happily. "Yes, coffee. So, Gigi, it's your big day. You ready?"

"Ready as I can get. Just a little nervous."

"Girl, that's a natural reaction. You're human. It's up to you how you react to it."

"Ok, Ms. Connie Angelou." Debbie grabbed four cups and fills them up with coffee

"So, what happens after you audition? Do they tell you if

you won on the spot? Or do they call and tell you?" Ms. Ruby stood pouring cream in her coffee

"So, from what I read, they call in ten people to audition. We all do the auditions, and from there they pick three people to go to the semifinals," Gigi said

"She blew on her coffee before taking a sip. "Well, I don't know who's going against you, but I know I can say the Lord is going to be with you, and you got this."

"Oh, ok, I had it wrong. I thought you just had to go this round and audition and if they like you, they'll bring you in the studio to record with a contract," Debbie said.

"You were close, Ms. Debbie."

"But you say you her manager." Ms. Ruby smirked at Debbie and chuckled.

"The contestants have to sing a song that the judges give to them. That is for the first audition. For the semifinals the contestants get to sing the song of their choice," Gigi said.

"Ok, that sounds fair. I am with Ms. Ruby on this one, Gigi, you got this. It was like you were born to sing," Connie said.

"Awe, thanks Connie." Gigi wrapped her arms around Connie's shoulders. "That's sweet of you to say."

"I told Lance and Rob they did not have to come in today. We're going to open for a few hours, then we are heading out to Gigi's audition," Ms. Ruby said.

"Yup let's knock out this rush, then we can be on our way. Gigi, can you roll that silverware that Lance left in the back?" Debbie filled the sugar caddies

After a few moments, the door chimed, and the Delivery Man walked in. "Hello, I'm looking for a Gigi." He took a towel out of his pocket and wiped his forehead.

"I'm Gigi, but I didn't order anything." Gigi walked up to the

Delivery Man with a confused look on her face.

"Here's the paper." He passed paperwork to Gigi. Debbie walked out from behind the counter, being nosy.

"Let me see the paperwork there." Debbie took paperwork from Gigi and looked it over.

"Where do you want me to set it?" Delivery Man said.

"You could set it right there in the back. Up against the wall." Ms. Ruby answered.

"Now, Ms. Ruby, you then went and bought a Juke Box." Debbie looked at the package.

"Will this be fine right here?" Delivery Man asked

"Yes, that'll be fine," Debbie said

"Ms. Ruby, you got a juke box for me," Gigi said.

"Yes, for you because when you get to making them records, I want to put all your music in there so people will know you started your life over here," Ms. Ruby said.

"And this is why I love y'all." Gigi started to tear up.

"I am going to unbox this and set it up for you ladies. Once I'm done, you will be all set to go. You can also program up to twenty songs to play automatically," the Delivery Man said.

"I like this thing already. I never had anyone to buy me anything." Gigi hugged Ms. Ruby again.

"You're all set. Here is the manual for the machine. I could quickly show you, ma'am, how to work and program it if you like," the Delivery Man said.

"You can show Gigi and she will show us." Ms. Ruby walked off and headed towards her office. "We have to get ready for this rush

The Delivery Man went over instructions with Gigi. "It sure smells good up in here. Can I see a menu so I can get something to go?"

"Sure!" Gigi passed the Delivery Man a menu. "Once you're

126

ready, just have a seat at the counter, and I will take your order." She seemed distracted, chewing on her thumbnail absentmindedly.

"Gigi, you ok?" Connie asked.

"Yes, the delivery man would like something to go so he's looking over the menu."

"Oh ok! We need you to be focused for tonight." Connie got up from the barstool and adjusted her apron. "I see my construction guys are about to come in so let me grab their drinks. Two coffees and two Cokes!" Connie filled up cups with drinks. As she did so, the door chimed and the construction workers enter.

"Hey fellows, have a seat and I will be right with you. I am getting your drinks now." Connie welcomed them and the four guys went to take a seat at a table.

"Are you all set to order, sir?" Gigi pulled out her notepad. "Yes, I would like the smothered gyro sandwich with the fries and drink special." He handed Gigi the menu back. "Can I please have my meat grilled and extra sauce on the side?"

Gigi walked over to the register to place the man's order. "Debbie, make sure you put extra sauce on the side."

"Heard!"

Connie rang in her order. "This should be a nice tip. Debbie, make all those steaks medium." Connie turned around, looking at Debbie in the food window.

"Oh, I see you got your regulars over there, and it's pay day too. That's about a twenty-dollar tip, if not more," Debbie said. "Yeah, they always tip good." Connie got a round of refills for the table

Debbie hit the food bell. "Smothered gyro special: up! Grilled with extra sauce."

Gigi grabbed the food order and put it in a to-go bag. "Here is your food, sir. Is there anything else I can get for you?"

"No, young lady. Thank you! Enjoy your day. The rest is

yours." He passed Gigi money for his bill and walked out.

"Gigi, you know how to program the jukebox, right?" Debbie asked.

"Yes, it's easy, I can show you."

"You can show me later, I got food on cooking now. How about you put a song on, then go check on Ms. Ruby."

Gigi put on Sade's 'Feel No Pain'. "Now this is my song." Gigi began to sing along.

"As Ms. Ruby will say, that girl has an old soul." Connie placed the dirty dishes in the dish window.

"Ms. Ruby fell asleep again, but she got up and she's in the bathroom now," Gigi said.

"I noticed she's been tired a lot." Debbie walked from the kitchen to the counter and grabbed the coffee pot. She poured two cups of coffee. "I'm going to see if I can get her in to go see the doctor to make sure everything is ok. Do not tell Scooter, Gigi. I don't want him worrying. I'm just going to take her in for a checkup."

"Child, I was on the prayer line helping to pray for folks, then I dozed off." Ms. Ruby took a seat at the counter

"I made some fresh coffee. Debbie set a cup of coffe in front of Ms. Ruby. "Look, Ms. Ruby, I noticed lately you been dozing off a lot. When was the last time you been to the doctor for a checkup? The last time I recall is when Vicky took you for your legs? That was a while ago. Damn near over a year ago."

"Child, I'm ok, just getting old. I been taking my meds for my arthritis and varicose veins." Ms. Ruby poured cream in her coffee. "Ain't no need for me to go to the doctor. I'm ok."

"I kind of agree with Ms. Debbie, Ms. Ruby. You have been seeming really tired lately," Gigi said.

"I said I'm ok." Ms. Ruby smiled genuinely at the two women, and calmly stirred cream into her coffee

"Ms. Ruby, you have health insurance, right?" Connie placed dirty dishes in the dish bin and walked to the register to cash her table out.

"I'm covered with BlueCross, but I'm covered by my God, so no need to go to the doctor. I just need to rest from time to time." "Ms. Ruby." Debbie bended down to look Ms. Ruby in the eyes. "If you don't allow me to take you to see a doctor, I will tell Scooter you ain't been feeling good, and you refuse to go to the doctor to get a checkup."

"Please, don't tell that boy anything, I don't want to have him worried."

"I won't tell him, but only if you agree to go. Now, I have your doctor's information. I will call and make an appointment now. Connie, can you make sure the tables are all set with fresh silverware and condiments? Gigi, can you make sure all caddies are filled up? The freezers and coolers are clean. After this, we'll be ready to head out. Gigi, once you are done, you should go into the offic restroom and change your clothes and freshen up before our ride gets here."

The doorbell chimed and Scooter walked in. He was sporting a blue Adidas suit with orange stripes and a pair of blue and orange Nikes. "Hello ladies. Hey Grandma." Scooter hugged Ms. Ruby as she sat on the barstool. "How's my favorite lady feeling today?"

"I'm feeling fine, Scooter. You looking and smelling nice." Ms. Ruby looked Scooter up and down.

"Now close your eyes, Grandma. I got something for you."

"Boy, it's not my birthday or nothing." Ms. Ruby closed her eyes. "Now, what'd you go and get then?" "You can open your eyes now."

"Scooter, this is beautiful." Ms. Ruby looked happy as she touched her neck looking at the necklace, with 'Ruby's Diner' inlaid in diamonds.

"Now, Ms. Ruby that is beautiful." Connie touched the necklace, examining the stones.

"Wait, where is mine, Scooter?" Debbie asked.

"I think I saw Caesar in the store looking for one for you." "Oh, real funny. You got me there."

"Where is Gigi? We need to be heading out." Gigi walked out the back wearing a red dress that fits every curve of her beautiful, thick body, with a pair of knock-off Red Bottom shoes with a designer black shawl.

"Gigi, you look..." His voice faded, lost for words for a moment.

"You look stunning. Like a model out off a magazine.

"She is beautiful." Connie grabbed her camera from her backpack and started snapping pictures of Gigi. "Now, you and Scooter get over here and take a few pictures together. After them, Ms. Ruby and Debbie, I would like all of you to get in so I can take a picture of us all. Now I'm going to put the camera timer on five seconds, so get ready." Connie set the camera and ran over to pose with the rest of the group as the camera took the shot.

"Ok, come on, Grandma. You riding shotgun." Scooter grabbed Ms. Ruby's hand. "I hope you don't mind, Gigi, if she rides up front. My grandma has leg pain so I don't want to put her in the back." Scooter opened the car door for Ms. Ruby and helped her in.

"That's fine with me, Calvin." Scooter looked at Gigi with a soft smile as he kissed her on the forehead. "I'll be reading over my music."

"Scooter, I would like to hear one song when we get in the car please," Debbie said.

"As long as it don't have all that cussing in it," Ms. Ruby said.

"No, Ms. Ruby, no cussing. I want to hear my Beyoncé. 'Drunk in Love'."

"You do know that's old, Debbie," Gigi said.

Scooter opened the door and helped Gigi in.

"What about me, Scooter?" She gave Scooter the Wanda face from the TV show In Living Color. "I'm still a lady."

"Ms. Debbie, you too funny. For real though, you should try out comedy. I think you'd be good at it," Scooter said.

"I can see you doing that too, Debbie." Connie got into the back seat.

"Scooter, this is nice and spacious. I never been in one of these. I love the leather. What year is this again, Scooter?" Debbie said.

It's a 2020." Scooter told Alexa to play Beyoncé's 'Drunk in Love'. The music started playing.

"Who is Alexa?" Ms. Ruby had a puzzled look on her face as Beyoncé's 'Drunk in Love' was playing. Everyone in the truck laughed. "It's a software you can speak to that tells you things. You can also control it to work with other apps such as music apps. So, if you ask it to play a song, it will play that song for you.

"Ms. Ruby, that's new technology these new millenniums are using. You know that 'Beam me up, Scotty' Star Trek shit—I meant 'stuff,' Ms. Ruby," Debbie said

"Debbie, don't think I'm too far away to swing this purse of mine back there." Ms. Ruby looked at Debbie through the rearview mirror, giving her a sinister frown.

"Now, Ms. Ruby, we don't need you swinging your purse all up in here like Esther off of Sanford and Son," she laughed

"Mmm-hmm. So, Gigi, it will play what you ask it to?" Ms. Ruby asked.

"Yes, Ms. Ruby. Just say 'Alexa,' then ask it to play what song you would like."

"Ok, let's give it a try." She paused. "Alexa, play "Work It Out."

Everyone laughed softly as Beyoncé continued to play.

"Grandma, it's set to be controlled by my voice only. Some of the guys get in my ride and try changing my music by saying 'Hey Alexa,' so I set it to only be controlled by my voice. I'll let you listen to your gospel another time, ok, Grandma? Right now, we have to get Gigi pumped for this audition."

"And the thing to do that is music. Turn it up some, Scooter." Debbie and the other ladies sang along.

"We'll be all night. Ohhhh. Ohhhh." Connie sang and bobbed her head to the music as Ms. Ruby bobbed along.

"Ok, I like this beat," Ms. Ruby said.

"We're here, ladies." Scooter pulled into the valet parking of the studio. The Valet Guy opened the door for Ms. Ruby and the ladies as Scooter walked around to hand him the keys.

"OMG, it's Calvin Walker." The Valet Guy looked on in amusement. "This our year, Mr. Walker. Super Bowl, here we come." He walked backwards, still looking at Scooter and the ladies. Scooter smiled and grabbed Gigi's hand.

"That's the plan," Scooter said.

"It's nice up in here." She looked around.

"Yes, look at all the singers on the wall. Such beautiful pictures," Connie said.

Ms. Ruby nodded her head in agreement. "I never been in a studio before. So, this where they do all the TV stuff?

"Some of it, Grandma."

"I never been in a studio before neither, Ms. Ruby." Gigi looked around, smiling ear to ear in amazement.

"Well, I guess this is all our first. So, Gigi, we need you to go in there and make history so when you write your memoir, this will be one of the first things mentioned.

"And what's that, Ms. Debbie?" Gigi asked.

"Your first time walking through the doors, your name

unknown. And your first time walking out the doors, your name known."

"I know that's right, Debbie. Speak it into existence," Ms. Ruby asked.

The group walked up to the counter in the lobby.

"Hi, may I help you? Lady at counter said. She smiled kindly. "Yes, I'm here for the audition for the show Your Big Chance." "And your name, ma'am?"

"I'm Gigi Garcia."

"Catchy name. May I see your ID?" Gigi passed her ID, and the Lady at the Counter scanned it.

"Yes, I see you have a 5 p.m."

She passed Gigi a name tag with her name on it, along with a number. "You will need to sign in, along with your guests. I will need to scan their IDs too for security reasons. Normally, you're only allowed two guests, Ms. Garcia. But since you're with Mr. Walker, you all can go up." She winked at Calvin. "Only one is allowed backstage with Ms. Garcia due to space and other contestants. The other guests may take a seat in the audience with the others."

Everyone passed the Lady at Counter their IDs. "Thank you all. Just please walk around the corner to the right 'till you get to Studio 7. You'll be given directions from there. And Ms. Garcia, good luck."

"Thank you," Gigi said.

"Did you see that heifer winking at Scooter?" Debbie said. "I'm talking about all up in his face," Connie said.

"Child, y'all stop that there. My Scooter don't care about no groupies. You see whose hands he's locked with?" Ms. Ruby looked pointedly at Scooter and Gigi holding hands as they walked down the hall.

"I know, Ms. Ruby. It just kills me how Hens always up in a

guy face knowing they got someone or seeing someone. Gigi, what y'all new millenniums call them now—THOTs?" Debbie said. "THOTs? What the heck is a THOT?"

"Ms. Ruby, I don't think you really want to know," Connie said.

"Ms. Ruby, it stands for "That Hoe Over There," like the one at the counter low-balling," Debbie said.

"You were right Connie," Ms. Ruby answered. "We're here," Gigi said nervously.

"Calm down, ma, you will be fine. Just go in there and sing to them like you been singing to me on Skype," Scooter said.

They approached a desk, with a Casting Agent sitting behind the counter.

"Hi I'm—"

The Casting Agent cut Gigi off. "Gigi Garcia. Nice to meet you." She stood up to shake Gigi's hand.

"Carmen was right, you do have a catchy name and are beautiful."

"Carmen?" Gigi asked.

"Yes, Carmen. The young lady that took your IDs. My name is Mary Jane, and I work with the casting department. May I have your portfolio?"

Gigi passed the portfolio as the lady looks through it.

"This is beautiful. Please make sure you put your name tag on. Also, you are only allowed one guest in the back with you while the others sit in the audience," the Casting Agent said.

"Y'all keep saying audience like she's auditioning live and will be on TV."

"Well, that's exactly how it is. They decided to switch it up this year. They figure if you can't handle this and you crack under pressure, you're not fit for this industry.

"Now that's some slick sh—"

"Debbie, shut your mouth," Ms. Ruby yelled. "Ms. Ruby, I was going to saying slick stuff." "Mmm-hmm.

"You mean to tell me I'm not just auditioning for three judges, but all of America?"

"Yes, that's correct. I understand if you can't do it, you wouldn't be the first.

She ain't say she couldn't do it," Debbie said.

"That's right, she wasn't born to do this just to walk away," Connie said.

"Live TV or not, this child is ready to show the world what she can do. Now, where's my seat, my legs getting tired," Ms. Ruby said.

The ladies all went to take a seat while Scooter went behind the curtain with Gigi and the other contestants.

"Hello everyone, there have been some changes this year opposed to how the show has been ran before." The Casting Agent walked into the center of the room, snapping her fingers at the group of contestants with an air of importance. "I know we asked you all to be here at a certain time but truth be told, we gave you guys all the same time. This year we twisted things up."

"How this will work will go like this." The Casting Agent walked back and forth as she talked to the crowd. "Two of you will go onstage. You will then flip the dice to see who gets the highest number. The person with the highest number will get the chance to sing the song given to them by the judges. Or they can pass the song to the next contestant, which is the person they are onstage with. The contestants with the highest dice then will sing the same song. "

"The judges will then decide who they think sang the song the best, and who will move on to the next round and who will be going home. That means five contestants will advance tonight, and five will go home. The five that advance tonight, will come back next week, but this time contestants can sing the song of their choice. Out of those five, only three will be selected to go to the semifinals

"Once at the semifinals, the contestants must write a song and sing it for a chance to win a recording contract with This That Production Recording Studio, along with one hundred thousand dollars."

The contestants began to clap excitedly.

"Before we get started, I'd like to thank you all for coming out. And for those who do not advance, remember this is not the end, but yet a beginning. Good luck! When we are ready for the first two, your numbers will be called," the Casting Agent said.

"How you feeling?" Scooter held both of Gigi's hands, giving her a big smile. "You need some water or something? They have refreshments I see over by the wall. I'll grab some if you'd like."

"Calvin, calm down. You more nervous than I am. Water would be nice." Gigi stood, looking into her notepad.

"Here you go, Gigi." Scooter opened up the bottle and passes it to Gigi. "So, two go on at one time and you don't know who you're going against until your number is called?" He opened a bottle of water for himself.

"Thanks Calvin. I mean I really do appreciate you and the others being here for me. It's been a long time since I felt the love Ms. Ruby and the others show me. Gigi smiles! And, I never really had a male friend like you. Someone who like me for me. Someone, I can be myself around and not feel scared. Thank you, Calvin." She kissed his lips softly.

Meanwhile, Debbie reached into her bag and grabbed some cashews, munching on them. "Now we've seen six contestants already, now when are they going to call Gigi up?" Debbie said. "Y'all want some?"

"I'll take a few." Debbie passed the nuts and Connie grabbed the bag, pouring the nuts into her hand before passing the bag to Ms. Ruby.

"Nah, I'm ok, I'm just getting a little tired."

"Now, I know at least two of them contestants knew they should have stayed home and they recording this too. They will never have a chance in the music industry unless they bring that Milli Vanilli back," Debbie laughed.

"A few of them sounded good though," Connie passed the nuts back.

"I agree with Connie, a few were good, especially that young guy who had the Barry White voice. Now, he blew my mind. You would have never known something that small had a big voice like that," Ms. Ruby said.

"Next up: Numbers 6804 and 5718!" the Announcer yelled. "That's Gigi number! 5718!" Debbie screamed.

Gigi and another young lady stepped up on the stage.

"Hello ladies, so how are you feeling?" Judge 1 asked.

"I'm excited, and I couldn't wait to get up here." Contestant 6804 said ecstatically.

"And your name, hun?" Judge 2 asked. "I'm Brittany."

"And you?"

"I'm Ginger Garcia but everyone calls me Gigi."

"Gigi, so, are you as excited as Brittany to be here?" Judge 3 asked.

"I think I'm more nervous than excited. I mean I'm excited— don't get me wrong—but the nerves have kicked in," Gigi said. "Hey, we all just want you two to do your best and have fun with it," Judge 3 said.

"Right, just relax and have fun and let your voices do the rest," Judge 2 said.

"So, Brittany, how long have you been singing?" The judge

sipped on a bottle of water that sat in front of him.

"You can say all my life. I sang backup for a few hit singers but I'm trying to branch out on my own and get my own recording contract."

"So, singing is nothing new for you?" Judge 2 said.

"Let's just say, singing is something that comes naturally to me."

"Ok, ok, we'll see how naturally. So, Brittany, what type of work do you do now? Since you've been trying to get your own contract?" Judge 2 said.

"I do real estate now," Brittany said.

"And what about you Gigi, how long have you been singing?" The judge sat back as she waited for Gigi's answer.

"I just sing around the house and around my job. I just like music and writing it. I never sang backup for anyone, but I do like writing music."

"So, you not only sing, you write your own music too? Now that's a talent to have, because if you can't sing you could always sell them to artists that look for songs. But come on, we're about to find out what you ladies can do," Judge 1 said.

"And what type of work do you do, Gigi?"

"I work for a place called Ruby's Diner as a server."

"Ok, ladies. Let's get started." The Announcer passed Brittany a blue plush die and Gigi a red plush die. "Now, we go by alphabet on who is going to roll first so, Brittany you will roll first. After you both roll, the judges will give the song to be sung, and if the person with the highest dice would like to pass, they can. If passed, the remaining contestant must sing the same song, and the judges will score one through ten on who sang the song the best. The contestant with the highest score advances on to the next round."

The audience clapped.

"Now, time to roll the dice." The Announcer stood in between Gigi and Brittany. "Brittany, it's your roll first. Please step up and roll the die."

Brittany rolled the die.

"It's a five. It's your roll now, Gigi." The Announcer extended his hand, gesturing for Gigi to roll. After a moment's hesitation, she rolled her die.

"It's a three," the Announcer said. "Damn!" Debbie said disappointed.

"Girl, hush 'fore you get us kicked out of here," Ms. Ruby said.

"Brittany, you win. Now it's up to you to sing the song first that we're going to give you or you can pass it on to Gigi.," Judge 1 announced.

"The song to sing is Andra Day's 'Rise Up'." Judge 2 said.

Ms. Ruby whispered, "She got this, with as much as she sings this song."

"Brittany, would you like to sing first, or pass it on?" The judge leaned in his chair with his hand on his chin.

"I'll sing this first. I sang this on my YouTube channel and got thousands of likes."

"So, this should come easy to you then." The Announcer escorted Brittany up to the microphone. Gigi took a seat offstage as she waited on Brittany to finish the song. A few minutes later, Brittany finished. The Judges all talked amongst each other

"Brittany, I will agree you need to come from behind the scenes and be seen. That was awesome," Judge 1 said.

"I agree, you sang that like I never heard anyone sing it before," Judge 2 said.

"Yes, that was an awesome performance," Judge 3 said.

"Ok, Brittany you got the judges agreeing with each other which is always a good thing. Lock your scores in, judges, as we get ready for Ms. Gigi," the Announcer said. "So, Gigi, how you feeling after seeing Brittany perform? Are you still nervous, or ready to go?"

"Brittany did a wonderful job, I'm just ready to show you guys what I can do." Gigi was escorted to the microphone by the Announcer. Gigi stood there singing her soul out emotionally. A few minutes later, Gigi's performance was over. The Judges all stood up and applauded Gigi, as they all teared up.

"Gigi, if this toupee was not pinned down on my head, you would've blown it back. Your voice is just so powerful and breathtaking," Judge 1 said.

"I can't stop pouring tears. You're the first person other than Andra Day who can sing that song to me. And Gigi, you sang that song," Judge 2 said.

"That was a mic-drop performance. You put on your big-woman draws and showed up on this stage. If you advance, I could imagine what we have in-store," Judge 3 said.

"Ok, judges, it's time for you to lock you scores in. And I must say, you ladies both did a splendid job—but there only can be one." The Announcer stood between Britany and Gigi. "And the winner to advance to the next round will be..."

The audience got quiet as the scores populates on the huge monitor.

"...Gigi! Ginger Garcia advances on to the next round."

Gigi held both of her hands to her face as tears rolled down her cheeks. Scooter ran on the stage and picked Gigi up. "You won, Gigi! You won. I knew you could do it."

"Congratulations Gigi, you move on to the next round," the Announcer passed her a card that says 'Advanced to Second Round'. "And I see your boyfriend is happy for you too."

The Judges and audience stood up and clapped for Gigi.

CHAPTER FIFTEEN

"This place been rocking hard ever since Gigi advanced to the second round." Debbie put in an order for one of her tables.

"Yeah, the child got people coming in here asking for her autograph and to take pictures," Ms. Ruby said.

"I know. That's why I had Connie bring her camera setup. If anyone would like to take a picture with Gigi, and get a signed autograph, they can do so in the back with the help of Andrew Jackson."

"Andrew Jackson?" Ms. Ruby looked puzzled. "Who is that?" "This man right here." Debbie pulled out a stack of twenty- dollar bills.

"I guess that was a good idea to charge for pictures. That's what stars do, and we have a star in the house." Ms. Ruby watched Gigi take a picture with some fans. "That child got a future ahead of her."

"Yeah, Gigi wants to get a laptop to put her music on. So, later on after we close, I'm going to take her up to Walmart."

"That will be nice. I know she mentioned wanting to get one before." Ms. Ruby sat down at one of the tables to enjoy a patty melt with French onion soup.

"That Gigi is a natural. The people love her already and my camera loves her too. Gigi takes shots like a model." Connie walked over to sit next to Ms. Ruby, showing her the pics Gigi had taken with some of her fans.

"These pictures look really nice, Connie. I see why you picked this camera back up. It brings joy to you. I see you taking pictures and just looking happy as can be as you snap away. Sometimes, when we lose things in our lives, it makes some of us lose our drive. I see picking that camera back up and snapping pictures of Gigi, you got your camara groove back. Sometimes, it takes just that for others to give you that strive to drive. Gigi found her strive. Now all she needs to do is drive."

"Thank you, Ms. Ruby and you're right. Sometimes, it takes just that for others to give you that strive to drive. And working with you guys, gave me that back." Connie held Ms. Ruby's hand, smiling gratefully. The door chimed, and Connie walked over to assist a guest, grabbing a menu along the way.

"Hi! Just one?"

"Yes, just one." The Lady said.

Connie escorts her to one of her tables. "Hi I'm Connie. May I start you off with something to drink?

Connie waited for the suspicious-looking woman's response. While she waited, she scoped the woman out. She was wearing a black hoody that covered her blonde hair, black jeans, and dark black sunglasses.

"Let me get a water with lemon."

The lady looked down at the menu. "I'll need some time to look over the menu."

Connie walked off as the woman continued to flip through the menu. "I don't know what's going on with that table I just got but she looks suspicious, like she's trying to hide from somebody." Connie grabbed a glass and filled it with ice

"All black, big sunglasses, hoody on. Yeah, she's hiding from somebody."

Gigi walked out of the ladies' room, drying her hands off on some paper towels and throwing them in the garbage. "Who y'all talking about?"

"My table I just sat. It seems like she is hiding from somebody."

Gigi looked towards the lady dressed in all black. "Wait, that look like Peaches—I mean, Felicia."

"You know her, Gigi?" Connie filled the cup of ice with water

"Yeah, she's one of Mean Mug's girls." Gigi's eyes got big. "Why is she here?"

"The pimp you told me about that had you out there? The same ugly dude that came in here irritating Connie?" Debbie asked.

"Yeah, that dude."

"Are you sure it's her?" Connie said.

"Connie, I can't see from here because of the hood but do she have blonde hair?"

"The little bit that's displayed hanging out is blonde."

Gigi grabbed the glass of water from Connie, and walked it over to the table. "Peaches—I mean Felicia, what are you doing here?"

Peaches looked suspicious. "Girl, I knew it was you when I saw you on TV." Peaches looked up at Gigi. "You looking nice, Gigi and I see you're still singing too. You blew them judges' minds." Peaches looked around suspiciously. Gigi set the glass of water on the table, then took a seat across from Peaches.

"What's going on, Peaches? How you been?"

"I been..." She sip on the water. "He's looking for me." "Who? Mean Mug? Why?"

"I told him I want out. I told him I'm tired." Peaches started to cry as she removed her hood and glasses.

"Peaches, did Mean Mug do that to you?" Gigi looked at the knots and bruises on Peaches's head and neck.

143

"He beat my ass when I told him I wanted out. I thought he was going to kill me, Gigi. All he talk about doing is getting you and putting you back on these streets." Peaches took off her glasses, displaying a black eye. "We were all in the house one day and the TV was on and that's when he saw you onstage hugging that football guy. That made him furious. He started hitting walls and shit, talking about motherfuckers taking his money. Look Gigi, be careful, he's after you."

"I'm not going to worry about Mean Mug no more. If he tries to come up in here, Ms. Debbie got them pistols waiting on him. Plus, we have our cook Rob who took out dudes badder than Mean Mug. If I keep running, I will forever have to look over my back. I'm done with them streets. You should be done too."

"I been laying low for a few days 'till I was able to get a car. I'm heading on out to Potato Town where my sister and her kids stay. She says she could help me get a job working in the beauty shop doing hair, so I'm heading there. I just wanted to stop by and tell you to be careful."

"Potato Town?" Gigi was puzzled.

"Idaho, Gigi. If I don't get away from that crazy motherfucker, he's going to kill me. He started snorting that shit too." Peaches shook her head as tears rolled down her face. "He thinks you had something to do with the house getting raided. He says you snitched to the police."

"I didn't do anything. When I saw them coming up in there, I climbed down the fire escape and left so I wouldn't get arrested. So, I don't know why he would think I did it."

"I think the bitch Trina did it. Once Mean Mug got locked up, she started working with Terrell and his crew. Running trap houses and shit. But the bitch was going to see Mean Mug while he was locked up, telling him, it was you who snitched to 12."

"I never liked that sneaky bitch anyways, but it wasn't me. Give me your number, Peaches, so we can stay in touch." Gigi passed Peaches her phone. Peached punches her number in and hit "Save."

"I have to make one stop to pick up some money my girl owes me, then I'm on the expressway and not looking back." Peaches stood up as she put her sunglasses back on. "Call me, girl, and congratulations. You always had a voice." Peaches hugged Gigi before she exited the diner.

"Gigi, is everything ok?" Ms. Ruby asked.

"Everything is just fine Ms. Ruby. Can I get you a refill?" "No, I'm ok, just finishing up my soup."

Gigi walked over to the counter where Debbie was sitting, traying up food. "Connie, your food's up." Debbie placed a bottle of A1 sauce on the tray.

"Thanks Debbie! Tell Rob to make the steak I just put in medium, not medium-well. The man changed his mind on how he wants it cooked." Connie took the tray of food to her table.

"Debbie, I was right. That was one of the girls who used to live in the house with me. She said Mean Mug thinks I snitched to the cops and had the house raided, but I didn't."

"Calm down, girl. We don't want Ms. Ruby seeing you like this. Now what happened? What'd the girl tell you?"

"She said he thinks I made him lose a lot of money due to the police raiding the house. She said he thinks it was me who did it when it wasn't. She said he said he's coming for me and he beat her so bad she's leaving town to go stay with her sister."

"Gigi, the police station is right around the corner. If he tries anything, they will be on his ass. Plus, I got these things." Debbie pointed under the register to the two guns hiding behind it. "And Rob is here too. There ain't nothing for you to be worried about. The only thing that should be on your mind is your audition. I have the cop's name and number who comes in here for breakfast, I can call him and you can get an order of protection if you are afraid—just to be safe."

"That sounds like something I should do. Yes, call him for me, Ms. Debbie. I'm going to go in the back and call Calvin."

"What's going on with Gigi?" Connie placed dirty dishes in dish bin.

"She'll be ok. That table you had with the lady; Gigi used to live in the same house as her. Gigi said the girl told her that the dude that got arrested thinks Gigi had something to do with his house getting raided and him getting arrested. The girl told Gigi, he said he was going to get Gigi for snitching to the police."

"Gigi needs to call the police," Connie said.

"I'm doing that now so she can get an order of protection against him just in case he tries to pull anything. Gigi said he beat that girl up pretty bad and she's scared and leaving town."

"That's why she was covering herself up." Connie shook her head. "I know how it is. She's doing the right thing by getting away from him."

"Gigi, will be ok, I promise that. We got backup up in here." Debbie cocked the gun, looking like Queen Latifah in Set it Off. "Don't say anything to Ms. Ruby, I don't want her to be worried."

"Well, I will keep my eyes open for him and anyone else looking suspicious."

"I'm going to play something on this jukebox and help Lance with the tables." Debbie walked out with the dish bin and started grabbing dirty dishes off the table

"Ms. Ruby are you all done?" Debbie grabbed the empty plate that sat in front of Ms. Ruby.

"Yes, Debbie, I'm all done. I just spoke with Scooter and he said he'll be up here in a few." Ms. Ruby stood up and stretched. "I'm going in the back to do the count. Tell Scooter to come back there when he gets here." Ms. Ruby walked to the back, then turned around to Debbie. "Ain't nothing going to happen to Gigi, God got her covered. Mean Mug or not." She turned and walked to the back.

"You can't get nothing past that lady." Debbie put the dish bin in the window for Lance to get. The doorbell chimed and Office Reed walked in, taking a seat at the counter.

"Hi Debbie! Where is the young lady who needs to file a report?" The officer placed his hat on the counte

"She's in the back, I'll have Rob get her." Debbie turned around and looked at Rob through the food window. "Rob, tell Gigi to come up here, please. She's in the back room."

"So, who is it she would like to get an order of protection against? An ex-boyfriend?" Debbie grabbed the coffee mug and poured the officer some coff

"It's for some dude named Mean Mug."

"Mean Mug, the pimp?" The office grabbed the coffee, pouring Sweet'n Low into it. "That dude's bad news. Thinks he's Nino Brown of the streetwalkers. How the hell she get involved with him?" "It's a long story and it's been a while since she's seen him. He got locked up and he thinks it's Gigi that snitched to the police and that's why they raided his house and arrested him."

"His real name is Gilbert Wright. He's a convicted felon and he's currently on parole. So, if he tries anything, his ass will be going back to the pen."

"Hi Office Reed." Gigi walked out from the back, standing behind the counter. "How's your day going?"

"Same old', same old'. Now Debbie, tells me you need to file a report on Gilbert Wright."

"Gilbert Wright?" Gigi looked puzzled as she stood leaning on the counter with folded arms.

"Gilbert Wright, aka Mean Mug."

"You mean to tell me that Mean Mug's real name is Gilbert?" "Yes. Now, I got the paperwork here for you. I just need you to sign your initials here, here, and here. Then sign your name here, and here." Gigi signed the papers.

Officer Reed tore the bottom copy off, and gave it to Gi

"Mr. Wright is to stay one thousand feet from you. If you see him, call the police and he will be arrested for violating the order of protection. I already had Judge Carlson sign off on it since Mr. Wright is a known criminal. Again, call if you need assistance." Office Reed passed Gigi his card. "And congratulations on your next round for your audition." Office Reed finished up his coffee and exits. As he was leaving, Scooter was walking in. Scooter walked towards the counter. "Gigi, you ok?" Scooter got closer, kissing her on the forehead.

"I'm ok. I feel much better now knowing I got this order of protection."

"That's good. I wish that dude would show his face around here." He paused. "Let me go say hi to my grandma and I'll be right back." Scooter went to the back to say hi to Ms. Ruby. There was a moment of quiet before a yell was heard, and something broke. Scooter came running back out to the front of the restaurant. Scooter facial expression was filled with worry as his hands were trembling

"Debbie, call an ambulance! Grandma's having trouble breathing." Scooter ran back to the office Debbie, Gigi, and Connie followed.

"Ms. Ruby, what's wrong? Tell me where it hurts," Debbie said.

"Child, I'm ok. I'm just having shortness of breath."

"Ms. Ruby, do you have any chest pain?" Connie kneeled down, looking at Ms. Ruby's eyes as she felt her pulse.

"Damn, Connie, you're an undercover doctor too?" Debbie said.

"No, I took CPR classes. Now, Ms. Ruby, are you having chest pains?"

"My chest was hurting earlier so, I took some   Alka-Seltzer and ginger ale.

Scooter was concerned. "How long you been feeling like this, Grandma? You have to open your mouth, Grandma, when something is bothering you. You're all I got."

Debbie yelled at Rob, "Watch the front! Ms. Ruby is not feeling too good and we have to call her an ambulance. Have Lance knock out them tables, and we will be closing up for the day."

An ambulance came and EMTs walked calmly into the Diner.

"Hi, we received a call of someone having shortness of breath," EMT 1 said.

Rob directed them to the back. They moved past him swiftly, and entered the back of the restaurant.

"Someone needs assistance back here." The EMT 1 looked down at Ms. Ruby.

"Yes, my grandma. She is having shortness of breath," Scooter said.

"Hi ma'am, can you tell me how long you been having this shortness of breath?" the EMT 2 opened a bag, taking out a blood pressure machine.

"You guys mind if we get a little room?" the EMT 1 pulled out his stethoscope, and placed it gently against Ms. Ruby's back. "Ma'am, can you take a good, deep breath for me?"

"Your pressure is low. Let's get you in the ambulance so the ER can take more tests to see what's causing the shortness of breath." An EMT brought in a cot and placed Ms. Ruby on it, strolling her out to the ambulance. Scooter and the others followed as Debbie set the alarm and locked the doors.

Hours Later, Scooter and Gigi were standing quietly together at the vending machines. Scooter leaned his forehead against the glass, while Gigi rubbed his back. Behind them, Debbie and Connie sat side by side in the waiting room, worried expressions plastered on their faces.

"I hope she will be alright." Scooter placed a few dollars in the soda machine and pushed the button for a Gatorade.

"She'll be ok. They got her taking an EKG now and they gave her something to bring her pressure up," Debbie said.

"She'll be ok, Scooter. All I can hear her saying is 'Have a mustard seed of faith'," Gigi said.

Debbie paced back and forth while she was on the phone. "Vicky, we are just waiting for the doctors to finish running her tests and then I will call you and Willie back." Debbie hung up.

"That was Ms. Vicky, huh, Debbie?" Scooter sipped on the Gatorade.

"Yeah, just letting them know what's going on with Ms. Ruby." "First Peaches shows up and tell me about Mean Mug. Then I make a police report. Now, Ms. Ruby." Gigi put her head against Scooter's chest as he held her.

"Gigi, you had nothing to do with this. Ms. Ruby been saying she's been feeling tired. It's a good thing now that she is here, and we can find out what's wrong," Connie said

The Doctor came out to the lobby.

"Hi, I'm looking for the Walker family."

"I'm Calvin Walker. Ms. Ruby is my grandma. Can you tell me what's going on?"

"They Calvin Walker? I didn't expect to walk out here and see you, son. Congrats on being the number one draft pick. Now, just get us there to the Super Bowl."

"Look not being rude, but enough of that. What's going on with Ms. Ruby?" Debbie walked up to the Doctor.

"Well, Ms. Walker's shortness of breath is being caused by a blockage in the artery to the heart. Her test shows she had a mild heart attack over a week ago that's why she was getting the chest pains."

"So, Doctor, what can you do to treat her?" Scooter asked. "There's a procedure I can perform called a 'coronary angioplasty'." The Doctor said.

"And what will that procedure do?" Debbie asked.

"Coronary angioplasty is a medical procedure in which a balloon is used to open a blockage in a coronary artery narrowed by atherosclerosis. This procedure improves blood flow to the heart. Atherosclerosis is a condition in which a material called plaque builds up on the inner walls of the arteries."

"Now, I would like to keep her here to monitor her vitals and to perform the procedure. After the procedure, patients usually can return home with the next twenty-four to forty-eight hours. I would like to watch over Ms. Ruby, considering her age."

"So, she will have to stay here overnight?" Scooter asked. "Yes," the Doctor said.

"Ok, I would like for her to have the best private hospital room there is in here."

"You will take that up with registration. I will get the paperwork ready for your grandma to sign and I can start the procedure tomorrow morning. Tonight, I just would like for her to get some rest."

"Can we see her?" Gigi grabbed Scooter's hand.

"Yes, but just for a few minutes. I need to get meds into her body for this procedure and she needs rest."

"Is that why she's been feeling tired?" Connie asked. "Yes, a clogged artery will cause that, along with the chest pains she's been having."

"I'm just glad we got her here," Debbie said.

"Again, please do not be too long. Ms. Walker needs her rest."

All of them walked in the room with Ms. Ruby.

"Now, Ms. Ruby, you can't be scaring us all like that. Got my pressure going up while you're pressure going down. Now, we both can't be laid up in here." Debbie bended down and kisses Ms. Ruby on the cheek.

"I'm glad you're ok, Ms. Ruby. You had me worried." Gigi grabbed Ms. Ruby hand.

"You had all us worried." Connie stood at the end of Ms. Ruby's bed, rubbing her leg.

"So, the doctor said you had a mild heart attack, Grandma and he will be performing a procedure tomorrow to unclog your artery. That's why you been having shortness of breath. How long you been feeling like this, Grandma?" Scooter said.

"Well, I never thought it was a heart attack. I thought it was gas from the cabbage I cooked the other day at home. I'm just glad the Lord got me here in time," Ms. Ruby said.

"Yes, I closed the diner down quickly just like the piano man in The Color Purple: Time to go!" Debbie said.

Ms. Ruby laughed. "Debbie, stop being scared and get your butt up on a stage and make them people laugh like you make us do. I agree with Scooter. You should try."

"Ms. Ruby, this is not about me now. We're here for you. We'll talk about that later. Right now, let's get you back right. After this, Ms. Ruby, you can stay home and rest up for a few days. We can take care of the restaurant."

"Yeah, that's what it seems like I'm going to be doing. Doctor's orders. But I want to go see Gigi perform."

"Grandma, I will record it for you. You need to be home. I know Gigi and Ms. Debbie are there with you. But I called my assistant and she will be getting you in home care to just help you out around the house."

"Scooter, I'm not handicapped, I just had a clogged artery. I'll be ok. I don't need no help."

"No Ms. Ruby, I agree. When my husband was home, I took care of him, but I still had a nurse come in to assist. Especially when I had to go into the office. I think it's a good idea," Connie sai

"I'll still be there too, Ms. Ruby, to help you. I promise," Gigi said.

"Child, the only thing I need for you to do is show up and show out for that second round and bring the card home." "The card?" Gigi asked.

"The semifinals card they will be giving you for making it to the finals.

"I will, Ms. Ruby. I will." Gigi hugged Ms. Ruby as her eyes teared up.

"Now Gigi, there's no need to cry. I'll be alright."

"I can't help it. You're the closest thing to a mother I've had in over a year. I just don't want to see anything bad happening to you."

"Again everyone, God took the wheel already. I'm good. Now y'all go on and get out of here and let me rest. I'll talk with y'all tomorrow. Debbie, open the diner and I will give you guys a call once I'm done with the procedure."

"I'll be here, Grandma. For you," Scooter said. "Me too," Gigi said.

"You sure, Ms. Ruby, about opening up the diner tomorrow? I want to be here for your procedure." Debbie grabbed Ms. Ruby's hand.

"Child, open up the diner. I know the officer and the construction guys will need coffee and lunch. Once y'all finish for the day, Scooter should have me home by then."

"Ok, Ms. Ruby, I'll do just that. I love you, and I'll see you tomorrow." Debbie kissed Ms. Ruby goodbye, followed by the others.

153

CHAPTER SIXTEEN

"I'm glad it wasn't a massive heart attack." Scooter opened the car door for the ladies.

"You? I think we are all glad. I'm just glad they are able to fix it. Some folks have a heart attack and don't live to talk about it," Debbie said.

"I'm just glad she will be alright."

"Yeah, I'm glad she's going to be alright too. Ms. Ruby puts hope back in people's lives like a breath of fresh air. A new start."

"Yes, she do. Now, I didn't want to talk in front of Ms. Ruby, but Gigi, everything will be ok as far as that Mean Mug dude. What I need you to concentrate on is advancing to the semifinals, like Ms. Ruby said. You are almost there."

"I agree with Debbie. Don't worry about that dude, the police will take care of him. If Debbie don't get to him first.

"I told Gigi, I got them things. Look just remember, don't mention this to Ms. Ruby. We don't need her worrying or having any more heart attacks—mild or not.

"So, Gigi, how you feeling about the audition? Are you still excited?" Scooter said.

"I'm not worried about that competition; I'm worried about Ms. Ruby and her health," Gigi said.

"One thing I have learned about Ms. Ruby is that she don't

give up on herself nor other people. She's a pusher," Connie said.

"Well, I'm going to drop you ladies back off at the diner to get your cars. I have practice tomorrow morning but I will let Coach know what's going on with my grandma so I can be there when she wakes up."

"You have always been her rock and she's always been yours. You're a good grandson, Scooter."

Scooter pulled up in front of the diner. "I already spoke with my assistant on the phone, and she hired a nurse from the assisted living center that works with elderly cardio patients. She will be there in the morning when I go see Grandma, and she will be coming back home with us. Debbie, I would like for you to show her around so Grandma can get some rest."

"The nurse will be a big help." Connie opened the truck's door and got out.

"I'll be there to help as well."

"I know you will be, Gigi, but you also have to remember you may not be there all the time due to your upcoming dates," Debbie said.

"Upcoming dates?" Gigi asked.

Scooter opened up the car door for Gigi helping her out. "Recording dates. You will be in the studio soon working on your first album. Plus, the nurse will also keep Ms. Ruby company," Debbie said.

"Speaking of company. I had a surprise to tell her before this happened, but I completely forgot because there's been so much going on," Scooter said.

"What surprise, Scooter?" "I bought her a puppy."

"A puppy. What kind?" Gigi inquired. "One of those little dogs. A yorkie."

"Those are beautiful . . . and expensive," Connie said surprised.

"Yeah, they are cute dogs. Gigi, I would like to go pick the puppy up and bring it back over to my grandma's house in the morning before I go to the hospital. I have the puppy stuff in my trunk. Can you set it up for my granny? There's a dog bowl, puppy training pads, leash, and puppy food."

"Yes, Calvin, that will be great. She's going to love it just as much as I will. I love dogs. I always wanted to have one," Gigi told him.

"That's real nice of you, Scooter. Now, Gigi, get the stuff. Caesar is coming over tonight to cook me dinner. I need to get home and freshen up so, I can give him this dessert after he's done with dinner," Debbie said.

"Well, I guess I'll be seeing you ladies tomorrow." Connie took her keys out of her purse and opened her car door. "Good night." She pulled off

"Gigi, thank you!" Scooter said.

"Thank you for what?" Gigi grabbed the bag with the dog supplies and Scooter grabbed the food. Thank you for caring," he kissed her on her lips. "That really means a lot to me especially if we're going to be dating."

"Dating? Are you asking me to be your girl Calvin Walker?" "

Y'all can talk about all that on that Skype or on the phone. I need to be getting home," Debbie exclaimed.

"Ok, Ms. Debbie. I'll see you tomorrow. Have fun. I'll talk to you in a few, Gigi."

CHAPTER SEVENTEEN

"Hey baby, you up here bright and early." Ms. Ruby opened her eyes, smiling up at Scooter, who sat up forward in the chair next to her hospital bed.

"Yes, grandma, I'm here. I saw the doctor and spoke with him. He says your blood pressure is back to normal and they are ready to prep you for the procedure."

"Can you please go to the cafeteria and get me some coffee before they take me for the procedure? You know I drink my coffee every morning."

"Grandma, you can have water, apple juice, or any other clear liquid. But you cannot have coffee until afterwards. Look Grandma, I have something to tell you."

"What is it, Scooter?" A look of worry crossed her face.

"Nothing bad, Grandma." Scooter held her hand as he sat on the stool. "My assistant got you a nurse and she'll be here in a few so you can meet her. She will be going home with you and assisting you until you can fully recover."

"Now, me and Debbie already talked and we both agreed that you will need to get some rest. I got you that new BET channel called BET+ where you can watch all your shows just like you like. They just added some new shows too. I also got another surprise for you but we'll get to that later."

"I thank God for blessing me with such a great grandson. I love you, Scooter."

At that moment, the Doctor walked in. "Good morning Ms. Walker. How is my favorite patient doing this morning?"

"I'm doing ok, Doctor. I just want my coffee and to get this over with so I can get back home to my bed."

"Well, those are the plans, Ms. Walker: to get you back home healthy. Now, I explained the procedure to you both. Are there any other questions you may have for me before we begin?"

"Yes, Doctor, can you please tell my stubborn grandma again that once the procedure is over, she is to take some time off from the diner? At least a week or two?"

"I see your grandson not only knows football, but he seems to know what's best for you too. REST. So, get plenty of it.

"Thanks Doc!" Scooter said.

"The orderlies will be up in a few to get you, Ms. Walker. I'll see you then." The doctor walked out. After a moment, there was a knock at the door.

"Come in," Scooter said.

"Hi I'm Nurse Betty. I'm looking for Ms. Ruby Walker." "I'm Ruby Walker."

The Nurse walked over to the side of Ms. Ruby's bed. "I'm Nurse Betty, from assisted living. I'll be assisting you from here on now. You must be Calvin Walker." She looked over at Scooter.

"Yes, I'm Calvin and this is my grandma. I received some good reviews from the assisted living management, and I believe you will be a good fit for my grandma. Plus, my assistant did a thorough background check and everything checked out."

There was another knock at the door, and the Orderly walked in. "Hi I'm here for Ms. Ruby. It's time to take you up."

"I'll be right here when you get back, Grandma." Scooter

kissed Ms. Ruby on her forehead before Ms. Ruby was rolled out of the room.

A Few Days Later, Scooter wheeled his grandma in the house.

"Hey there, Ms. Ruby," Debbie said.

"It sure is good to see you back," Ms. Ruby said.

Debbie walked over to Ms. Ruby's chair and gave her a hug.

"And I must say, it feels good to be out of that place and back home." Ms. Ruby opened her arms, hugging Debbie back. "I see y'all here."

"I'm happy you're back too, Ms. Ruby." Gigi bended down and gave Ms. Ruby a hug.

"I think we are all glad your home, Ms. Ruby." Connie hugged Ms. Ruby too.

"What a great welcome-home present, coming home to those that love you," Nurse Betty said.

"Debbie, Scooter must told you what I said because I smell real food. That hospital food was terrible, private room or not." Ms. Ruby tried to get out the wheelchair as Nurse Betty moved to help her. "Ms. Ruby, would you like to go lay down?" Nurse Betty helped Ms. Ruby up.

"No Betty, I been laying down since I got in the hospital. But I would love to go sit on the couch." Ms. Ruby started walking towards the couch. Scooter grabbed her arm to try to assist.

"Boy, I don't need your help, I can walk."

She pushes Scooter away as she sat on the end of the couch, resting her arm on the armrest. "So, Debbie, what you cook that smells so good?"

"Well, I made some baked chicken, with some greens and yams. I cooked using Mrs. Dash too, and I must say it's still delicious, but without all the salt. We don't need you having any blood pressure problems around here."

"Ms. Debbie, your food always tastes good. Even the bowls of cereal you make," Gigi said.

They all laughed.

"Nah, but for real, Ms. Debbie. You do your thing when it comes to the food. Anyways, Grandma, remember that surprise I was telling you about?" Scooter said.

"Yeah. Thank you for making sure everyone was here and that Debbie cooked me something to eat. Lawd knows I'm starving," Ms. Ruby said.

"Grandma, I didn't make them be here. They're here because they love you. I got another surprise for you."

Ms. Ruby sat up and looks around. "So, what is it, child? Hurry it up, my stomach is starting to get loud over here."

Everyone laughed as Ms. Ruby looks on with anticipation.

"Close your eyes, Grandma."

"Now, it's not my birthday, Scooter. What do I need to close my eyes for? Boy, just hurry along so I can eat. "

"Ok Grandma, once you close your eyes..." Scooter ran out to the back returning with the dog. "Open your eyes, Grandma."

"What in the fur ball do you have there?" She looked up at Scooter holding the puppy in a blanket. "Lawd, it's a puppy." A big smile appeared on her face as Scooter set the dog down on her lap.

"You got me a puppy. He's too cute." Ms. Ruby picked the puppy up as she rubbed his nose with her own. "He's adorable, Scooter."

"I'm glad you like him, Grandma. He's potty-trained but I bought him some puppy pads for when he's in the house while he's still training."

"I love him, I love him. I never would have thought you would have bought me a dog." She petted the dog as he sat in her lap.

"How you know it's a boy, Grandma? Gigi, you told her?"

Scooter looked at Gigi with a smirk on his face.

"Boy, Gigi ain't told me nothing. I do know the difference between a male and female dog." Ms. Ruby started to chuckle. "Do he got a name?"

"No Grandma, you get to name him." Scooter sat next to her rubbing on the puppy.

"I'm going to name him Tripp."

Scooter was confused, "Tripp, Grandma? Why Tripp?"

"One, he's so small, I have to watch out for him walking around so I won't trip over him. Two, while I was in the hospital, I was thinking I should take a vacation somewhere relaxing, you know? Do some sightseeing and shopping." A trip is what I need.

"That sounds good to me, Ms. Ruby. So, when we going?" Debbie stood up from the couch. "We should go to the Virgin Islands, or the Dominican Republic." Debbie walked out to check on the food.

Ms. Ruby chuckled, "That child always making it about her." "That do sound nice, Ms. Ruby, a vacation. I would love to see other parts of the world," Gigi said.

"Gigi, your chance is coming. Once you knock them semifinals out and get that recording contract, you'll be on your way to perform in places like London, China, and Africa. You know all them places Beyoncé performed in too. It's coming, child, it's coming. Now, Gigi, after dinner, please go grab the mail for me," Ms. Ruby said.

Debbie alerted everyone that dinner was ready as she placed silverware on the dinner table for everyone.

***

"Ms. Ruby looked so happy last night at dinner."

"Yeah, you can tell she was feeling better too, and she loved the puppy. She gave him the perfect name. I was going to the bathroom last night and he was in my room laying on the carpet and I almost tripped over him. I ordered a collar from Amazon and it will be delivered today. I let Nurse Betty know," Gigi said.

"Well that's good. Her face did light up when she saw the dog," Debbie said.

Connie walked into the diner. "Hey ladies. You ready to kick some butt tonight, Gigi?" She walked behind the counter and took her purse off her shoulder, placing it under the counter

"Yes ma'am, as ready as I'll ever be," Gigi said. "Ms. Ruby doing ok this morning?" Connie asked.

"Yes, she was up making her some coffee when we were leaving out. The nurse was walking in too when we were leaving, so she's fine," Gigi said

"Well that's good she seems to be feeling better. Look, Gigi, sorry but I won't be able to make it tonight. My daughter will be home and she needs me to help her with a project for school. I know you'll do just fine without me there. You'll still have Scooter and Debbie rooting you on,"

"That's fine, Connie. I understand. And you're right, I'll have Ms. Debbie." Gigi looked over at Debbie, smiling. "And Calvin will be there." She blushed.

A Few Hours Later, Gigi took a seat at the counter on a barstool. Debbie stood nearby at the cash register. "It's been one busy morning. I'm starving."

"What would you like me to order for you?" Debbie asked her.

"I don't want anything big, just something light."

"I got the right thing for you." Debbie keyed in the order. "Rob, that's for Gigi."

"Well, that table finally left." Connie sat counting her tips. "Debbie, can you please pour me a cup of coffee?

"Debbie, can you also pass me my bag? I got some mail but

haven't had time to look it over," Gigi said.

Debbie passed Gigi her bag as she turned around to grab the coffee pot. The door chimed, and the Delivery Man entered. He was holding a vase full of red roses.

"Hi, I have a delivery for a Debbie."

"I'm Debbie." She walked around from behind the counter.

"Can you sign here please?" He passed Debbie a clipboard, and waited while she signs. "Thank you!" After signing for the roses, the Delivery Man left.

"Those are beautiful," Connie said.

Yes, they are." Debbie smelled the roses.

"I see y'all getting serious, huh, Debbie?" Connie sipped on her coffee

"You can say that." Debbie walked behind the counter and placed the roses on the end by the window, where the sun was shining through.

"They are beautiful. I like Caesar." Gigi said. Debbie smiled, "He is a good man."

Rob rang the food bell. "Gigi, food up!"

"Ok Gigi, this is something I would like to try on the menu for those who would like something light but tasteful." Debbie passed Gigi the plate.

"Ms. Debbie, now this is what I'm talking about. I haven't had no asparagus in years." Gigi picked up a asparagus, chewing on it. "And the glazed chicken looks good too. Thanks Rob!"

Rob hit the food bell. "You're welcome, Gigi. knock 'em out tonight." Rob flipped the stainless-steel spatula in the air and caught it like a professional chef.

"Those the plans. Now, Ms. Debbie where you get this recipe?" Gigi cut through the chicken with her fork.

"I was watching the food network one night and this lady was putting it together but hers just looked plain. So, I decided I will try it with a twist and see how it will sell on the menu. The new menus will be in next week with the picture display."

"It's tasteful too, Ms. Debbie and the glaze on the asparagus brings them out."

"I'm glad you like it. That means others will too."

"Who don't like what you cook?" Connie looked at Gigi's plate. "That do look good. I'll be taking two of those home tonight for dinner tomorrow. It's pizza tonight."

"Your daughter will like it, especially if she likes asparagus."

Gigi bit into the chicken.

"Yeah, she will. She loves both chicken and asparagus. So, Gigi, I see Quincy hooked your hair up again." Connie looked over at Gigi.

"Yes, he came over last night and curled my hair and brought me this outfit he made a while ago that's just been hanging in his closet."

"Wait he made the dress for you?"

"No. He said he made it for one of his clients, but she never came back to get it."

"Oh I remember who he's talking about. He's talking about that girl named Sherry. She got popped off trying to use somebody's credit card and Quincy got stuck with the dress," Debbie said.

"It's a beautiful dress. I can't wait to put it on," Gigi said.

"Yeah, the dress is beautiful. The turquoise one with the white rhinestones, right, Gigi?"

"Yes, that's the one. And the shoes I bought from the mall last week goes perfect with them."

"I bet you will look beautiful tonight. Please take a lot of pictures and I can convert them for you professionally," Connie said. "I'll make sure I do just that, Connie. Debbie, can you give me some sweet tea please?" Gigi said.

Debbie passed Gigi the iced tea as Gigi looked in her bag. Gigi smiled, "He wrote me back." Gigi hugged the letter. "You talking about your brother?" Debbie asked.

"Yes!" Gigi pushed her empty plate to the side, opening the letter.

"That's great news, Gigi. I know you said it's been a while since you heard from him," Connie said.

"He says he's going back to court because his conviction can be overturned due to dirty cops putting drugs on him."

Debbie shook her head, "I had that happen to one of my girlfriend's son some years ago. They put some drugs on him when they pulled him over saying he fit the description of a known gangbanger wanted for murder. The boy told them they had the wrong person and they beat his ass and put some drugs in the boy's car."

"My girlfriend hired a lawyer and come to find out, these cops had a lot of complaints against them. Majority of them from minorities, but nothing was done to them because the chief was dirty too. It was on the news and everything. So, all them boys those dirty cops locked up, the state had to let a lot of them go and the state was sued. This here with your brother sounds like a lawsuit to me too."

"I'm just glad he will get to come home." "Where will he stay once he comes home, Gigi?"

"His father. He always stayed with his daddy. I'm just going to be happy to see him. I can't wait."

"Did you tell him about the audition?"

"Yes, he knows. Well, Scooter, he'll be here in a few to pick me so I can go get dressed at home. I wanted to take a shower before I got dressed." Gigi got up and puts her empty plate in the dish bin.

"Yeah, I will meet y'all back at the house. I'm going to help Connie with resetting the tables then I'll be on my way to get dressed too after I stop and get a bottle of Cîroc," Debbie said.

"Now, that Cîroc sounds good. Maybe I'll grab a bottle of that tonight too," Connie said.

The door chimes, and Scooter walked into the diner, "Hey ladies, you about already to go, Gigi?" Scooter walked over to Gigi and kissed her softly on the forehead.

"I'm ready, Calvin." She grabbed her bag off of the counter. "I'll see you later, Debbie. Bye Connie."

"Bye ladies." Scooter opened the door for Gigi and they left.

CHAPTER EIGHTEEN

On the night of the audition, Scooter was sitting in the front room with Ms. Ruby as she watched the black version of Steel Magnolias, playing with Tripp. Gigi walked out into the front room.

"Child, you look beautiful. That color brings your skin tone out. Turn around, child, let me see you." Ms. Ruby got up from the couch, looking Gigi over from head to toe.

"She do look beautiful, Grandma." Scooter swallowed deeply. "That's going to look good with the surprise I have for you."

"Surprise?" Gigi said.

"Scooter, take that fancy phone of yours out of your pocket and take a few pictures of us together." Ms. Ruby posed with Gigi as Scooter touched the screen, taking pictures. "Well, y'all best to be getting out of here so you won't be late." Ms. Ruby bended down and picked up Tripp. She set him on her lap as she sat back down on the couch.

"We just waiting on Ms. Debbie. She just texted and said she's putting on her makeup," Gigi said.

Debbie came walking through the back door.

"Ok, Ms. Debbie, I see you. I like that."

"That suit is hot, Debbie, especially with the wedges. Are you sure, you not related to Jill Scott in real life, because you do favor her," Gigi said.

"Honey, I'm older. Do you mean could she be related to me?" She chuckled, "Quincy made this suit for me some years ago but I gained some weight and had to put it to the back of my closet. But since I lost weight these past few months, I can wear it again and I don't have to squeeze into it," she laughed.

"I've never seen you in a blue jean suit, but it do look good on you, Debbie." Ms. Ruby pet Tripp as he played with her fingers. "Scooter, take a picture of us ladies." Ms. Ruby held Tripp in her arms, standing between Gigi and Debbie. Scooter took a couple pictures of them. "Thanks, Scooter." Ms. Ruby sat back down.

"Debbie, can you take some pictures of Gigi and me?" Scooter passed Debbie the camera. She took a few pictures of the two of them together.

"Ok, y'all best be going. And Gigi remember, a mustard—" Gigi recited it with Ms. Ruby, "A mustard seed of faith is all it takes."

"She's rubbing off on you, I see," Scooter said

Ms. Ruby's doorbell rang, "Who could that be?" Ms. Ruby moved to get up.

"Grandma, sit down. I got the door." Scooter opened the door to a Limo Driver, dressed in an all-black suit, wearing a chauffeur's hat.

"I'm here for a Ms. Ginger Garcia," the Driver said. He took his hat off placing it under his arm

"I'm Gigi—I mean, Ginger."

"Your ride awaits you." The Limo Driver pointed at the Cadillac limo truck.

"Calvin, you got me a limo?" Gigi grabbed Scooter's cheeks and looked him in the eyes, smiling.

"This what I'm talking about, we going in style. Cadillac too. I hope they got cocktails." Debbie looked on. Gigi started to walk towards the limo, but Scooter grabbed her hand, holding her back.

"Get in, Ms. Debbie, I bought a special bottle for you. You say you like Cîroc?"

They all walked to the limo together.

"Cîroc, Peach, Pineapple, Mango . . . I like the 'roc." Debbi stepped into the limo. "Oh my God, when did you—"

Caesar cut Debbie off. Scooter and Gigi stepped into the limo. "Scooter gave me a call and asked if I would like to join you guys this evening."

Debbie took a seat next to Caesar kissing him. "Gigi, did you know about this?"

"Nah, Gigi didn't know. I didn't want her to crack under the pressure of trying to keep it from you," Scooter said.

"Well, I'm just glad you invited my boo." Debbie kissed Caesar again.

"Calvin, this is really nice of you." Gigi grabbed Scooter's hand.

"The bottles are over there, Ms. Debbie." Scooter pointed to the mini bar.

"Baby, which Cîroc would you like? We got all flavors," Caesar said.

"Can you fit in a bottle?

"Ms. Debbie, we still got young ears over here," Scooter laughed.

"Let me get peach, baby. Gigi, have a cocktail, it won't hurt."

"Nah, I'm ok, Ms. Debbie."

"Girl have a drink, this your night."

"It's ok baby, one drink will be fine," Scooter said. "Ok, I like the peach, but with ice."

"Peach it is." Caesar made Gigi a drink and passed it to her.

"Scooter what you drinking?" Debbie asked.

"I'll have some of that Hen, Caesar."

Caesar poured himself and Scooter a drink. "Who would've

thought, I'd be hanging out with such beautiful women tonight along with Calvin Walker?"

"I'll toast to that." Debbie took a swig of her drink. "Ok, Caesar, you hooked this up smoothly."

"I did a little bartending before, back in my college days." "I haven't had one of these in a while, and it is good." Gigi sipped on her drink.

"After Gigi wins tonight, we're going to celebrate at Club NuNu," Scooter said.

"Scooter, I see you know your clubs. That's a nice club there where all the stars be."

"What you know about that club, Caesar?" Debbie sipped on the Cîroc.

"Well, I remodeled the place after they had that fire last year. Plus, I also know the owner."

"Ok, my baby plugged too around this here city," Debbie said.

"Scooter how do you know—" Gigi said. Scooter cut Gigi off

"Mustard seed of faith," they said at the same time. Scooter and Debbie both laughed as the Limo Driver pulled up in front of the studio. The Driver got out first and opened the door for them to get out. Scooter stepped out first and grabbed Gigi's hand and Caesar and Debbie followed. The valet guy opened the studio door for the group to walk in together, arm in arm.

"Hi, Ms. Garcia, glad to see you back. Hi Mr. Walker, glad to see you as well. Again, I must scan IDs in for security purposes. After, you guys can head to the back where the casting team awaits with the other contestants," the Lady at front desk said.

They all passed the lady their IDs, then head to the back to Studio 7. As they walked in, they could hear the other contestants talking and singing. A Casting Team Member sat at the desk.

"Hi I'm Ginger Garcia, I was told we are to sign in here."

"Yes Ms. Garcia, please sign in here. We will be starting shortly," a casting team member said.

"So, this is how it looks back here with all the tension in the air. Eyes staring hard at you, Gigi, when we walked in," Debbie said.

"They staring at Calvin." Gigi looked around the room.

"Nah, honey, they staring at you, especially that one chick in the blue over there looking like the penitentiary Remy Ma."

"Ms. Debbie, stop."

"Baby, that Cîroc got you talking about folks," Caesar said. "Nah, I'm just saying she was staring Gigi down. Giving Gigi that Mommy-said-knock-you-out look," Debbie threw her fist in the air like she was boxing.

"Ok all, quiet down, quiet down. Welcome back to the second and final round to the semifinals," the casting team member said. He walked back and forth as he speaks. "As you can see, there's a few of us team members around and if you need help with anything, please feel free to ask. As always, refreshments are against the back wall. I wish you all good luck. Now, again, only one person is allowed back here with the contestants, and the others will be escorted to sit in the audience."

"That's our cue, Caesar." Debbie walked over to Gigi. "Girl, hurry and get this over with so we can go party. Oh, and if it's that Remy Ma chick you got to go against, sit her blue peacock ass down. Looking like the NBC Mascot."

"Ok, baby come on. Good luck, Gigi," Caesar pulled Debbie away.

"I'll be waiting on you to receive that gold card." Scooter hugged and held Gigi close in his arms as she laid on his chest, smelling his cologne and smiling. Scooter looked in Gigi's eyes, smiling and holding both of her hands. "Go get 'em."

Later the Announcer said, "Hello all and welcome back to

Your Big Chance."

The audience applauded.

"Today we have our five contestants returning trying to move on to the semifinals. But there can only be two that will advance on to the semifi als. The winner of the semifinals will win a record deal along with one hundred thousand dollars."

The crowd applauded again.

"Contestants, are you ready? Oh, I forgot to mention that we changed something again..."

The audience looked on in anticipation.

"In this box that sits on this table, lay five pieces of paper. On each piece of paper will be two songs. You will choose one song off the paper. Hopefully you'll know the song." The Announcer smirked. "The catch to this is, you do not unfold the piece of paper until it's time for you to get up here and sing. You'll announce the song from the paper you would like to sing and the other song will not be revealed."

The audience went wild clapping.

"Now, what did also change is the numbering system. I know you guys at home and in the audience are wondering what the numbering system is. Well, the numbering system is when each contestant pulls out a number from the box, which will determine the lineup. I will walk up to you with the box and you pull out a piece of paper. That piece of paper will have a number on it. The person with Number 1 goes first and we follow in suit until we get to Number 5.

The Announcer walked to each contestant as they pulled out a piece of folded paper, "Please reveal your numbers," the Announcer said.

Each contestant held their number in front of them. Gigi held Number 5. The girl that stared Gigi down held Number 3. After all, the contestants sang, it was time for the Announcer to say who would be advancing to the semifinals. "Judges, anything else you would like to say before the semifinal contestants are announced?

All the Judges congratulated the contestants, who were standing nervously, waiting to see who would advance to the semifinals

"And the first person to advance to the semifinals is..." The Announcer pulled the card out the envelope. "...Ginger Garcia."

Gigi fell to the ground on one knee, holding her face, and bouncing back up as tears roll down her face.

"The second to make it to the semifinals is..." The Announcer pulled the card out the envelope. "... Rachel Blue.

The girl that had stared Gigi down walked up, a hand over her mouth as she cried too, looking over at Gigi.

"So, ladies, now that you know who you will be facing in the semifinals, how are you feeling?" Judge 1 said

"I'm feeling so excited. I've waited all my life for something like this to happen. I'm very competitive and I look forward to the competition," Rachel said. She looked over at Gigi, posing like Janet Jackson from the video 'Control,' throwing her hair back.

"Ok, Ms. Rachel, giving them all that finesse in that blue dress." He looked Rachel over before he looked over at Gigi. "And Ginger, how do you feel now, knowing who you are up against in the semifinals?

"I'm feeling thankful and humble at this time. I'm honored to be sharing the semifinals stage with Ms. Blue for she's a talented singer."

"Well, let's give it up for both ladies." The Announcer began to clap.

A Little Later, Debbie and Caesar met with Scooter and Gigi in the hall of the studio.

"I knew you were going to have to go against Miss Stare Me Down." Debbie walked up to Gigi, giving her a hug. "Her last name is Blue, and she wore that blue dress. Gigi, going to have her looking blue after them semifinals.

"Congratulations, Gigi. I always heard you sing over the phone, but you sang really good in person. You did a great job," Caesar said. "Girl, you blew my mind. I never ever heard you sing that song.

You had Caesar over there shaking his head and patting his knee like he was at a Charlie Wilson concert," Debbie said.

"I never heard a woman sing that song like that. Charlie, my guy and you tore that up. You had the audience rocking back and forth singing along too," Caesar said.

"She, had you too. So, Gigi, I'm curious to know what the other song was you passed on."

They began to walk towards the valet.

"I passed on Vivian Greene."

"'Emotional Rollercoaster'? That's my song. I hear you singing it at times around the diner," Debbie said.

"Yes, I love her music but as you just said, Ms. Debbie, I sing it at times. I wanted a challenge and that was to sing Charlie Wilson's song, opposed to Vivian's. Because it was made and sung by a man and I wanted to prove to the audience that I can sing men songs just as well as I can sing female singers' songs."

"That's my Gigi." Scooter grabbed her hand.

"Ok, ok, you did the reverse audience judge move," Scooter said.

"The what?" Gigi looked confused.

"When you flip the script. See, the judges and audience was expecting you to sing a song by a woman, but you flipped the script and went with good old' Charlie," Debbie said.

"And she made the right decision by doing so. That was a smart move, Gigi. Now the world knows you can sing a mixture of both male and female artists," Caesar said.

"Baby, you sounded great." Scooter grabbed her and kissed her passionately. The limo pulled up.

"Now, let's go get our party on."

The limo driver opened the door, escorting the ladies into the limo.

"It's time for a cocktail, baby." Debbie pulled her compact out of her purse and looked over herself in the mirror. "This time let me get the mango Cîroc. Gigi are you having—the same?"

"Let me try the mango too." Gigi rubbed on Scooter's leg.

"I remember when I was your guys' age," he said smiling. "I met my wife when I was around your guys' age, rest her soul. My point is you guys look good together and you both give off good vibes. Congratulations to you both for having a bright future."

The limo pulled up in front of a club. Outside, there was a long line of folks trying to get in.

"Ok, I see it's about to be cracking up in here." Debbie finished her drink. "Club NuNu, here we come."

"Calvin, look at all these people. This place must be bumping." Gigi sipped on her drink. The Limo Driver stopped and got out to open the door. Scooter stepped out first, reaching for Gigi's hand. A flash of cameras started snapping

"It's Calvin Walker!" A girl in crowd yelled.

"And Debbie Fox," Debbie said. Debbie and Gigi stepped out the car, looking at the crowd as they snapped pictures. Scooter grabbed Gigi's hand, holding her close to him.

"You ready to have fun, baby?" He kissed her as they walked into the club. The club owner walked up to them as they walked into the club doors.

"Calvin Walker and Caesar Palace, nice to see you fellows again," Owner said. He shook both men's hands. "Hello ladies." He kissed both Gigi's and Debbie's hands.

"Welcome to Club NuNu. I hope you all enjoy. Mr. Walker, I have your VIP tables set up right over there. The host will seat you, and serve a bottle of champagne on me." The host led Scooter and the others to the VIP section.

"Now, this is what the hell I'm talking about in real life." Debbie bobbed her head to the music as they walked to the VIP section.

Scooter said to the host, "Can we please also start off with some chicken wings with both ranch and blue cheese? We need to put something on our stomachs before we dive deep into the liquor." "Yes, I'll put that in for you, Mr. Walker. Your bottle of champagne is on its way." The host walked away.

"Now, this is off the chain. I always heard about this place, but I never been in here. I love the diversity. There's all types of people in here," Gigi said.

"Yeah, this place be rocking. When I first got drafted, some of the guys on the team brought me here a few times."

"Yeah, this is a moneymaker right here, for real. One hundred dollars to get in and I think the cheapest beer is about ten dollars a bottle," Debbie said.

"Well, I'm glad we were invited, and we don't have to worry about buying drinks," she laughed.

"Standup comedy Ms. Debbie, standup comedy," Scooter said.

"The dance floor is packed. The DJ's doing his thing," Gigi said.

House music played. Debbie sang along.

"Yeah, the DJ's going way back. 'It's time for the percolator, it's time for the percolator'," Debbie said.

"That's my jam too, Debbie." Gigi started to move around in the seat.

"Well, show me what you got Gigi." Scooter got up and pulled Gigi onto the dance floor. Scooter, Gigi, Debbie, and Caesar danced all night.

"It's getting late Scooter, and I'm tired." Gigi grabbed Scooter's hand, leading him back to the table. They sat and watched Debbie and Caesar as they continued dancing.

"Me too. Debbie got that liquor in her and can't sit down. Let me get up and let them know we will be leaving in a few." Scooter walked off, headed towards the dance floo

Gigi sat at the table playing with the olives in her cup with the straw as someone came up and took a seat next to her. Gigi turned to look at him. A stunned expression quickly came over her face.

"Hello baby girl," Mean Mug said. He touched her leg under the table, gripping it tightly. "I see you all up in here with your little boyfriend toasting it up. So, bitch, you snitched on me to the police and all I ever did was try to be good to you by providing you with a roof over your head and feeding your ass too. And you pay me back by snitching to the police. And not just that—getting me locked up too." He squeezed her leg tighter. A pained expression came over her face.

"Mean Mug, it wasn't me. I didn't tell the police anything. I promise." She teared up, trying to pull her leg back. "I jumped out on the fire escape when they came in. It wasn't me that snitched about anything."

"Bitch, you lying. Trina told me it was you." He looked her in the eyes with a hateful stare. "I not only lost you and money, but Peaches too but that was that bitch's fault. You singing and shit, I see. All on TV and shit. Them people don't know who the fuck you really are, do they Ginger."

He releases his grip on her leg, "I want what belongs to me. And that's lost wages, plus the money you owe me. I'll be seeing you around." Mean Mug got up and disappeared into the crowd, as Debbie and the others approached the table.

"I haven't danced like this in such a long time." Debbie sat down, pouring herself some champagne. "You ok over there, Gigi? You look like you spaced out."

"I'm ok, Ms. Debbie, I'm just tired. It's been a long night full of surprises."

"We're about to leave now, ma. Let me pay the bill and we out," Scooter pulled a few hundred dollars out his wallet as the host approached. "Can you please get our limo?" He placed the bills in the host's hand. The host left, signaling to the valet to get the limo. Scooter helped Gigi up from the table, as Caesar helped Debbie up. They began to all walk towards the front of the club.

"You sure you ok, Gigi?" Scooter asked.

"Yes, just tired and ready to take these clothes off and get in the bed." They all made it to the front as the limo pulled up. The valet driver opened the limo door, escorting them all into the limo.

"This night was wonderful. I haven't had fun like this in so long," Debbie said.

"Yes, we had a ball," Caesar said.

"Scooter, can you please stay over tonight? I'm not feeling too good all of a sudden," Gigi said.

"You sure it's not the liquor?" Debbie asked.

"No, Ms. Debbie, it's not the liquor. My stomach just feels upset all of a sudden."

"Sure, I'll stay. You sure you're ok though? Your whole attitude changed. I thought you'd be happy to make it to the semifinals." "I'm ok, Scooter. I'm just not feeling too good."

"Ok, just trying to make sure you're good. We can talk for a minute, then I'll go sleep in my room," Scooter said.

"And Caesar could sleep in mine." Debbie pulled Caesar's leg closer to hers with a sexual grip. Gigi laid on Scooter's chest as the limo driver entered the expressway.

CHAPTER NINETEEN

"We had a ball this weekend." Debbie walked over to the jukebox and inserts a few quarters. "I been thinking about this song ever since Caesar left my house."

The song 'Happy Feelings' started to play as Debbie stepped through the diner, two-stepping.

"I see somebody's feeling happy." Connie made two fresh pots of coffee

"I see you, Ms. Debbie."

"Nah, I see you." Debbie grabbed Gigi's hands and started stepping with her. "What you know about stepping, Gigi?"

"My mom used to step all time, especially when we had birthdays, family get-together, and barbeques. That's when we used to have fun until she met her husband and started drinking."

"Well, you got me to step with from now on. Whenever you're ready, I'm here." Debbie released Gigi's hands and walked behind the counter, getting herself a glass of water.

"Looks like someone getting up in age. You tired, Debbie? I have Tylenol," Connie said.

"Nah, Connie I'm good. It's just been a while since I danced." Debbie grabbed Connie and stepped with her. "What you going to do with it, Connie?" Debbie moved Connie side to side, pulling her body into hers, then out.

"I'm not new to this. I did ballroom dancing," Connie said.

Debbie laughed, "Well, this is what we call stepping." Debbie spun Connie around.

"Ok, I'm dizzy." Connie took a seat, fanning herself with her hand and laughing.

"I want to be just like y'all when I grow up." She giggled. "Nah, we trying to get where you going," Debbie said. "And where is that?"

"Rich Valley. You got a fan base already. They got you all on YouTube with over one hundred thousand followers," Debbie said. "I didn't know you were into YouTube. But yeah, Scooter showed me last night. I was shocked."

"I don't see why; your voice is unforgettable when you sing. You got that Millie Jackson mixed with Angie Stone voice," Connie said.

Gigi jerked her head back, looking at Connie, "Now Connie, what do you know about Millie Jackson and Angie Stone?"

"My husband used to play Millie when we used to cook in the kitchen together. Millie was one of his favorite singers. I told y'all I was married but I didn't mention it was to a black man."

"Ok, Connie, so you like the wood too." Debbie started to do a dance, grabbing the barstool and moving her body in a stroking motion.

"Ok, Connie, I see you got a whole lot of secrets coming out." She smirked. "I'm going to call Ms. Ruby and check on her."

"I just did. Nurse Betty is with her. She's taking a bath now." Debbie grabbed cash out the register, putting it in a money pouch. "I'm going to take this to the back." Debbie walked away.

"Where is the remote control? The guys in the corner would like for me to turn the afternoon news on," Connie said.

Gigi walked behind the counter and grabbed the remote, handing it to Connie. "Here you go, Connie."

"Thanks, Gigi." Connie walked over to the guys and asked what channel they would like to watch.

"Fox News will be fine. Can we also get two cups of coffee with extra creamer and sugar?" One of the guys said.

"Yessir. Two coffees with extra creamer." Connie walked back to the counter.

"I see you got the two grumpy old men over there. They asked you to turn on the news, and to bring extra creamer," Debbie said.

"Yes ma'am, and extra sugar," Connie said.

"I've served those guys a few times. Now the old man with the Kangol, watch him, he likes to fill his pockets up with creamers and sugar." Debbie swept the floor behind the counter. Connie walked behind the counter next to her. She opened the pie container, cutting off two slices of sweet potato pie

"That pie do look good," Gigi said.

"Gigi, can you please take this over to the two old men? I have to use the ladies' room," Connie said.

"Sure!" Gigi grabbed the two slices of sweet potato pie and walked them over to the table. "Hi, I have your two slices of pie."

The men were looking up at the news as Gigi approached the table. She put the pie down and looked up at the TV.

"Where they say they found her body at?" Old Man 1 said.

"In the damn garbage can. Whoever did that to her, sure didn't give a flying fuck. Just tossed the lady's body in the garbage can." Old Man 2 said.

Gigi looked up at the TV and froze when she saw a picture of Peaches's face flash on the TV

"If anyone has information, please contact the Chicago Police Department," she heard the TV Announcer saying.

"Oh my God, I don't believe this." Gigi ran to the back of the diner into the bathroom and threw up in the toilet. "Peaches, he killed Peaches." Gigi looked at her reflection in the mirror. "He killed Peaches." Tears fell down her face.

"What's wrong, Gigi?" Connie flushed the toilet and walked out. She looked into the mirror, washing her hands. "Why are you crying?" Connie grabbed paper towels and dried her hands.

"Peaches is dead." Gigi leaned back on the wall. She bended over, her face in her hands, crying.

Connie was worried, "Peaches who?"

"The girl that came in here the other day wearing all black, that was sitting at your table."

"Oh, now I remember. What the hell?" Connie grabbed Gigi trying to comfort her.

"She just was telling me that she was going to leave town to go stay with her sister to get away from Mean Mug, now she's dead. Gigi sobbing. I bet he killed her. I have to get out of here." Gigi opened the bathroom door, walked behind the counter, and grabbed her purse.

"Gigi, what's wrong girl?"

"I need to get out of here Ms. Debbie. I just need to leave before he comes for me."

"Before who comes for you?" Debbie asked.

Connie walks in behind Gigi, "She's talking about the pimp. Gigi thinks he killed the girl that was in here the other day dressed in black."

"Killed her? What the hell you mean killed her?" Debbie looked up, as she stopped wiping the counter.

"She's dead, Debbie. My friend that came in here the other day."

"The girl in all the black?"

"Yes, I just saw on the news that she was found dead in a garbage can."

"In a garbage can?" Debbie shook her head as she frowned.

182

"Gigi, come have a seat and calm down." Debbie grabbed a cup of hot tea for Gigi. She reached in her bra and pulled out a small bottle of cognac, pouring it in Gigi's tea. "Now, that's some horrible shit, somebody dumping a body in the garbage. That there sounds like some personal shit. Like they were trying to make a statement."

"Did they say how she died?" Connie grabbed the coffee pot. "Honey, could we get some refills?" One guy said. He waved at Connie, holding his cup up.

"Yessir, I'm getting the coffee pot now." Connie walked off to the table, pouring the old men refills. "Would you care for anything else? More pie? The check?" Are you trying to kick us out of here?" the other guy said. "No, sir, I'm just trying to make sure my customers have what they need. If you care not to order anything else, I can drop the check." "I'm just messing with you, baby." The man added creamer to his coffee. "You can bring the check; I have to be on my way to dialysis. You know coffee helps to improve the vascular functions for people like me on dialysis."

"We'll take the check, honey." One of the old men grabbed Connie's wrist. Connie snatched her arm back.

"Excuse you!" She yelled.

"He's partially blind the other man said. So, when he talk to women, he be trying to be on that Ray Charles felly shit. You know, grabbing the woman's wrist to tell her size." He laughed.

"Well, this not the Ray Charles movie." Connie pulled their receipt out of her apron as Guy 1 passed her a twenty-dollar bill and told her to keep the change. Connie walked off behind the counter. "I can't believe that old man just grabbed my damn wrist." Connie cashed the check out at the register. Yeah, he did that to me before and I checked him on the spot, Debbie traying up an order.

You see, they didn't want to sit with me. He know I will curse his old Bengay-smelling ass out. Trying to get free fills and shit.

"I tell you about these old men. I need to call Scooter, so I can tell him what happened." Gigi pulled her phone out.

"He Gigi, how's my new superstar doing?" Scooter said. "Calvin, I'm scared."

Scooter said frantically, "Scared of what? What happened, Gigi? What's going on?"

"The girl I told you about that came in the diner the other day..."

"Yeah, the one you said that dude beat up really bad."

"Yes, Peaches." Gigi wiped away tears as they roll down her face. "She's dead. They found her body in a garbage can."

"Oh Gigi, I'm sorry to hear that. I'm on my way, baby. Let me tell the fellows I'm leaving." Scooter hung up.

"Do you want me to call Office Reed so you can let him know what she said before she was murdered?"

"No. Oh, no. I'm not about to do that, Debbie, and put my life in stake. Not just my life but everybody's life in here. He will do something bad to one of you just to get to me. No, I'm not calling the police."

"Gigi, you have semifinals in two weeks. We have to think of something," Connie said.

"I told Rob what's going on and the man pulled a nine clout out, talking about he wish that nigga would show up. Back there looking like the black Lone Ranger."

The food bell rang. "I'm not playing, I'll kill that nigga if he comes up in here and I won't even feel bad about it." Rob displayed his nine glock.

"Now, Rob, I hope you have a Concealed Carry," Debbie said.

"I'm ex-military. I fought for this country, so, I am Concealed. I'll treat that little punk like he's the enemy and take his ass out, but on some self-defense shit. I'm military, I'm not stupid." Rob hit the food bell again.

"Ms. Debbie, I'm done with the dishes and the bathrooms." Lance stood, popping his neck.

"Now, Lance, you could leave," Debbie said.

"Ok, I'm going to punch out, Ms. Debbie." He walked behind the counter, clocking out.

"Gigi, are you ok?" Lance walked over to her, handing her a paper towel.

"I'm ok, Lance. I just got some bad news." Gigi wiped her eyes with the paper towel.

"Well, I got a new bike. Would you like to see it?" Lance grabbed Gigi's hand. "I bought it with my checks from Walmart. It got big wheels just like the motorcycles. I can take you for a ride if you like. I think that will make you smile." Lance and Gigi walked outside.

"Maybe next time, Lance. This is a cool bike. The wheels are big." Gigi looked at the bike as Lance unchains it from the tree. "The girls are going to like this." Gigi touched the handlebars.

Lance stuttered, "I got a girlfriend already." He blushed. "Ok, and what's your girlfriend's name?"

"Her name is Billie."

"Oh, like the singer Billie Holiday."

"How'd you know? You know my girlfriend?"

"No, Lance. Billie Holiday was a famous singer. So, I assumed maybe her mom named her after the singer or after her daddy if his name was Billie. I'm just saying. Look, be careful, Lance. I will see you later."

Lance hugged Gigi, then got on his bike.

"Gigi, congratulations. You're going to win." He pulled away as a black pimpmobile 1970s–looking car with twenty-inch rims and tinted windows drives by slowly. It stopped at the stop sign, letting the back window down. Gigi looked at it in shock.

"Bitch, didn't I tell you I could pull up on you anytime?" Mean Mug said. He played with a toothpick in his mouth. "I saw you made it to them semifinals. That's the only thing stopping me from fucking you up. Now, like I told you in the club, bitch you owe me interest, plus the motherfucking money I lost when you got me popped off.

Gigi tried to turn around and run into the diner.

"Bitch, I'll shoot your ass right now if you move another motherfucking foot."

"Gigi froze, looking scared.

"Mean Mug, I told you I didn't snitch to the police. Why would I do that? I was making money too. Why, would I want that to stop."

She stood there, swallowing, looking nervous. "I jumped out the damn window onto the fire escape when 12 came in there.

"Bitch, you don't think I've seen Law and Order before? I've seen how them motherfuckers be setting niggas up. Becoming C-eyes and shit, fucking informants. So, I'm not trying to hear..." He continued in a whiny voice, mocking her. "...I jumped out the window shit onto the fire escape." He continued in his normal voice. "Bitch, I don't trust you. You ain't come see me one motherfucking time when I was locked up so diss me with that bullshit."

"Mean Mug, it wasn't me."

"Well, bitch, this right here is about to be you. You going to go in them semifinals and win that motherfucking one hundred thousand dollars. Once you cut that check, you're going to give me half of that and that's just to keep your ass alive plus my wages and losses."

"I don't know if I'm going to win. What if I don't?"

"Bitch, you better sing like a motherfucking opera singer mixed with a fucking fantasia. I don't give a fuck; you better make them lungs blue or I'm going to blow your motherfucking head off Or do you want me to come to the old lady's house and blow that motherfucker up? Yeah bitch, I been knowing where you were living and bitch, I got your number too." Mean Mug started to raise the window up with a sawed-off shotgun sticking out of it about to pull off before he lowered the window back down. "Get my money, bitch, or everyone you know will feel this steel, including her."

Mean Mug grabbed a handful of hair of a person in the passenger seat, forcing her head up, displaying Gigi's mother who looks all doped up. "Yeah, this bitch sucking on both my dicks, this dick." He displayed a glass crack pipe and grabbed his balls. Mean Mug pulled off as Scooter pulled up. Scooter parked, and jumped out of his car.

"Hey Gigi, you ok?" He walked up to her caressing her in his arms, looking down in her eyes. "Who, was that you were talking to? Those twenty-inch rims were nice."

"That was nobody. They were looking for directions to Hyde Park. Some out-of-towners." Gigi grabbed Scooter as they walked in the diner.

"There goes my favorite little nephew," Debbie said.

"Oh, I'm your nephew now?" Scooter gave Debbie a hug.

"Hey Scooter." Connie took her apron off and stuffed it in her bag. "Tell your granny I'll call her back tonight. I'm about to get out of here. I have to shoot a pet funeral."

"Shoot a pet funeral? What the hell? Who the hell have funerals for dead animals? I'm just saying my granddaddy's dogs died and he just buried them in the yard," Debbie said.

"That's what some of us white folks do. I'll see you guys later." Connie grabbed her bag and left. They all laughed.

"So, Gigi, tell me what happened?" Scooter asked her.

"I'll tell you once you get me back to Ms. Ruby's." Gigi grabbed her bag.

"Ms. Debbie—"

Debbie cut Scooter off, "Just take her home. Rob and I are

going to lock up. I'll be there shortly." Debbie hugged both Gigi and Scooter. Scooter walked over and peeked through the food window.

"What up, Rob?" He paused. "Ok Debbie, we'll see you later." Scooter and Gigi left together.

"Thank you for coming. I just got spooked when I saw the news saying Peaches was dead. I mean, I just saw her the other day now she's dead."

Scooter grabbed Gigi's hand as they drove down the expressway. "Yeah, that's some real fucked-up shit especially if that dude did that shit. I think you need to go to the police, Gigi, seriously. Let them know what's going on."

"I'll be ok as long as I have people around me that will help to protect me." She squeezed Scooter's hand. "He's a low-life–ass dude. I'm sorry, Calvin, but I'm pissed. He's a nothing-ass nigga. Living off motherfuckers he know ain't got shit."

"I'll protect you." Scooter looked into Gigi's eyes. "But I still think you need to go to the police."

"I already put an order of protection in place. If he comes around me, he'll be arrested."

CHAPTER TWENTY

When they arrive at Ms. Ruby's Home, Scooter laid his car keys on the kitchen table. "Hi Nurse Betty. Where's my granny?" He took his jacket off

"Hi, Nurse Betty. "Gigi walked towards her room.

"Scooter, I'm going to take a shower, then change my clothes. Give me a few." She walked in her room and closed the door.

"Hey Grandma." Scooter walked over to the couch where Ms. Ruby laid, and bent down to kiss her on the cheek. "I see you spoiling Tripp." Scooter picked Tripp up from Ms. Ruby's lap, rubbing his nose against the dog's nose.

"That's my baby. I fell in love with him from the first time I saw him. I'm glad you got him for me." Ms. Ruby rubbed Tripp's belly. "So, what's going on with Gigi?"

"She's upset. She just found out one of her friends was murdered."

"Murdered! What friend?" Ms. Ruby sat up on the couch. "Some girl that was in the diner the other day. One of the girls she used to stay with in that house."

"The girl who came in dressed in all black. She's dead now? How?"

"Gigi said they found her in a garbage can." Scooter grabbed the toy ball and threw it across the floor while Tripp chased after it

"Oh my Lawd! They put her body in a garbage can?" Ms. Ruby shook her head in disgust. "Gigi must be shaken up."

"Yeah, she's pretty hurt. She thinks that guy Mean Mug murdered her. She told me Debbie called one of the officer that comes to the diner to eat to help Gigi get an order of protection."

"So she got an order of protection? That's good."

"Ms. Ruby, dinner should be ready in a few. I made my favorite meatloaf with homemade mashed potatoes and corn.," Nurse Betty said.

"I hope you made enough for me. I'm starving," Scooter said. "There's more than enough, Mr. Walker," Nurse Betty said. "Call me Calvin." Scooter smiled at her as he tossed the toy ball from hand to hand.

"Betty, it smells good too. Gigi is here to, but I don't know if she is up for eating. Can you make a plate for her and just set it in the microwave, once the food is ready?" Ms. Ruby said.

"Sure!" She walked back to the kitchen.

A Half an Hour later, Gigi was sitting on the loveseat across from Ms. Ruby with her notepad.

"Hi Ms. Ruby. How are you feeling today?"

"I'm feeling ok, child. Scooter told me what happened. Are you ok?" Ms. Ruby sat up to pat Gigi's knee.

"No, I can't completely say I am. I'm scared. I can't believe Peaches is dead. Not only that, they put her body in the garbage can like she was a piece of trash."

"Honey, that's just pure evil. Look Scooter said you think that guy Mean Mug had something to do with her murder."

"I know Mean Mug. I know he did this or had someone do it. When Peaches was at the diner talking to me, she was telling me that she was leaving town and going to Idaho to move in with her sister and start doing hair. But she had to make a stop at one of her friend's

190

house to pick up some money. That was the last time I saw her." A sad frown passed over Gigi's face.

"I was telling my granny, the same thing I was telling you. You still need to go to the police." Scooter continued to play with Tripp.

"The police don't care about girls like Peaches. The same girl I used to be." Gigi shook her head. "People look at girls like Peaches, like me, and just automatically judge us. I didn't want to be out there in them streets but when my mom kicked me out, I had nowhere to go. I would've went over to my brother's house but he's locked up. So, that's when I met Peaches and she invited me into her home. She told me that her and a few more women stay there but I can stay too if I help to pay the bills. I was like "I don't have a job," and that's when I was introduced to that lifestyle known as Mean Mug."

"Well, that's behind you. You did what you needed to do to survive. But men like Mean Mug prey on young girls like yourself. You were vulnerable and he took advantage of that. Child, you're young, this shall pass," Ms. Ruby said.

"Thanks, Ms. Ruby." Gigi smiled at Ms. Ruby. "I see Tripp loving his new place."

Tripp was on the floor at their feet, playing with one of his stuffed toys

"Well, I don't know about y'all, but I'm hungry." Scooter stood up, rubbing his stomach.

"I didn't know if you were hungry or not Gigi, so I had Betty put you up a plate in the microwave," Ms. Ruby said.

"It smells good. I could eat." Gigi stood up and stretched her arms out.

Scooter yelled to Nurse Betty, "Is the food ready, Nurse Betty?" He helped Ms. Ruby off the couch

"Yes, everything is all ready now. Are you guys ready to eat?"

"Yes, can you please bring the food in the living room at the family table? I'll be right back; I'm going to wash my hands." Ms. Ruby walks off into the bathroom

"Me too." Scooter went into his bathroom off of his bedroom and washed his hands. Tripp bit at his pant legs, yanking on them playfully. Gigi's phone rang and an unfamiliar number appeared. Gigi hesitated, then answered it.

"Bitch, you better have my money or I'm going to kill all you motherfuckers, including that dog." The phone disconnected and Gigi ran to the window. She looked out to see Mean Mug's pimpmobile pulled off. Ms. Ruby shuffled back into the ro

"Now I'm ready to eat." She took a seat.

"Yeah, this looks really good." Gigi took a seat at the table as well.

"I told you, Grandma, Nurse Betty got skills." Scooter reached for the meatloaf and Ms. Ruby hit his hand.

"Anything else you need for now, Ms. Ruby?" Nurse Betty placed the potatoes on the table along with a gravy boat.

"No, child, we ok. Thank you for preparing dinner."

"No problem, Ms. Ruby. That's what your grandson pays me to do." She winked at Scooter. "If you won't be needing anything else, I'm going to head out. I'll see you tomorrow morning."

They all said good night to Nurse Betty as she walked out the front door.

"Let's say Grace." Ms. Ruby bowed her head to say Grace. "Lawd, bless this food that we are about to receive. In Jesus's name, amen."

CHAPTER TWENTY-ONE

On the semifinals day, Debbie and Quincy walked into the kitchen of Ms. Ruby's house. They're dressed in jogging attire, both breathing like they were out of breath.

"Ms. Ruby, we had a nice run today." Debbie and Quincy walked into the kitchen of Ms. Ruby's house, grabbing paper towels and rubbing the sweat off their face and neck

"Ms. Ruby, I see you all up in here." Quincy looked around the kitchen, admiring the stainless-steel appliances. "Now, this refrigerator is what's happening. You can sit in your kitchen cooking or eating and got a whole TV to look at on the fridge. Now that's hot."

"Hey Quincy, what you doing over here?" Ms. Ruby reached up from her chair to give Quincy a hug.

"I'm going to do Gigi's makeup and bump her curls and send her out on that stage looking impeccable." He posed like RuPaul with both hands on his hips.

"I know you are."

"Ok, Ms. Debbie, I got my dress and things." Gigi stood holding a Dolce & Gabbana Lamé one-shoulder cocktail dress with a DG belt. "Gigi, that dress is hot." Quincy grabbed the dress, looking it over. He held the dress close to his body. "This is something Quita would wear. Wait, girl, this here was some coins. How much it hit you for?"

"It was a gift from Calvin." Gigi smiled.

"It's beautiful, Gigi. I had Scooter program the TV, so when the semifinals come on it will automatically turn to it so I won't have to be fumbling with that remote," Ms. Ruby said.

"Ms. Ruby, you do know that remote you have, you just push the button at the top and tell the remote what you would like to look at, and it will go to that program for you," Debbie said.

"Ms. Ruby, you living fancy up in here. You have TV's you can talk to. Well Gigi, let's go knock this out." Quincy walked over to Ms. Ruby. "It was nice to see you again. Whenever you are ready for me to do your hair again, Ms. Ruby, I'm here. Quincy grabbed a bag from Gigi as they left leaving out the back.

"You need anything, Ms. Ruby?" Debbie stood up.

"Nah child, I'm good. Nurse Betty will be here in a few. We're going to watch the show tonight together. Look Debbie..." Ms. Ruby grabbed Debbie's arm. "Keep an eye on Gigi. She has a lot on her mind with her friend being murdered and all."

"I got her, Ms. Ruby. Let me go get myself together too. Scooter will be here to pick us up and I want to look just as immaculate walking up in that place like I'm the semifinalist," Debbie said

Gigi sat in a highchair as Quincy curled her hair.

"Girl, you better kick some ass tonight, bitch. And bring that one hundred thousand dollars back." He looked at her in the mirror, giving her a grin.

"Nephew, Gigi got this." Debbie poured her a cup of Moscato.

"You drinking by yourself, Auntie, or do you not see me over here?"

Debbie poured Quincy a glass of wine. "Would you like some wine, Gigi?"

"I'll have a glass, Ms. Debbie."

Debbie passed them both a glass of wine.

"So, girl, what you going to sing tonight? Some Beyoncé, or

194

some Alicia Keys?" He blew the curling iron off before placing it in Gigi's hair.

"No, I'm going to sing a piece of music I written. Give them me, Gigi."

"Ok, ok, original. Well, I'm done bumping your hair, let's get this makeup going. I have the perfect colors to match your dress." Quincy opened his suitcase and took out his makeup. "Bitch, I want to try these new lashes on you." He pulled out a pack of long Diana Ross–looking lashes.

"These are hot. I was looking for some of these, but I couldn't find them nowhere.

"Girl, maybe because them damn boosters stole them all. I have some boosters on speed dial depending on what I'm looking for. If I need lashes, I'll call Keisha with the big butt. If I needed some food stamps, I'll call Rhonda. All, I'm saying girl is, if you need it, I can get it," Quincy said.

"After she win tonight, Nephew, she's going to be set for life. Living like them divas Mary J. Blige, Faith Evans, Erykah Badu. She's going to be on their levels. Now, Gigi, don't forget about us little folks when you win tonight."

"I will never forget you, Quincy, Connie, Calvin, and especially Ms. Ruby for opening up her doors for me giving me a chance. She didn't have to do that."

"That's Ms. Ruby being Ms. Ruby. She is always trying to help and save folks. And you're just one of many to come. That lady has a big heart. I was nervous when she had to go have that procedure done. I'm just glad she's feeling better and doing alright. She'll be back in the diner next week," Debbie said.

A few hours had passed, and Gigi and Debbie were dressed.

Gigi stepped out from changing in the bathroom.

"Gigi, you look beautiful. Nephew hooked your makeup up."

Debbie pulled her phone out, snapping pictures of Gigi.

"Yes, girl, that dress is hugging that ass. Honey, if I was into the fish, I'd try to holler," Quincy said

"Holler what? Girl, you don't want me to give you my switch up, because I could switch up," Quincy said.

Quincy posed like a thug, standing with both legs spread out, with his arms folded across his chest.

"No, Nephew," Debbie laughed. "That don't even look right on you."

"You looking good too, Debbie." Gigi looked at Debbie in her heels with her black fitted slacks and red floral shirt. "You wearing them shoes."

"Gigi, we in there on some Tupac shit. All eyes on us." "Debbie, I also wanted to tell you that I really appreciate everything you have done for me too—your words of encouragement. You're like the mother I wish my real mother could be and I just wanted to tell you that I do appreciate you. If I do win tonight, you're most definitely in my corner."

"That is sweet of you to say, Gigi. Now, I don't need to be crying, I don't want to mess my makeup up." Debbie hugged Gigi. "Now, get you another drink and let's walk over here so Ms. Ruby can see us. Scooter should be pulling up in a few minutes. Caesar can't make it this time. He has an event he's taking his daughter to. Father and Daughter Dance."

"Aww, that's sweet. I always wanted to do a Father and Daughter Dance, but my dad left when I was younger. I don't even really remember him too much," Gigi said.

"It's ok, girl. I didn't have no daddy neither. I mean I had daddies, if you know what I mean," Quincy said.

Gigi laughed, "You always find a way to make me laugh, Q.

"That's what I do. I'm going to also tell you this. Stop worrying about your past for you cannot walk into the future holding baggage. Let that shit go, because if you don't, it's going to enable you. What your mother did, that was fucked up, but look at you now." He grabbed Gigi by the shoulders, holding her as they both look in the mirror. "Like you said in your song, I see a broken bird whose wings are healing and ready to fly, so go then." Quincy hugged Gigi. They all walked out back over to Ms. Ruby's place. When they arrived, they enter through the back door.

"Hey ladies! Gigi, you wearing that dress. And, Debbie, girl you looking good too. I must say, I love them heels," Nurse Betty said. "Thanks, Betty. What Big Freedia say? We came to slay," Debbie said.

"Ok Auntie, what you know about Big Freedia?" Quincy said. "Betty, this is my nephew, Quincy."

"Nice to meet you, Betty. If you need anything done as far as your hair, nails, or makeup I can hook that up for you." He pulled out a business card and gave it to Nurse Betty.

"Ok, so you do it all, I see. I am looking for a new beautician, mine moved to Atlanta,"Nurse Betty said. "Call me," Quincy said.

The doorbell rang.

"That must be Calvin." Debbie opened the front door.

"Hey Debbie, you ladies ready? Y'all all up in here looking enticing." Scooter walked in with an all-black tuxedo on. He walks up to Gigi and kissed her softly on the forehead. "Hey, here. I got something for you." Scooter pulled out a beautiful orange and beige corsage that matched the exact colors of her dress.

"Calvin, this is beautiful."

Scooter put the corsage on her right wrist.

"That is beautiful, Calvin." Ms. Ruby said as she got up to look at Gigi and Scooter taking pictures with Debbie's camera, Quincy's camera, Gigi's camera, and Scooter's. Pictures were just snapping everywhere.

"Grandma, I bought you something too." Scooter pulled out a picture frame with him and the Chicago Bears team.

"Look at my grandson. Didn't I tell you God will do it? Mustard seed of faith, baby, mustard seed of faith. I'm going to put this right here on my fireplace with the rest of your trophies," Ms. Ruby said

"Ok, enough for the pictures, we have to get out of here," Debbie said.

"Ok, grandma, I set the TV for you so the show will automatically turn the TV to the channel for you. You also got the voice command on the remote," Scooter said.

"Yeah, Debbie told me about the feature, and I like it. All this different technology. Gigi, go show them what a mustard seed of faith will get you," Ms. Ruby hugged Gigi.

"Nurse Betty, you got my number if you need to call," Scooter said.

"Y'all about to step in that place showing out. I must say Ms.

Ruby, your grandson wears a tux well," Quincy said. "Thanks dude, now let's get out of here."

"Quincy, are you staying at my house or are you going home?" Debbie said.

"Nah, Auntie, I'm going to ride out. I have a date tonight. I just came to hook y'all up," Quincy said.

"Ok, we out. Love you, Grandma."

They all walked out the door getting into the car.

"Scooter, when the hell did you get a freaking Rolls-Royce? It got your initials all on the headrest," Debbie said.

Scooter helped the ladies into the car. "Ms. Debbie, this what happens when you get a nice-ass contract, plus a bonus."

"Damn, and y'all going in style. Maybe I should go. Nah, I'm just messing, I'm not dressed, but y'all have fun. Gigi, bring them coins home." Quincy popped his car trunk. He puts his suitcase in his car, then gets in the driver's seat.

"Good luck, girl," Quincy said as he pulled off

"This is nice. I never rode in a Rolls-Royce." Gigi sat in the front, rubbing her hands on the seats of the car.

"Me neither, but I'm about to ride now," Debbie said.

"Ms. Debbie, hit that button right there in the middle," Scooter said.

Debbie hit the button and a cabinet opened, revealing bottles of liquor.

"I knew that would make you happy."

"Boy, I could kiss you."Debbie grabbed a bottle of D'Ussé, cracking it open.

"Gigi, you want a shot?"

"Nah, I'm ok for now. I'm just ready to go in here and see what Ms. Blue going to bring to the table."

"I know you not worried, are you?" Scooter grabbed Gigi's hand softly.

"No Calvin, I'm just ready to get this contract." She looked at him with her soft eyes.

"And you got ice back here too. I could get used to this lifestyle." Debbie leaned back in the seat, crossing her legs and sipping on the D'Ussé. "Now, Gigi, that girl Blue, trust me, she been preparing for this day too. Now, don't get me wrong, the girl can sing and she is going to try to bring it hard."

"Yeah, I agree with Ms. Debbie on that. She had fi e in her eyes on that stage."

"She got fire, but Gigi lungs. Now, you pumping me up back here, Ms. Debbie.". "I guess I will take a shot." Debbie poured Gigi a shot of D'Ussé.

"Scooter, you're our designated driver. No drinking for you tonight."

"I'm good, Ms. Debbie. The night is about Gigi."

"Hell, me too. I will be managing her after we win tonight, right, Gigi?"

"Ms. Debbie, I promise you if I pull this off, you can manage me."

"Great choice. Did I tell you I also have my Business Degree from DePaul University? Not only that, when I used to cater, I would cater to some of the number one radio stations in Chicago. WGCI, V103, and 106 and Park. So, I know folks in the business. But once you sign that contract, you should be good from there too. Especially if we're going to be able to sign with ROC Nation."

"Hell yeah, that will be nice. I'll get to meet Beyoncé, Jay-Z, and Meek Mill."

"That's right—talk it into existence."

"We are here, ladies." Scooter pulled up next to the valet stand of the building.

"OMG, look at all these people out here. There is the announcer!" Gigi said.

"Baby, this is semifinals. It's shine time," Debbie said

The Valet Guy opened both the back and front door for Gigi and Debbie. Scooter took Gigi's arm as Debbie grabbed his other. "Let's walk in this bitch with style." Debbie walked up with a sexy strut, waving to everybody like she's the one singing tonight. "Ladies and gentlemen, it's Ms. Gigi," Announcer yelled. The crowd applauded.

"So, Gigi, how are you feeling? Are you nervous?" The Announcer moved the mic closer to Gigi. "What will you be singing tonight?"

"I'll be singing a piece of music that I've written, and I hope you guys like it."

"I'm quite sure we will. But tell me what's going on here with you and Calvin Walker—Chicago Bears number one draft pick,"

Announcer said.

"This is not about me tonight, it's about my baby Gigi. So, let's keep this about her and not us." Scooter grabbed Gigi by the waist as cameras snapped pictures.

"And this here is my manager, Debbie without whom I couldn't have been here, and a few more that believed in me," Gigi said. "So, Ms. Debbie, do you think Gigi is going to win the semifinals tonight?" The Announcer placed the mic in Debbie's face.

"Did Prince like purple?" Debbie said and then walked on. "Ms. Debbie, did you just walk off like that?

"That's how you do it, keep it moving so folks don't get the impression you're nervous or scared."

They made it into the studio to the Lady at the Counter.

"Good Evening, Ms. Garcia. You and your guests can head straight to the back, they are expecting you," lady at counter said.

"Oh, no IDs this time?" Debbie said.

They all walked to the back to Studio 7.

"Hi Ms. Garcia, we have a dressing room waiting for you. Tonight, you are allowed two guests to come out onstage with you, opposed to one as before. Please follow me." A Cast Member walked Gigi to her room. "So, tonight we will have the previous winners come in and sing a song, then it will be the grand finale, which is the semifinals for you and Ms. Blue. You can see the show from back here on this flat screen TV. We'll call you when we are ready. Good luck." He walked out, closing the door behind him.

"Ok, this is nice. The room, the TV, the snacks." Debbie grabbed some meat and cheese that sit on a platter. "I see they have waters, canned teas, coffee—but I don't see the D'Ussé.

"I don't think they want the semifinalists drinking before the competition." Scooter hugged Gigi from behind, giving her a kiss on the cheek.

"That's ok." Debbie opened her purse. "I brought some Debbie walked over to the table. She placed some ice cubes from a bowl on the table into a plastic cup, and poured the D'Ussé.

"Ok, Ms. Debbie, now we don't need you getting drunk on us," Gigi said.

"Oh, no baby, I'm not on that. I just want a few cocktails to set the mood." She sat down on the couch, with a small plate of meat, cheese, and crackers.

An Hour Later a Cast Member arrived, "Ms. Gigi, they will be ready for you to make your appearance and to tell what song you will be singing for tonight."

Gigi walked backstage with the Cast Member, where she spotted Ms. Blue.

"Hi Gigi, nice dress. I see we have the same taste in fashion too," Ms. Blue said.

"Nice dress you have as well." Gigi looked Ms. Blue up and down in disbelief. Gigi and Ms. Blue were wearing the same damn dress. Gigi's was orange and beige, while Ms. Blue's was green and gold. "I see you're just missing a corsage." Gigi said.

The Cast Member rushed backstage to find the two girls. "Ok, ladies, the announcer will call both of you out and ask both of you a few questions and then we will go into commercial break. Once we come back, that's when you will get on the stage and sing the song of your choice. Good luck, ladies." The Cast Member walked out.

"Audience, give it up for our previous singers," the Announcer said to the audience.

Five previous singers took the stage. They song a well-rehearsed song together, moving the audience. The Judges watched with admiration, whispering in hushed voices about their favorite winners from previous seasons. The song ended, and the singers bow before they were escorted off the stage

"Alright ladies and gentlemen the semifinals you all have been waiting on." The audience and all Judges clapped. "Let's bring out Ms. Rachel Blue and Ms. Ginger Garcia."

Gigi and Ms. Blue walked out on stage.

"Hello ladies, you made it to the semifinals. Judges, anything you would like to ask Ms. Blue or Ms. Garcia before we start the semifinals?" the announcer said

"I see you both know your fashions. How is it that the both of you have on the same design by Dolce & Gabbana, but different colors?" Judge 1 asked them.

"I thought the same thing when I saw Ms. Garcia. The only thing I can say is we both have the same taste in designers," Ms. Blue said.

"Ok, and what a good taste it is. You both look lovely. I hope you both sound as lovely as you look," Judge 2 said.

"So, Gigi, what song will you be performing tonight" Judge 3 said.

"I wrote a song that reflec s on my past life, and I would love to share it with the audience and those looking from home," Gigi said.

The audience applauded

"So, Rachel, what will you be performing?" Judge 1 asked.

"Like Gigi, I wrote a song too that tells the story of my journey to get here."

"Well, you both sound like you have a story to tell through your music. Audience and judges, are you ready?" Announcer said and the crowd and Judges all applauded. "Alright ladies, on this round, a coin will be flipp d, and you call heads or tell. The person that hits the target will get the chance to say if they would like to perform first or last. So, ladies, heads or tails?" He flicked the coin into the air. "Tails!"

"That leaves you with heads, Rachel." The coin flipp d in the air. Gigi and Rachel watched as it hit the floor

"It's heads. So, Rachel you can pick if you would like to go first or pass it on to Gigi?"

"Well, since Ms. Garcia said she is honored to share the stage with me, I will give her the honors to go first.

"Ok audience, when we come back, we will hear from Ms. Gigi Garcia." The Announcer put his arm around Gigi's shoulder, the mic in his other hand. "Gigi, are you ready?"

"You'll see once we get back from commercial break," Gigi said.

"At the same time, Ms. Debbie's phone rang. She pulled out her phone, checked the Caller ID, and passed it to Gigi.

"So, Ms. Blue going to give you first. Now, don't be nervous, just go out there and do what you do every day at the diner and at home. Sing your ass off, but sing it with your heart. Let it flow and come natural," Ms. Ruby said.

"Hey child, remember a mustard seed of Faith. You got this." Ms. Ruby hung up.

"Baby, this is your big chance to show people what you're really made of. The song is beautiful, you will have the audience eating out your hands." Scooter gave Gigi a hug and kissed on her forehead. "We'll be here."

"Gigi, we'll be back live in one minute, get ready," Announcer said.

Gigi nodded and got ready to take the stage. A minute passed and the announcer said, "We are back. Are you ready, audience, for

Your Big Chance? Are you ready, judges?"

The audience and Judges all applauded.

"Ok Gigi, can you tell me the title of your song you will be singing, and what inspired you to sing it?"

"The name of my song I've written is called 'Spoken Truth.' I wrote this song because of past abandonments in my life and I would like to share it with you guys."

"The title is great with how you explained why you decided to sing this song," Judge 1 said.

"Well, let's see what you got, Ms. Gigi," Judge 2 said.

"Well, if it sounds like the way you sang before on this stage last time, I think you will be alright," Judge 3 said.

"Alright Gigi, please take your place," the announcer said.

The audience applauded as Gigi walked over to the mic. Gigi began to sing her song.

"I remember the day it was all so clear,
The day my heart was crushed,
Like a truck hitting a deer
Just like a baby bird
Alone in the nest,
With no protection,
but pushed to fly away
Abandonment has embraced me
I feel like dead weight
But yet in my dreams
My arms stretch out for you yet in my dreams
My heart beats loud in search of you
I wish it were me you loved
Just as I love you

But yet, I wake up
And I'm hit with the truth
I was that chick that felt all alone
Who was pushed out my nest and kicked out my home
But as time passed my wings strengthen to fly
The dead weight dropped off for I'm flying high.
Doors are opening, and I'm walking through

Thanking the lord for seeing me through
But yet, my arms still stretch for you."

Gigi, stood crying as she finished the song, wiping the tears away as they rolled down her face. The Announcer walked over to Gigi, with tears in his eyes.

"That there was beautiful and really deep. You got the audience all standing and tearing up. So, judges, what do you think?" Announcer said.

"I'm lost for words. I used to feel like that bird that was pushed out the nest, so I could relate," Judge 2 said.

"Beautiful, is all I can say. Beautiful," Judge 3 said. "Standing ovation is all I can say," Judge 1 said.

The Judges continued to applaud, standing. "Thank you, Ms. Gigi," Announcer told her. Gigi walked offstage

"Gigi, that was lovely, baby." Scooter hugged Gigi tightly. "After tonight, everything will be alright from here."

Debbie shook her head as tears rolled down her face. She grabbed Gigi and hugged her. 'Girl. I heard you sing this at my house, but you didn't do it like this with such passion and meaning."

"So, you guys think I did good?" Gigi paced, trembling. "I could use that D'Ussé now, Ms. Debbie."

Debbie made Gigi a drink. "You put on an amazing performance." Debbie's phone rang as she passed Gigi the drink. Debbie answered, she's right here, passing Gigi the phone.

"Hi Ms. Ruby."

"You just planted that mustard seed. Faith goes a long way, baby. Your time is now."

"Thanks Ms. Ruby."

Debbie snatched the phone back. "Ok, Ms. Ruby, we have to go so we can hear what Ms. Blue got to bring after what Gigi just put on them."

Debbie hung up the phone as the Announcer talked with Ms. Blue as they all looked on from behind stage. After Ms. Blue sang her song and talked with the Judges, the Announcer called Gigi back to the stage. The audience and Judges all applauded.

"Well, ladies I must say you both did a magnificent job but there can only be one winner," the Announcer said.

Gigi walked over to Ms. Blue and smiled at her as she embraced her hand.

"And the winner to take home one hundred thousand dollars, plus receive a contract with This That Production Studios is..." The two ladies held each other's hands tightly.

"Ginger Garcia."

Confetti began to fall as Gigi fell to her knees, holding her face with her hands as tears flowed down. Scooter and Debbie ran out on the stage. Scooter picked Gigi up from the ground, giving her a hug. He spun her around, kissing her passionately before setting her down on her feet softly. Ms. Debbie ran up to Gigi crying and hugging Gigi to as she held the bottle of D'Ussé in the other hand.

"So, Gigi, how are you feeling right now that you have won the one hundred thousand dollars and a contract to record music for This That Production Studios." The Announcer placed the mic closer to Gigi. "This is your time."

"First and foremost, I would like to thank God and a lady named Ms. Ruby for giving me back my faith and telling me that a little mustard seed of faith is all I needed to believe in myself again."

"I will also like to thank my new boo, Calvin, but y'all may know him as the number one NFL draft pick and our new quarterback for our Chicago Bears."

The crowd cheered.

"Last but not least, I would like to thank my manager, Ms.

Debbie, for letting me see that I was that lion from the Wizard of Oz who didn't have the courage. But with the help of those that surrounded him, he was able to feel strong again, and that's what Ms. Debbie was able to bring out in me what I have suppressed for so long: my courage, my strength, my wings. Oh, and my stylist and makeup artist, Quincy."

Gigi waved at the camera. The audience applauded as the Announcer brought out a giant check, written out for one hundred thousand dollars.

CHAPTER TWENTY-TWO

Everybody was at the diner that following Monday in celebration of Gigi winning the Semifinals. The diner was packed with people coming in to eat and to also get a picture and autographs signed by Gigi.

"I hired a catering service to help with the food today. Now Nephew, for every autographed picture, that will be twenty-five dollars and if they want to take a picture with Gigi, that will be fifty dollars. Now, just because she won that money, doesn't mean she can't make more," Debbie said.

"Auntie, I got this. I'm also including my business card for makeup, hair, and nails. Gigi said it was ok that I let people know I'm Quincy, her makeup artist. You see the cards I made?" Quincy passed Debbie a card. She read it out loud.

"All-in-one stylist from makeup to nails, fashion to hair. If you care to look as beautiful as GIGI, call to schedule yourself an appointment. Sorry, no appointment, no service." Debbie looked at the card, shaking her head. "I guess your salon is about to blow up too."

"Quincy, here are copies of the photos of Gigi." Connie passed the photos to Quincy. "This should be more than enough. I made over five hundred copies. If they want to take one with her, just snap the picture with the camera and hit print, and it will print out on the printer here."

"Connie, believe it or not, I used to work in a club taking pictures for folks' parties, events, hell, baby showers too, so I am familiar," Quincy said.

"This is so overwhelming; I feel like a light has shone down on me. I wish Ms. Ruby could've been here, but I understand her doctor's appointment comes first. I'll just see her at home tonight," Gigi said.

"Girl, you're a star now, get used to it. Because trust me, there's going to be more to come, especially since you announced that you and Calvin are a couple now too and he's worth millions," Quincy said.

"Yes, the hens are going to be trying to knock at Scooter's door every chance they feel you are not around. Hell, some will do it in your face. Sometimes, it will get under your skin because your new lifestyle will be in the spotlight now. It's up to you how you choose to deal with it, especially when it comes to the rumors of the hens and media," Debbie said.

"Girl, y'all the new Russell and Ciara of the NFL, there's going to be plenty of haters. Speaking of Mr. Football, where is your man, Gigi?" Quincy said.

"He's on his way, he said he had to make a stop really quick and he should be here shortly."

"Ms. Gigi, would it be ok if my son took a picture with you? After seeing you sing last night, my baby said that he wants to sing just like you one day," a diner guest said.

"Sure, no problem." Gigi bended down to take a picture with the fan when the door chimed, and Scooter walked in.

"Where is my new star Gigi at?" Scooter spread his arms open and picked Gigi up, wrapping her in a hug.

"Hey, baby." Gigi gave Calvin a kiss. "So, what did you have to pick up?" Gigi laid back in Scooter's lap as he sat on the barstool.

"It's coming in now."

The door chimed as someone walked in, holding a handful of balloons and a handful of flowers. The Delivery Man talked from behind the balloons, his face covered.

"I'm looking for a Ginger Garcia, I have a special delivery for her," guy with balloons said.

"I'm over here." Gigi waved at the man to walk her way. "Aww, Calvin these are lovely."

Gigi took the balloons from the guy and looked up at the ceiling. She let the balloons fly up and they covered the ceiling of the diner. Gigi looked back over at the guy that brought the balloons and flowers. She covered her mouth and began to cry, walking over to the guy and giving him a tight hug.

"Oh my God, is it really you?" Gigi hugged him again.

"Yes, it's me sister. I'm home, they let me out I'm free," the man said. He put the flowers down and hugged Gigi as Quincy snapped pictures. "If it wasn't for the help of Calvin, I wouldn't be here. He told the NFL commissioner my story and got me a new lawyer the next thing you know, I'm out and was offered a nice-ass settlement.

"Everybody, this is my brother George. George, this is Connie, the one I told you that did my portfolio. And this is Ms. Debbie, my new manager. This is Quincy, Debbie's nephew. He's my new stylist, and the one I told you who hooked all my makeup, nails, and hair up."

"Hey, George" Quincy said, flirty

"I see you met my boo already. You too were all quiet about this one, I was not expecting none of this. Thanks baby." Gigi hugged and kissed Calvin.

Lance said, smoothly, without stuttering, "Gigi, I told you that you were going to win. I'm proud of you." Lance put the dish bin down, and gave Gigi a hug and a kissed on her cheek.

"Thank you, Lance." She hugged him back.

"Hi Calvin, I'm still coming to one of your games, right?" "Of course, Lance." Scooter playfully hit Lance in the arm. "I'm going to go use the bathroom," Gigi said.

"So, Scooter have you spoken with Ms. Ruby?" Debbie sipped on a bottle of water.

"Yeah, she said the doctor said things are looking good so far and she can come back to the diner. But just not six days a week."

"I told Ms. Ruby she didn't have to be here all six days but with you not being there, she made this place her priority. Now that I'm here, I can take on more. I know once I start managing Gigi, Rob will take over as manager because we trust him, and we will also be hiring a few more servers. Scooter, we got this. I know this Ms. Ruby's baby, but this my baby too," Debbie said.

"I know you do, Ms. Debbie. Hey George, you want a beer? There's a store a few blocks down the street we can get some beer there," Scooter said.

"Hell yeah, I would love a beer."

"Debbie, tell Gigi we went to go grab some beer. And I already know, Ms. Debbie, bring you something back to drink too."

"And you know it."

Scooter and George exited the diner, heading to store across the street. The door chimed. A lady walked into the diner wearing a pair of yellow sunglasses, orange thigh shorts, yellow shirt, with orange pom-pom ball socks with a pair of see-through sandals. Debbie walked over to greet the lady.

"Hi ma'am, will you be dining in today?" The lady looked around and said nothing at first. Debbie watched her suspiciously

"I would like to talk to Gigi. She's my daughter. I'm her mother," the lady said.

Debbie swallowed hard as her face drops, looking at the frail lady that stood before her.

"Gigi is in the bathroom. I will get her for you. Please have a seat here at the counter. Nephew, please give Ms. Garcia something to drink. Whatever she likes, I'll be back."

"So, your Gigi's mother?" "Yes, I am."

"I'm Gigi's stylist. So, what can I get you to drink? We don't have liquor in here, just an FYI," Quincy said.

"Coffee will be fine," Ms. Garcia continued to look around the diner.

Quincy grabbed a cup and poured Ms. Garcia a cup of coffee. "So, what brings you here to see Gigi?" He bended down to look Ms. Garcia in the face as he poured the coffee. "Considering you kicked her out of her home because you thought she wanted your husband. But it was your husband that was hitting on Gigi and raping her. That child tried telling you and instead of listening, you turned your back on her and kicked her out. Now look at you."

"Gigi has a future now and people that care for her. Damn if you feel you can come back into her life because she won some money and a recording contract. Nah, mommy or not, she is not going to be supporting your drug or drinking habit. I can smell you now." Quincy smelled the air, then shook his head. "You smell like premos. You nor anyone else is not about to stop this girl shine."

Quincy walked over to the jukebox and put on the clean version of Missy Elliott's 'Throw It Back' and dances to the beat. He looked over at Gigi's mom. " Throw it back." He pointed at the door, gesturing for her to get the hell out.

Connie walked over to the counter, placing dishes in the food bin and talking to Quincy. "Quincy, what are you doing?"

"Oh nothing, just playing a song for a guest I thought that needs to hear it. Plus I love me some Missy Elliott."

"What guest?" Connie looked around.

"Oh Connie, let me introduce you to Gigi's mother, Ms.

Garcia. Yeah, I guess she heard about Gigi winning that money. Now, she wants to pull a 'I know I haven't been in your life, but I'm here now.' I told Ms. Thing, it ain't happening in our camp. Gigi has too much support behind her to let you come in trying to fuck her up. I will get like Big Freedia on that ass to protect that girl from the shit you and your husband made her have to go through. Hell! Out there on them streets, hoeing to eat, no place to go," Quincy said.

Debbie walked out to the front with one hand around Gigi's shoulders. Gigi's mother stood up as she saw Gigi coming from the back. Debbie and Quincy stood looking at Gigi's mom as she walked up to Gigi. She tried to hug Gigi, but Gigi pulled back.

"What are you doing here? Why are you here?"

Gigi's mother tried to grab her hand, but Gigi snatched her hand back.

"Answer me, why are you here?"

"Baby look, I wanted to see you to tell you I saw you on TV and you sounded beautiful. I remember when you were a kid and how you used to walk 'round the house singing. Especially when we used to bake cookies and cakes, and especially on Christmas you used to sing all the holiday songs. Look, I'm sorry for putting you out. I'm didn't know he was pushing up on you and trying to sleep with you."

Gigi walked up to her mother, looking her in the eyes. "I told you and instead of you believing me and putting him out, you kicked me out. All you ever cared and worried about was him, your bottle, and your drugs. Now, you want to come all up in here like we're supposed to have this reunion."

"Look, I'm trying to apologize to you. But like always, you always seem to want all the attention. You walking around the house in those tight-ass shorts and tight-ass pants, sticking your young titties out. Who was I to believe when you were doing all that?"

"I dressed like any regular teenage girl. I was not dressing in

214

tight stuff, especially not around him. And regardless of what I wore, he had no business trying to touch and force himself on me. Pulling out his penis, talking about "Feel it." And you know what, mommy, I could've sworn one night you were laid out drunk and I was in my room asleep. And he came in there masturbating over me while I was asleep. I turned around and caught him, and I could've sworn you stood there watching."

Debbie told Quincy to make sure he played a few songs on the jukebox, so others in the diner couldn't really hear what was going on. "I don't know what you're talking about." She folded her arms, looking at Gigi. "You never told me that neither."

"I didn't have to tell you; you were standing right there."

"Look, I was drunk back then."

Debbie whispered, "You still look like a drunk to me."

"Look, I didn't come in here for all this. I just wanted to know since I'm your mother if I can get a few dollars to, you know, help me get back on my feet. You know I lost my place since he left me. I lost my job and lost my car. I have nothing now. All, I'm asking is for a few thousand to get me an apartment and, you know, to try to get clean."

"How many times have I heard you say you're going to get clean? At least George knew who his daddy was. I wish I did too, to get away from you back then. Like they say, you can pick your friends, but you can't pick your family. Please leave now, please."

Before Ms. Garcia could open her mouth, the door chimed. Scooter and George walked in, laughing. All heads turned to look their way.

"Man, that was too funny. I've never seen a grown-ass man run from such a small-ass dog," Scooter said.

Ms. Garcia's eyes bulge, and she ran over to George. "George, oh my God. I haven't seen you in forever." She hugged George. "I don't believe you're out. When did you get out?"

215

George removed her arms from around him. "Hold on, hold on. What are you doing? You haven't tried writing me one time since I got locked up. I've written you plenty of times, but you never written me back. Now you want to be hugging all on me, like you miss me or something. What are you doing here anyways?"

The door chimed and Mean Mug walked in, interrupting them. "She's here to collect my fifty thousand dollars Gigi owes me."

Mean Mug walked up to Gigi's mother, pulling her over to him. "See, this my HOE." He pointed at Gigi's mother. "This been my HOE way before Gigi was born. As a matter of fact, HOE." Mean Mug pulled on Gigi's mother's arm, pushing her behind him. "Did you tell Gigi, I'm that bitch's daddy?"

"My daddy?" Gigi looked at her mother. "What the hell do he mean he's my daddy?"

"Oh, she ain't tell you, you were a trick baby. Yeah, the HOE came to work for me when she was let go by her first baby daddy, I guess that was this nigga's daddy." Mean Mug looked towards George. "She became one of my HOEs and I tore that pussy up every day. Nice pussy too." He looked back at Gigi's mother. "Well, back then."

Gigi's mother stood behind Mean Mug, with a saddened frown on her face.

"See Gigi was a good BITCH, she brought me other BITCHES. The more BITCHES, the more MONEY. Now, she took that away from me when she snitched to the police and had me arrested. So, I lost money doing time locked in the pen, now I'm here to collect what I'm owed."

"I got your, bitch." George leaped towards Mean Mug but stopped in his tracks when Mean Mug displays a gun that sat in the front of his pants. "Be froggy if you want nigga." Mean Mug patted the gun. "Now, like I told Gigi, if she don't have my fifty thousand dollars I will be here to see her. And here I am. SURPRISE."

216

"Dude, Gigi don't owe you shit. You were bogus as hell for beating on her and pimping her out like that." Scooter looked at Mean Mug angrily, his fists balled up at his sides

"Mr. Number One Draft Pick. Boy, I advise you to shut the fuck up before all them dreams and endorsements go down the drain with one shot." Mean Mug pulled out the Glock 9. "I could've took you out a long time ago if I wanted to. I been to your grandmother's house. Ask Gigi."

"What the hell he mean he's been to my granny's house, Gigi?" Scooter said.

"Yeah, Gigi, what the hell he mean?" Debbie asked.

All eyes turned to Gigi.

"Scooter, that day you pulled up and asked who I was talking to, and I told you it was someone asking for directions. It was Mean Mug. He was telling me he knows where I've been staying, and he knows I've been seeing you. And if I don't give him fifty thousand dollars, he will come to Ms. Ruby's house and kill her, you, and me."

"And you forgot to mention this to me." Scooter looked madly at Gigi. "He threatened my grandma."

"You never told Calvin; he's been threatening you?" He looked at Gigi with serious concern on his face.

"You fucked with the wrong dude when it comes to my grandma." Scooter looked at Mean Mug with a sinister look on his face. Lance came walking out of the kitchen. He tripped over the mat and dropped the dish pan, causing Mean Mug to look up. As Mean Mug looked up, Scooter rushed him. But not before Mean Mug could pull out his gun, shooting it multiple times. The few people that were left in the diner scramble under the booths and tables. Scooter was able to get Mean Mug to the ground, punching him repeatedly as teeth popped out of his mouth. Debbie screamed as she ran over to Gigi and George who both lied on the ground bleeding.

"Call 911, call 911!" Debbie screamed. She held Gigi in her arms, crying and shaking at the same time.

Gigi's mother fell to the ground shaking her head over and over, crying. "Why? Why? I'm sorry I failed you two as a mother." She grabbed Mean Mug's gun and shot herself in the head, falling over on Mean Mug's beat-up body. Connie gave CPR to Gigi. Having heard the commotion, Rob came running out of the kitchen over to George, giving him CPR. The EMTs rushed in, putting oxygen masks both on George and Gigi. They began to try treating their gun wounds they both sustained. One EMT examined Gigi's gunshot wound.

"She was shot in the lower stomach, we'll need a bus," EMT 1 said.

Another EMT crew came in. "Here! We need a bus for this one too."

The other EMTs worked on George, getting him on a bus, working on him as they began to wheel him out to the ambulance.

"He was shot in the chest."

"One, two, three, lift!" The two EMTs got Gigi onto the bus as they wheeled her out to the other ambulance. Scooter, Debbie, and Quincy headed towards the front door and left. Debbie paused in the doorway, and turned.

"Connie, you and Rob take care of things here with the police. We're going to the hospital. I'll call you."

CHAPTER TWENTY-THREE

"I don't believe this shit here. Let's just pray she will be alright. Now, don't go calling Ms. Ruby yet, Scooter. Let's wait to find out what's going on."

Scooter leaned up against the wall, with a blank stare on his face. "I don't believe he shot her; I don't believe this." He stood up and shook his head as Debbie tried to comfort him by giving him a hug.

"I don't believe this either. And to think, Mean Mug is the girl's daddy."

"And her brother. All he had to go through, being wrongfully accused of something, then being able to get out of jail just to get shot. This is sad. I feel sorry for the both of them. I'd never seen anyone take their own life. I can't believe her mother killed herself. That was guilt, that's all I can say it was," Quincy slid down the wall and sat on the ground. He looked at Gigi's pictures in his phone as he cried.

"Debbie, I know we ain't been together long but it seems like we have a bond. I knew something was wrong with her. I knew she was holding something back. I even asked her if there was anything wrong. She said no," Scooter said.

"How was she supposed to tell you all this? If it was difficul for her to handle, how do you think it may have felt for her to tell you? Maybe, she just wanted to get the money to pay him off to keep Ms. Ruby and you safe. All I'm saying is, she was not thinking this would happen, hell none of us were." Debbie paused. "All we can do now is wait and see what these doctors have to say."

They all waited in the waiting area. Debbie stared at the Doctor as he walked through the doors hours later.

"I'm looking for the family of Ms. Ginger Garcia." He took his glasses off, and placed them in the pocket of his doctor's coat. Scooter jumped out of the chair.

"We're her family. What's going on with her, Doc?" "And you are . . .?"

"That's her fiancé and I'm her auntie. Now, Doctor, can you please tell us what's going on?"

"Yes, please," Quincy said. He showed the doctor a picture of all them together. "Is Gigi going to be ok?"

The Doctor looked at all them as he took a deep breath, placing his hands in the sides of his doctor's coat. "Ms. Garcia had some internal bleeding that we were finally able to get under control. But when the bullet entered, it split off, hitting her in the spine

"So, what are you saying, Doc, she won't be able to walk again?" Scooter inquired.

"I'm sorry, but it seems like Ms. Garcia may be paralyzed from the waist down."

"Paralyzed! As in, can't-walk-again paralyzed?" Debbie grabbed the Doctor. "No, that can't be true. The girl's young, the girl's future just beginning."

Quincy pulled Debbie off the Doctor. "Doctor, is there a possibility that she'll be able to walk again?"

"Yes, Doctor, is there a possibility?" Scooter crying.

"There could be a sixty-forty chance, but that's just a possibility. She will need intense rehabilitation therapy to try to get her to even take baby steps, if possible."

"Intense therapy, huh?" Scooter shook his head. "I know the

best rehab therapist in the business. Gigi will get the best, I promise that."

"And what about George?" Debbie asked. "George?" The doctor was confused.

"Yeah, Gigi's brother. The other gunshot victim that came in with her. How is he doing?" Scooter said.

"Sorry to say, he did not make it. The bullet hit him in a major artery in the chest where we couldn't stop the bleeding. Ms. Garcia is in intensive care now and will need all the rest she can get. She will be heavily sedated over the next twelve to twenty-four hours. You guys could come back tomorrow if you like. Right now, she needs to rest."

"Can I just stay with her now? I promise, I won't be loud. I won't make a sound. I just want her to know I'm here for her." Scooter begged the Doctor as tears rolled down his face.

"Tomorrow, son. I'll tell you this though. Ms. Garcia is a fighter." The Doctor patted him on the shoulder and walked away

CHAPTER TWENTY-FOUR

Two Years Later, Debbie, Ms. Ruby, Scooter, and Gigi all sat in the living room watching the Grammy Awards as the Announcer announced that Gigi was the winner for best R&B song and best R&B album of the year for the album she wrote as she went through her battle of being in a wheelchair and getting through rehab.

"Gigi, can you tell us how you felt to win not one, but two Grammys in the same night?" He looked into the camera, speaking to Gigi via video cam.

"I feel ecstatic. Hello all."

The crowd stood, applauding, as Gigi waited for them to quiet down.

"I just want to thank God first, God second, and God third for giving me the opportunity to still be able to sing and breathe another day. I could have died when that bullet changed my life. Without him, none of this could have been possible."

"I also would like to thank my fiancé Calvin, and his grandmother Ms. Ruby, who is like a mother to me. And my Ms. Debbie, who is like an auntie to me. Without their words of wisdom and them helping me to keep my faith, this would not be possible. Last but not least, I would like to thank all my fans..."

Cheers erupted from the crowd.

"...who believed in me when I didn't. I would like to say thank you all so very, very much, and I love you."

"Here to accept these awards for Ms. Gigi and to sing a tribute to her, here is Ms. Rachel Blue Singing "My Truth" written by Gigi."

Ms. Blue walked out on the stage wearing the same beige and orange dress Gigi wore the night she won the semifinals, along with the same color corsage.

"When I first met Gigi, we were both trying to win a record deal on the TV show called Your Big Chance. I will admit, when I heard Gigi sing before me because I asked that she go first, I was behind the curtains bawling my eyes out because her voice was so breathtaking to hear."

"She won that semifinals and the one hundred thousand dollars, but I just wanted to let her know she inspired me in ways no other young singer has in my life. She taught me to be myself if no one else and, Gigi, this tribute is for you." Ms. Blue blew a kiss in the camera. Gigi sat in the wheelchair and began to cry.

"You ok, baby?" Scooter bended down on his knees, looking her in the eyes.

"I'm ok, I'm just surprised. I wasn't expecting to see Rachel sing my song and I did not know I was an inspiration to her. Her words were heartfelt." Gigi clutched her chest tearing up as the tears rolled down her cheek.

EPILOGUE

A Year Later, Scooter won the NFL MVP award for the third time in a row and his team and team management decided to throw him a gala.

"This is nice here." Debbie sat at the round table with Scooter, Ms. Ruby, Gigi, and Caesar. "This what you call fancy for real," she said in a low voice to Caesar. "Baby, pour me some of that champagne."

"Yes, this is lovely. I can't believe my Scooter won his third MVP. That's one for every year he's been in the NFL. I say ain't God good?" Ms. Ruby touched Scooter's hand softly.

"I'm going to roll on to the bathroom really quick to freshen up my makeup. I'll be right back." Gigi took the lock off her wheelchair

"Baby, I can help you there," Scooter said.

"Gigi, you want me to go with you?" Debbie sipped on the champagne.

"Baby, I'm ok. Thanks Debbie. I'll be right back," Gigi said. "You sure you don't want anyone going with you, Gigi?" Ms.

Ruby looked over at her.

"No. I'm ok. Just need to freshen up." Gigi rolled herself out. "I hope she's ok," Debbie said.

"She's fine. She hasn't been around a lot of people lately, so this could be overwhelming some. But she'll be fine," Caesar said

"Yeah, you could be right Caesar. She haven't been around

anyone but us and the rehab folks so this could be a bit much for her," Ms. Ruby said.

There was a man on stage, holding a trophy. "Now, since we got through all you guys' busted-ass lame jokes and watered-down drinks, let's bring our quarterback, my guy, and our MVP up here: Calvin Walker aka Scooter, Scooter, Scooter!"

"The man chants Scooter name as Scooter walks over, and bends down to hug his grandma. Scooter walks on the stage, grabbing the trophy as the man passed it to him and shook Scooter's hand. The crowd stands and chants "MVP, MVP, MVP!" Scooter looks around the crowd."

"First and foremost, I would like to thank God, and my grandma for always pushing me when I wanted to give up. Second, I would like to thank my fans and my coaches for believing in me to be the quarterback of this team. Without you guys, I wouldn't been able to get us to the Super Bowl."

The crowd cheered loudly.

"I would like to thank my fiancée too, but she had to be excused for a minute, But if she could hear me, I would like to say, thank you for being the woman of my dreams, and I can't wait to make you my wife one day."

"And I can't wait to become your wife." Gigi rolled herself close to the stage. Scooter began to walk her way until she gestured for him to stop.

"And as your wife, I want a big house with a white picket fence, with two dogs, and a playset for our kids."

Scooter looked deeply at Gigi. "I promise, when you're Mrs. Walker, you can have all that."

"Then I promise to marry you then and be the perfect mother to our kids." Gigi got up out of the chair and walked on the stage. Scooter fell to his knees, crawling on them to Gigi. He reached up and hugged her around the waist, looking up into her eyes. The crowd applauded as Gigi passed Scooter a home pregnancy test that showed 'Positive.'

Gigi whispered, "You're going to be a daddy, Calvin." "Scooter picked Gigi up and hugged her gently. After a moment, he set her down, and looked at the pregnancy test.

"You could walk baby? When did this happened? And you say I'm going to be a daddy? I'm going to be a daddy." He grabbed Gigi by the arm, closer to him, hugging and kissing her as tears rolled down his cheeks. Ms. Ruby and Debbie both got up and walked on the stage to join Scooter and Gigi. Gigi grabbed Ms. Ruby.

"A mustard seed of faith and you guys believing in me got me here. I love you guys," Gigi said.

"I'm going to be a great grandma. Thank you, Jesus! Thank you, Jesus," Ms. Ruby said. She hugged Gigi and Scooter.

"And I'm going to be a great auntie." Debbie went around hugging them all as tears of joy rolled from her eyes, gesturing for Caesar to come onstage.

ANALOGUE

After George's death, Gigi started a nonprofi called WeLiveOn2, where all lives matter. A place that helps those who have been wrongfully incarcerated. George won a settlement from the state for being wrongfully accused, which Gigi donated to other programs that help those who have been wrongfully incarcerated.

Nine months later, Gigi gave birth to a set of fraternal twins: a boy and a girl. The boy they named George, and the girl they named Georgia. Gigi goes on to win an American Music Award and two Billboard Awards two years after, for Best Record for a Musical and Best Female Artist. She also went on to become a great singer, mother, and wife. She performed all over the world until she passed away from and aneurysm she sustained over time from the years of abuse from Mean Mug and other Johns that beat and raped her.

If you are a victim of abuse, don't wait, get help now, for later may be too late. All you have to do is pick up the phone, and help will be there on the other end.

Abuse Hotline:

If you are a sex worker or the loved one of a sex worker in an abusive situation, our advocates are here to talk with you by chat and phone every day from 6 a.m.–2 a.m. CST. Call us at 1-800-799-7233 (1-800-787-3224 TTY).

Additional resources:

- The HIPS Hotline helps those impacted by sexual exchange and/or drug use due to choice, coercion, or circumstance by phone, 24/7 at **1-800-676-HIPS**
- FORGE offers anti-violence support for members of the trans community and can supply referrals to local providers by phone at **1-414-559-2123**
- The Northwest Network and The Network/La Red provide support services to LGBTQIA+ survivors of sexual abuse and assault
- The Rape, Abuse & Incest National Network (RAINN) has a 24/7 hotline at **1-800-656-HOPE (4673)** and also offers an online chat
- After Silence and Pandora's Project are useful websites offering support for survivors of sexual violenc
- Male Survivor is a great resource for male survivors of sexual abuse and assault
- The Planned Parenthood Chatline offers support and education to anyone with questions or concerns about their reproductive health

Help is only a call away.

The End

Made in the USA
Monee, IL
13 April 2023

31565344R00128